THE WATERMEN

Patrick Easter

LARGE PRINT

Oxford

First published in Great Britain 2011
by
Quercus

Published in Large Print 2013 by ISIS Publishing Ltd.,
7 Centremead, Osney Mead, Oxford OX2 0ES
by arrangement with
Quercus

CIP data is available for this title from the British Library

ISBN 978–0–7531–9224–5 (hb)
ISBN 978–0–7531–9225–2 (pb)

Printed and bound in Great Britain by
T. J. International Ltd., Padstow, Cornwall

For Sara

There is a glossary of historical and nautical terms on page 347.

PROLOGUE

April 1798
Wapping, London

Joseph Boylin, landlord of the Queen's Head in Griffin Street, Shadwell, leaned against the wall of a house and wiped the sweat trickling down the side of his large, bulbous nose. Even for a man in early middle age, his health was not good — had not been since the day he'd been flogged. His face clouded at the memory of the injustice, still fresh despite the passage of the years. Hardly a day passed when he didn't think of it, and of the man responsible. And then his back would itch where the blows had fallen and a trembling rage would overcome him.

A muffled cry intruded on his thoughts. He looked down to where the woman lay, his eyebrows arched as though surprised by her presence, by the shuddering sob that escaped from under her ragged blue shawl and which seemed to draw the life out of her wasted body. The anger left him, driven away by the physical effort of the beating he'd given her, as though one were a necessary precursor of the other. He regarded her for a

1

moment, irritated by her behaviour, keen to be gone. He'd done what needed to be done. She'd not repeat her mistake.

It began to rain, gently at first but gaining in strength, the raindrops varnishing the bricks of the ramshackle buildings that stood on either side of the alley. Boylin turned up the collar of his coat and shuffled along the uneven surface towards the Thames, his thoughts returning to the day of his humiliation and to the man he still feared and loathed in equal measure. He'd not forget — nor forgive — that day as long as he drew breath.

The roar of the late-night crowd grew louder as he neared the junction with Wapping Street, the silhouette of the mob appearing as a confused blur of movement in the light of a shop-door lantern. He stopped at the sight of his reflection caught in the glass of a window, and stared at the smooth, marble-like sheen of his face, the skin drawn tight over his cheekbones, the engorged nose criss-crossed with a thousand lines of bloody purple.

He shrank back into the shadows, holding a hand in front of his face shielding him from the stares of strangers, his fingers playing with a canvas patch over his right eye. He remained still for a moment, smelling the dank perfumes of the river, the scent of rope and wood and tar and the odour of decaying fish. Then, thrusting himself into the amorphous throng, he was swallowed up in the night.

Of the woman, he thought no more.

★ ★ ★

In the narrow confines of that nameless alley off Wapping Street, a mile or so east of the City, an hour elapsed before Hannah Pinkerton dared to move. Every bone in her body ached. She put her hand to her mouth and felt the blood that had trickled from her broken nose and cut lips. She'd lost count of the number of times he'd struck her. Only money would satisfy him and save her from his beatings.

But she had none to give him.

Not since the pain had come; the searing agony that erupted deep within her every time she worked. She had known its meaning, of course, and of the foul stench of the mucus emanating from her. Even if she hadn't, there were others who would have told her. The pox was common enough in these parts.

She stifled a cry as a fresh bolt of pain spread from between her legs, waiting for it to subside. Only then did she climb to her feet and begin limping away, leaning an outstretched hand against the walls of the houses for support as her faltering steps took her further into the labyrinth of muddy, rat-infested alleys. When she could stay awake no longer she'd find somewhere to rest for an hour or two. But not yet. There was work still to be done. She drew her blue shawl about her battered face and forced herself to smile. The clients liked to see her smile. Without a smile, there'd be no money — and she knew what that meant.

And still the rain fell.

CHAPTER ONE

One month later
Limehouse Reach, the Port of London

Captain Tom Pascoe, late of His Majesty's Navy, stood on the quarterdeck of the West India barque the *Swansong*, enjoying the feel of the warm, spring breeze coming off the Isle of Dogs. He filled his lungs, breathing in the scented cocktail of wet grass and the tangy odour of sheep grazing the flat acres off his starboard beam.

This was journey's end.

In five, perhaps six weeks, it would all begin again and he would leave this place and head back to the open sea. He sighed and watched the scene slip by, savouring the moment. From somewhere behind him, he could hear the murmured instructions of the pilot and the answering grunt of the helmsman, the sudden flap of a sail and the groan of hemp under strain. He squinted up through the rigging, to the billowing white of the topgallants as a freshening breeze filled the canvas and gently pushed the *Swansong* through the tangled mass of shipping moored on either side of the reach.

"We're about ready, Captain, another two or three minutes . . ." The pilot's voice seemed far away.

"Thank you, Mr Pilot." Tom looked over his shoulder and caught the eye of the ship's mate. "Carry on, Mr Simmonds, if you please."

"All hands bring ship to anchor." Tom winced as the mate's piercing yell reverberated up and down Limehouse Reach.

Instinctively, he listened for the answering stamp and scurry of feet that would signal the men swaying up the rat lines, heading for the dizzying heights of the upper yards.

"Man t'gallant clew lines, fore and main. Look alive, you jumped-up, never-come-down, useless bastards." The stream of orders went on seemingly without interruption as though silence, or even the merest hint of it, might bring the mate's authority to an abrupt end.

Tom eased himself up onto the balls of his feet, feeling his aching calf muscles stretch and the throbbing pain fall away. He was a tall, well-built man, his face lined and weather-beaten from years at sea, his straw-coloured hair worn long and tied at the nape with a black silk ribbon. Now he watched the frenzied activity of the crew as the forward movement of the barque slowed to a crawl. He had, he thought, seen better seamanship on a Newcastle collier, although he could hardly blame the mate for that, not since the Navy had pillaged his finest men almost within sight of home. He stole a glance at the pilot, hoping the fellow hadn't noticed the crew's shortcomings.

"You may, sir, bring her up into the tide as soon as you wish." The pilot appeared too engrossed in his task to take much notice of the captain or his concerns.

Tom nodded and cast a practised eye along the crowded reach. There would be no room for error. He glanced over the side, checking his speed. Too fast, and the *Swansong* would stop with an embarrassing crash when the anchor was dropped and the cable tightened; too slow and she'd not swing up into the tide quickly enough to stay out of the way of other shipping. He stood back from the rail, his hand shielding his eyes from the sun, his thumb tracing the faint outline of a long, vertical scar close to his right eye.

"You may let go the anchor, Mr Simmonds, if you please."

"Aye, aye, sir. Stand clear of the starboard cable," shrieked the mate, his bowed shoulders, trembling with the exertion, his clenched fists held close to his side. "Helm a-lee. Let go the anchor."

A low rumble and the *Swansong*'s cable snaked its way out through the starboard hawsehole. Great sheets of spray shot upwards into the sunlight as the anchor hit the water and the barque began to swing up into the flood tide. Gradually, the soft gurgling sound along the hull petered out, leaving an eerie quietness disturbed only by the occasional creak of timber and the familiar muted bellow of the port.

Tom smoothed the wrinkles in the grubby blue uniform coat he still wore. Its double row of gold buttons dulled with age, its hem threadbare. At one shoulder a patch of deeper blue showed where once had hung the single gold epaulette of a master and commander: his rank in the Navy. Three years of exposure to the elements had failed to obscure the evidence; three years since he'd joined the swelling ranks of officers placed on indefinite shore leave for lack of a seagoing command. He'd been compelled then, for the sake of an income, to seek employment with the Committee of the West India Merchants and Planters as master of the *Swansong*.

He turned aft and walked to the taffrail, curling his thick, stump-like fingers round the larboard backstay as his eye swept the Rotherhithe shore, empty but for a clutch of buildings spewing black smoke into an already sootladen sky. The scene reminded him, if only for its contrast, of the windswept shores of Northumberland where he'd grown up, with the pale green waters of the North Sea as his constant companion.

He smiled at the memory of those far-off days when he'd often stand on the high dunes and watch the frothing rollers crashing onto the rocks below Bamburgh Castle, the sun glinting off the white, wind-tossed crests in the vast expanse of blue. Then he'd lift his eyes and look out beyond the Holy Isle where, as like as not, he'd catch sight of the distant fishing fleet travelling south with the herring. It was during those long-ago summers that he'd realised the sea was in his blood.

His chance had soon come. At the age of eleven, he'd left home to join the colliers tramping between Newcastle and London for a life brutal even by the standards of seamen. He'd been at sea when, a year later, his father had died of the fever, leaving Tom's mother to raise the two youngest children — both girls — on her own.

Now twenty-eight years old, Tom had not been home since. He wrote, of course, and from time to time he'd receive a letter in reply, giving him news of the family and of the boys on the boats and those who worked in the nearby lime pits. They were all men now, those who'd survived. He sometimes found it hard to conjure up their faces: his mother and his sisters and the boys he used to know.

His mother married again after the old man's death but Tom had never met the new husband, nor had he any real desire to do so — not even when his mother had written to tell him that he had a new brother. He'd be eight now.

"Be a man before he knows it . . ." he murmured to himself.

"What's that, Captain?" said the pilot, raising an enquiring eyebrow.

"Nothing." Tom felt a twinge of embarrassment at having been caught daydreaming. "I was just thinking aloud."

"Ah, well, I'll be leaving you now, sir."

"Very well." Tom eased a sodden plug of tobacco to the side of his mouth. "Thank you for your assistance. Mr Simmonds will see you to your gig."

He watched the man clamber over the side and make his way down the companion ladder.

"Are the men ready to be paid off?" Tom asked, as soon as the mate had returned.

"They are that, sir. Ready and waiting," said Simmonds, eyeing a small group of men and boys standing expectantly, abaft the main mast.

"What about the pay of those who were pressed?"

"Each man was paid before he left the barky, sir. All fair and square."

"Very well, you may let the rest go as soon as they've been paid."

CHAPTER
TWO

Two days later, Joseph Boylin heaved his sweating, forty-one-year-old frame onto the upper deck of the *Swansong*. There he stopped, his chest rising and falling, a laboured, hissing wheeze erupting from deep within his throat. He grasped the rail and steadied himself.

"And you are . . .?" asked a voice, close to his ear.

Boylin scrutinised his questioner.

"Who'll it be that's asking, mister?"

"Don't you get clever with me, you Irish bastard. I'm the mate aboard this 'ere barky and nothing moves without I say so."

"The mate, is it? Well fancy that." Boylin tilted his hat to the back of his head and levered his considerable bulk away from the rail. "Since you's asking now, just you be telling the captain that Joseph Michael Boylin will be wanting a word with him."

"You looking for me, Boylin?"

The publican spun round at the sound of the familiar voice and stared, open-mouthed, as though doubting what he saw.

"Will it be Captain Pascoe?" he managed at last.

Tom folded his arms and looked at the man in front of him.

"It's been a long time, Boylin. I heard you were about. Can't say I'm happy to see you, but now you're here you can state your business and leave."

"I carry the scars from the last time we met, Captain," said Boylin, recovering himself. "Three years it's been. I'll not easily forget . . ."

"You were, if I remember aright, sentenced by a court martial." Pascoe's jaw muscles tightened. "You got what you deserved."

"No man deserves two hundred lashes, Captain," said Boylin, surging animosity flooding his brain and choking the words he wanted to scream out loud.

"Your business?" said Tom.

Boylin's breathing quickened and his hand dropped to the hilt of a knife hidden beneath his apron. For one mad second he thought of using it, of evening the score, of plunging the blade deep into Pascoe's heart. It was what he wanted, what he'd dreamed of for so long, but he hesitated, his desire for revenge tempered by a dread of its consequences. He let go of the knife.

"Sure, you'll be wanting your ship unladed," he said.
"And?"

"You're on my patch, Captain. All the ships in this part of the reach are mine to unlade, yours included."

"Your patch?" Tom spat a plug of tobacco over the rail and stared at the mate of the *Swansong*. "Is that right, Mr Simmonds?"

"Well, sir," said Simmonds, shifting his weight from one leg to the other. "All master lumpers have their

12

own stretch of the port for lading and unlading. Can't say as I know this cully, but seems likely he's telling the truth."

"Aye, it's the truth, right enough, Captain. It's me or nobody," said Boylin, a slow smile of satisfaction crossing his despoiled features.

The eastern sky was no more than a glimmer of light in the hour before the dawn when, the following morning, three boats approached the *Swansong* from the direction of the landing stairs at Limehouse Hole.

"About time," muttered Tom. "Mr Simmonds! Make ready to receive the lumping gang if you please. I believe the revenue cutter is also approaching, is it not? Pray make sure the officers have everything they need."

He leaned his hands on the ship's rail and peered down into the gloom of the pre-dawn light, watching the newcomers scramble up the side. One after the other the lumpers, coopers, riggers, and the rest, reached the rail and dropped down into the waist of the barque, their pinched, sallow faces unsmiling, their hands and necks caked in filth, their clothing in tatters.

"A motley crew, Mr Simmonds," said Tom, observing the new arrivals. "I never thought to see such wretches as this in England. It's a wonder to me they have the strength to work. Don't they eat? Or wash?"

"Truth to tell, sir, I ain't given it no thought," said Simmonds. "Most of them is lumpers, and lumpers 'ave always looked the same to me. Irish savages, sir. Don't have nothing to do with 'em. I ain't seen a sober one yet, sir. Ain't surprised mind, not when you consider they work for the likes of that villain, Boylin."

Simmonds paused. "Was you shipmates, sir? You and Boylin? He seemed to know you, when he saw you, like."

Tom nodded. "Aye, we were shipmates. I was his commanding officer when I had the *Minot* — sixteen guns — a few years ago."

"That a fact? He don't seem to like you none, Captain."

"No, I don't suppose he does," said Tom, grinning. "Fractious little foremast jack, he was."

"Pressed man, I'll warrant."

"Aye, and of the worst kind," said Tom, watching the *Swansong*'s lower yards swing round in preparation for unlading the ship. "Got tipped out of Newgate onto a holding hulk and from there to me. I could have done without him. He was trouble from the day he was shipped aboard; hadn't been with us five minutes before he was caught stealing the people's rations. He was lucky not to be tossed overboard. He was charged and brought before me, but he wasn't prepared to accept my award and chose a court martial instead. It cost him two hundred lashes and he was thrown off the ship's books."

"Christ!" exclaimed Simmonds. "The flogging must have damned near killed him."

"He wasn't a pretty sight when they cut him down, that's for certain."

"Still don't look too pretty, do he?" said Simmonds. "What with the scars on his face an' all."

14

"He didn't get that from us," said Tom, rubbing the three-day stubble on his chin. "No, I've a feeling it was quicklime that did that. When I knew him he was a handsome specimen and quite the lady's man."

"Oh, aye?"

"Saw the effects of lime often enough when I was a lad watching the men in the pits," said Tom, more to himself than to Simmonds. "Just a slip of the hand and the stuff would be all over you . . ."

He paused and stared out over the reach. "It's a terrible thing to watch a man burning like that, to hear him scream and watch him try to claw the lime from his skin. I'll warrant there's many a limey-man paid dearly for his lack of attention."

"It don't seem to stop Boylin none," said Simmonds. "Struts about like a crow in the gutter and that's a fact."

"Aye, you're probably right," said Tom. "I've heard his name talked on by some of my fellow captains. Seems our Master Boylin has got himself quite a reputation in these parts. Mark you, I was still surprised to see him. I'd not realised he had a stretch of the port to himself."

He stared out over the Rotherhithe Marsh towards Wapping, then went on, "As for the lime, I reckon he's still working with the stuff. I could smell it on his clothes. Ah, the revenue, at last. Be so good as to see to the officers, Mr Simmonds, if you please."

Tom turned and walked to the ship's rail, thinking about Boylin and remembering the look in his eye: the same look the Irishman had given him three years before when they'd cut him down from the grating. He glanced up at the sound of approaching footsteps.

"If you please, sir." Mr Simmonds touched his forehead. "Unlading is ready to commence."

"Thank you, Mr Simmonds. You may carry on. I'll be in my cabin should you be wanting for anything."

Tom headed for his cabin door. His encounter with Boylin probably meant nothing . . . Suddenly, a loud cracking sound like splintering wood stopped him in his tracks. He spun round, caught a glimpse of a movement below the forecastle break, and saw the outline of two men.

"Mr Simmonds!"

"Aye, sir."

"Bring those confounded men to me at once." Tom squinted into the glare of the sun as the men emerged from the shadows.

"And your name is . . .?" said Tom, staring at the first of the two, a stooped, cadaverous figure in his late thirties, with grime filling the creases of his skin, rimming his deepset, bloodshot eyes.

"Sure my name is Gabriel. Gabriel Newman, your honour. It's the foreman-lumper I am." The voice was sly, ingratiating.

"What were you doing, Newman? You and this fellow with you?"

"Sure we was only looking at yon barrel, Captain. On account of it's stove in."

"Mr Simmonds —" Tom half-turned to the mate. "Be so good as to inspect that hogshead and let me know what you find. And you, sir. Your name, sir."

16

Tom jutted his chin at the squat, bull-necked man standing immediately behind Newman.

"Murphy." The man sniffed and drew a sleeve across a broken nose.

"And what is it you — Yes, Mr Simmonds, what did you find?" said Tom, interrupted by the sight of the returning mate.

"If you please, sir, the barrel appears to have been freshly damaged."

"Thank you, Mr Simmonds. What have you to say about that, Murphy?"

The lumper's eyes hardened and he looked away, saying nothing.

"You heard the captain, mister." The diminutive figure of the mate stepped forward. "Answer this instant or you'll be the sorrier for it."

"Damn your eyes," said Murphy, turning on his heel and heading for the starboard rail. "I answer to no man."

Simmonds lunged forward and caught the lumper's shoulder with his outstretched hand. He got no further. With a speed that belied his bulk, Murphy reached for an adze lying on top of a nearby barrel and aimed it at the mate's head. Simmonds ducked, but it was too late. The razor-like edge of the ship-builders' tool caught him a glancing blow on the left side of his temple, gouging skin and flesh and exposing the white bone of his skull. His eyes widened in surprise as his knees buckled and he sank slowly to the deck.

"One more step and I shoot." Tom's icy tone cut through the ensuing silence, his pistol pointing at Murphy's chest.

"Shoot and be damned, Captain, but be holding your pistol straight, else you're a dead man," said an infuriated Murphy, leaping towards the captain, the adze slashing the air between them. Tom felt the swish of air as the heavy length of steel sang past his face.

Then he pulled the trigger.

CHAPTER
THREE

Gabriel Newman, the foreman-lumper, remained seated until the waterman had brought the small boat to a halt alongside the river stairs. Fear gnawed the pit of his stomach at the thought of what lay ahead. He knew there was no avoiding a meeting with Boylin. The publican would hear about the shooting soon enough. Newman's hands shook as he rose to his feet and climbed out of the wherry.

"Will you be telling Master Boylin I'll be along later?" he said, following the others up the river stairs. He avoided their questioning looks, afraid they'd see through his mask of confidence; recognise the fear behind his bluster. "Sure, I'll not be long."

He waited for the men to walk away, hardly aware of the hammering din from the adjacent shipyard or the shouts and whistles of the river workers coming and going about their business. He thrust his hands deep into his pockets and thought about the questions, the recriminations, the threats he knew would come. As if the Murphy incident was his fault, something he, as foreman-lumper, could have prevented.

But there was nothing he could have done. He kicked at the dust in the alley and watched it carry away on the breeze. Somewhere in the distance a church bell tolled, its monotonous clanging an echo of Newman's despondent mood. He wanted no part of this, of Captain Pascoe, of Boylin, of Murphy's shooting.

He ambled along Limehouse, unsure of where he was going or why except that each step brought him closer to Boylin. In Narrow Street, he came to an alehouse he'd not been to before and went in. He found himself a seat over-looking the river and sat there for some minutes, unable to move. It was as though a heavy weight was bearing down on him, depressing his spirit and sapping his strength. There seemed no way of extricating himself from Boylin's grasp: his own existence dependent on the publican's whim, his life a downward spiral of hopeless despair.

The pot-boy set down his beer and left without a glance.

They'd grown up together, he and Boylin, boys from the same village, within sight of the Wicklow Mountains. Even then they'd not been close. While the older youth had, from time to time, shown signs of friendliness and even charm to those with whom he came into contact, these periods of comparative ease had never lasted and those around Boylin did his bidding out of fear rather than friendship.

Newman had never given those days any thought. At least not then. It was just the way things were. And when the others drifted away he'd remained faithful to Boylin, choosing the path of acquiescence over the dangers of confrontation: a decision he'd come to regret bitterly.

He stared at the table, tracing a path through a puddle of spilt beer with his forefinger. It was Boylin who had persuaded him to join the cause of republicanism, to take up the pike and the scythe in a murderous assault on the British — and many of his fellow countrymen. Too late had he regretted the destruction they had inflicted in the name of a free Ireland, his involvement shaping the course of his life ever since.

Within weeks of their joining the United Irishmen's cause, Boylin had seen fit to draw a blade across the throat of a drunken militiaman they'd found lying at the roadside. Frightened as never before, Newman and his young brother, Jacob, had followed the fleeing Boylin to England.

Within a year, Boylin had been caught stealing and committed to Newgate, from where he'd found himself unceremoniously pressed into the service of His Majesty aboard a man-of-war. His absence at sea had coincided with a period of comparative calm in Newman's life that was not, alas, destined to last. Expelled from the Navy, Boylin had returned to his old stamping ground in and around Wapping and Shadwell and quickly reverted to his violent ways. One day, in a fight with another man, he'd slipped and fallen into a lime pit.

Newman closed his eyes. He could still hear Boylin's screams, still see him clawing at the dripping, smoking mess trickling down his face, burning through the flesh

21

of his cheek and his lips, eating the membrane of his eye. He'd heard people claim that Boylin's violence had become worse, his republicanism more entrenched since that day, but he doubted that. Boylin had always been violent, always enjoyed the sight of fear in another man's eyes. He'd probably seen it several months later when he caught the man with whom he'd fought. He'd beaten his adversary senseless, before rubbing slaked lime into his eyes, and watched as the unfortunate creature called on the Almighty for his deliverance.

Then he'd strangled him.

In the years that followed, Boylin's merciless reign of terror had spread his power and influence throughout Wapping and Shadwell, as far as Ratcliff to the east and London Bridge to the west. Few dared to stand in his way, and those that did quickly learned to regret their defiance; their bodies washed ashore off Cuckold Point or, further south, amongst the ships of the King's fleet at Deptford.

Outside the alehouse window, a seagull flapped its wings, cried, and soared aloft. The strident call startled Newman. He watched the bird for a moment before picking up his beer mug and draining the contents. He couldn't put off meeting Boylin forever.

It was late afternoon on the same day by the time Tom Pascoe strode through the iron gates of the London Hospital and headed towards the western end of the building. Rounding the corner, he descended a flight of stone steps and entered a large, rectangular room, brightly lit by a row of windows that occupied the whole of one wall. On the opposite wall, several doors led to smaller rooms, each of which bore a label indicating its purpose: Surgeon's Consulting Room said one, Physician's Consulting Room announced another, Inquest and Surgeon's Room noted a third. A wooden bench ran round the other three sides of the main area and on this sat fifty or sixty people staring vacantly into space or resting their heads against the wall, apparently asleep. Others squatted or lay sprawled on the stone floor or on makeshift stretchers. Still more wandered about as if movement would hurry the moment of their release, anxiously looking about for some sign that their concerns had been noted.

Tom stopped in the doorway and let his nostrils adjust to the smells of the sick and the dying, his ears oddly alert to the sounds of physical pain that came towards him in unseen waves. He swallowed hard and forced back the nausea rising in his throat as he searched for his injured shipmate. Catching sight of him lying on a stretcher on the floor in the centre of the room, he hurried over. Simmonds opened his eyes.

"How goes it, Mr Simmonds?" Tom squatted beside him, doing his best to sound cheerful. The greyish-white skin of the mate's brow was all but hidden beneath a swathe of bloodied bandage.

Simmonds blinked but said nothing. Tom glanced at the nearest consulting room. It was empty, as was the second. In the third, two men were examining a patient. He got to his feet and was about to interrupt when he heard the older of the two men speaking.

". . . you will observe, sir, the object's extreme debility, his pale complexion and the bloated and spongy nature of his gums. There's no doubt, sir, the fellow's got scurvy." The speaker paused and gestured towards the patient's bare torso. "See here, the livid spots on the skin and the foul ulcers from which he suffers . . ."

Tom turned away and looked for someone else who might help. In the far corner a nurse was binding a child's arm; the youngster's terrified cries unsettling. He waited until the nurse had finished and then made his way over to her.

"Miss . . .?"

She turned towards him with an enquiring look. She was, he supposed, about twenty-two years of age, slim and of medium height with a pale, oval-shaped face and raven-black hair that was now almost completely hidden below a white cotton mobcap.

"My friend over there is in need of help." Tom gestured towards the injured Simmonds and then looked back at the nurse. A wisp of hair dropped from under her cap and he watched her push it away with the back of a bloodstained hand.

"Your friend was examined this morning by the assistant surgeon." She smiled at him, her tone gentle but firm. "He's to be received into the house as an accident case."

"Thankee! I was —"

"Don't worry too much about your friend," she said. "He's in good hands. The assistant surgeon has already referred his case to Mr Blizard."

"Who?" said Tom.

"Why, Mr Blizard!" She sounded surprised. "The gentleman over there. Surely you've heard of him."

Tom felt absurdly confused. He looked furtively in the direction she was indicating, at the man he'd overheard a moment or so ago. "No, I regret I have not."

"Well, no matter. Mr Blizard has given instructions that he'll see your friend tomorrow, when he performs his rounds. There's no cause for immediate concern. I regret . . ." She paused before continuing. "I regret the same cannot be said for your other friend, the one who was brought in at the same time. He is not expected to live."

"Murphy?" said Tom. He'd forgotten all about the lumper.

"Yes, Mr Murphy." She smiled again, a small, polite smile signalling the end of their conversation. She turned to leave.

"Miss."

"Yes?"

"May I see him tomorrow? My shipmate, I mean. After the surgeon has made his examination, Miss . . . er —?" He was unusually hesitant.

"Tompkins. I am Miss Tompkins," she said. "As to whether you may see your friend, that is a question for matron, but I daresay if he has recovered sufficiently by tomorrow or the day after, then you may see him at any hour before seven o'clock of the evening."

Her manner did not invite further dialogue and, in truth, he'd not the appetite for it. He watched her walk away, her graceful movements a vivid contrast to the sick and injured patients with whom she dealt. Then he turned and looked at Simmonds. The mate appeared to be sleeping. He sat down on one of the benches, suddenly tired.

"By your leave, sir." Tom's eyes snapped open. Nurse Tompkins was standing in front of him. He must have dozed off. "The porters are here to take your friend to the ward. Perhaps you would like to return tomorrow or the next day to see him. For the moment there is nothing for you to do."

Tom glanced at the retreating porters, Simmonds' stretcher between them.

"Thankee, Miss, but should you have no objection, I shall accompany my shipmate to the ward," said Tom, getting to his feet.

"I regret it extremely, sir, but —"

"I'll not be long," said Tom, smiling as he headed for the door through which the porters had passed. He checked his pocket watch. It was just after eight. He'd already been away from the *Swansong* for longer than he'd intended and time was pressing. Soon, the two customs officers on board would leave for the night. He paused at the entrance to the surgical ward and considered the risk.

Then he pushed open the door and went in. He'd be back in good time.

In the cellar of the Queen's Head, Joseph Boylin sat on a low stool, his head resting in his hands. So Tom Pascoe was back . . . He felt a rush of anger, the skin of his back beginning to itch. Three years had passed since he'd last set eyes on his old captain, the memory of what had happened seared into his mind as if with a branding iron.

He saw himself back on the upper deck of the frigate, strapped to the grating, a leather wad jammed between his teeth. He could hear the sharp bark of orders, the roll of drums, the muted coughing of the men drawn up to witness his punishment. He felt the first stinging lash touch his skin, winding its way round his naked torso. Then came another and another . . . He clenched his fist, each stroke, each fiery lick shredding the skin of his back, leaving it hanging and bloody, like ribbons soaked in wine. And with each downward sweep, the exquisite pain coursed through his body, to meet at a single point within his brain.

He put his fingers to his ears, trying to blot out the grunts of the bo'sun's mates and the faint whistling that preceded each savage blow. In those infinitesimal moments of time, his body had arched and stiffened — and waited. He had tried to number the blows; reached seventy before losing count, his eyes blinded by the salt of his sweat, his mouth dry, his tongue swollen, and his fingernails driven deep into the palms of his fists.

And into his head came a single name, a name he'd never forget.

Boylin stared into the dark shadows of the cellar, his fingers clawing the edge of a barrel, his whole body shaking. He'd all but died under that rain of blows, his health and his strength broken. Now he sat chewing the knuckles of his hand, the germ of an idea forming in his

27

anguished mind. For a while longer he considered the matter. Yes, it could be done, he could even the score with Pascoe — if he but had the courage. He hesitated. Much as he loathed the captain, he wasn't blind to the man's ruthless streak, his willingness to meet violence on its own terms, to enforce his own vision of the truth.

Boylin stared into the gloom, a vision of his Nemesis before him. Slowly his hand fell away from his mouth. There might still be a way. He mounted the steps from the cellar, his heavy breathing keeping time with the clump of his boots on the wooden treads. At the top, he opened the door and entered the taproom at the precise moment Gabriel Newman came in through the street door.

"It's a word I'll be wanting with you, mister," said Boylin.

The sun was sinking fast over the distant spires of the City as Tom Pascoe left the London Hospital. He glanced up and down an almost deserted Whitechapel road, stepping back into the gateway as a funeral procession passed by, the tiny group of mourners led by black-cloaked pallbearers carrying sprigs of rosemary. The sight reminded him of the countless deaths he'd witnessed over the years, of shipmates whose existence had been cut short by war, of the seeming pointlessness of their lives and the terror of their last moments.

He turned away, his sudden movement catching unawares a sallow-faced youth of around eighteen who seemed to have been waiting for him but who now darted out of sight down the side of a building opposite. Tom waited a second or two for him to reappear and then walked on, turning left into New Road and left again into the broad thoroughfare of the Ratcliff Highway.

It was packed as usual, the heavy press of people weaving between the barrows and stalls that populated the centre of the carriageway. Some gathered to gawp at dancing bears, others stood idle outside a score of drinking houses, talking to one another out of the corners of their mouths, their hands in their pockets, their darting eyes scouring the street as hungry dogs might hunt for a bone.

Tom trod warily. He knew all too well how brittle was the peace, how easily it could be broken. The counterfeit laughter and forced jollity did nothing to hide the brooding and pervasive fear, the infectious loathing that each man seemed to harbour for his fellows in this dismal street of cheap shops and cheaper brothels. He dropped behind a noisy group of sailors and followed them as they crossed to the south side of the carriageway, their discordant voices crooning a line or two of some sea shanty that ought to have been familiar to him but was not.

He left them and turned into Fox's Lane, a long, straight passageway leading directly to the Thames. It was a narrow place, not more than eight feet wide, its narrowness accentuated by the tall buildings on either side that appeared to meet high above his head, dimming the last of the evening light. Here and there women sat on stools washing clothes, their voices deep-throated and guttural, their long, unkempt hair shining with an over-abundance of grease, their faces pitted with open sores or marked with the bluish-black of healing bruises. Most had dispensed with their gowns and sat in sweat-stained underclothes, their half-laced stays as black and as filthy as the adjacent door-posts. Around them, oblivious to the settling flies and the nauseating reek of putrid effluvia rising from the open cesspits of the houses, small children played barefoot, their rickety limbs eloquent testimony to the sordid quality of their lives. The women stopped talking as he approached and watched him with sullen, mistrustful eyes as he passed by.

A creature, more dead than alive, her clothes ragged, her smell offensive, lurched into his path and would have fallen against him had he not reached out and steadied her. Tom smiled, gently disentangling himself as she mumbled her thanks, looking up at him from under a blue shawl drawn tightly about her head. She was little more than a child, her cheeks stained from the tears that flowed down her face. She returned his smile, an empty, lifeless grin that was the mark of her profession and then, seeing no hope of work, was gone, the sound of her hacking cough receding into the distance.

Tom watched her go before resuming his way, his thoughts on the morning's events. The lumper, Murphy, had died. That meant an inquest. His stomach gave an unpleasant lurch. There was no telling where that might end.

Suddenly he was aware of the sound of running feet drumming on the hard-packed earth of the alley, close behind him. He tensed and stepped aside, his hand sliding to his sword-hilt. A youth rushed by, his shoulders hunched. Tom thought he saw him glance towards the door of the Three Foxes tavern as though to some unseen person. There was something familiar about the boy. It was the same youth he'd seen loitering outside the London Hospital only a short while before.

He drew level with the front door of the tavern and stared into the gloom, his heartbeat quickening. A cat emerged from the shadows, its extended paw scratching amidst some discarded waste, its bones protruding through an emaciated frame, its tail twitching. Tom glanced at it and let his hand fall to his side. His imagination had got the better of him. The boy had gone, disappeared into an alleyway.

Tom relaxed.

Then the blow struck him in the small of the back.

He arched backwards, riding the punch. Another blow, this time to his neck. He stumbled and pitched forward, his fingers groping wildly for his sword. He yanked at it as a third blow struck the back of his skull. In the split second before the blackness of insensibility descended, he caught the acrid stench of lime.

CHAPTER
FOUR

At the London Hospital, Peggy Tompkins watched the course of Simmonds' fever with some alarm. She looked round, thought for a moment of asking the opinion of her fellow nurse on the ward, and then changed her mind. Charity Squibb was not the sort of person one asked for advice in the medical line. In fact, thought Peggy, she was not the sort of person to ask about anything. She watched despairingly as her room-mate stood talking to a newly arrived patient, the palm of her hand held out in front of her. It wasn't the first time she'd demanded money from the patients and withheld food and care from those that would not or could not oblige. Peggy was reminded of a comment she'd once overheard describing her fellow nurses as too drunk, too dirty, too stolid and too bad to do anything else.

She bent down and laid her hand on her patient's pallid forehead as his head thrashed from side to side, sweat running down his cheeks and onto his neck. The skin felt hot to her touch.

"Miss Squibb," she called out, her voice betraying rising panic, "I should be obliged to you was you to call Mr Blizard. He is, I believe, the duty surgeon. Ask him to come directly, if he's at leisure. I fear for the condition of this object."

Five minutes later Peggy heard the sound of running feet in the corridor outside the ward, quickly followed by a scrum of young men bursting through the door, each one seemingly intent on being first into the room. The leading youth wavered, saw Peggy and trotted towards her, closely followed by the others. Behind them, and occupying the places of honour on either side of the tall, austere figure of the principal surgeon, came the dressers, each carrying an instrument case as though it were a mark of their importance. This second group now also advanced to where Peggy stood by the bed of the unsuspecting Simmonds.

"What, pray, seems to be the trouble?" William Blizard's tone was severe at the best of times.

"This object, sir, is in a state of stupor and showing signs of distress," said Peggy. "I've applied a cold compress to his forehead but the fever is not reduced. And I find that while his left pupil is enlarged, the right one is constricted."

"Thank you," said Blizard, cocking a surprised eyebrow. "Mr Snodgrass, I would be grateful to you, sir, was you to avoid murdering my patient before I have examined the nature of his discomfort. Get off his stomach, man. Right, gentlemen . . ."

The group squeezed itself into a tight knot round the bed, leaving a discomfited Peggy with no room to escape. Hardly daring to breathe, she stole a glance at the black-clad figure of authority standing beside her. He seemed not to have noticed her as he cradled

Simmonds' head in both hands, his fingers probing the frontal and temporal areas of the skull. At last, he straightened his back and stood looking thoughtfully at his unconscious patient.

"I suspect that the object's cranium may be fractured," he said, addressing the group. "I cannot be certain until I've scalped the lid but you are to observe that the removal of the skin will allow me to better judge the matter. If it is as I suspect, it will be necessary to trephine the skull in order to relieve the pressure. Pray observe the patient is presently without his senses, which is to our advantage as it will be to his, poor devil. I shall therefore cut him presently. Perhaps if any of you is at leisure, you might like to draw the curtains and hold the object steady."

There was a scramble as many a willing hand caught the insensible Simmonds, holding his head in a vice-like grip while others pinioned his arms and sat him upright on a chair.

Removing his coat, Blizard rolled up the sleeves of his loose-fitting silk shirt and turned towards his instrument case. "I'll have the —"

His eyes widened a fraction as he saw his mother-of-pearl-handled scalpel being offered to him by a female hand.

"Are we ready, gentlemen?" He glanced up at the expectant faces and then, placing the blade of the scalpel at a point well forward of the patient's right ear, he brought it, in one swift movement, round the back of the head to the nape of the neck and back up over the opposite ear. The incision completed, he drew the scalp over the top of the skull and down in front of Simmonds' face, exposing the bone.

"Mr Snodgrass, be so good as to wash my scalpel and see to it that it is dried proper before returning it to its case." Blizard was now wholly absorbed in his work. He examined the wound carefully. "There you have it, gentlemen. Mr Miles, perhaps you could tell us what we are looking at and its meaning?"

Mr Miles looked uncomfortable. "I . . . I'm not sure, sir."

"I sometimes wonder, sir, why you trouble to attend my rounds," said Blizard. "Gentlemen, in cases where a fracture of the skull has occurred, blood leaks out under the scalp producing a large, boggy swelling and, as in this case, discoloration in the temporal area. It is an excellent aid to your diagnosis. I suggest you remember it."

Blizard looked round the group. "What treatment does that suggest to you, Mr Kirby?"

"A trephine, sir?"

"Quite right, Mr Kirby," said Blizard. "I'm glad someone was listening. Perhaps —"

Once more, Peggy had anticipated his requirement and held out the required instrument.

"Should you be ready, gentlemen," said Blizard, a look of faint surprise still evident in his arched eyebrows, "I shall begin the next stage of this procedure."

Gently and very carefully, he placed the locating pin of the trephine directly over the discoloured bone. Then, drawing a deep breath, he began turning the handle at the side of the instrument, driving a circular metal saw down through the skull. A slight movement warned him that Simmonds was regaining consciousness.

"Be sure to hold the object's head still, gentlemen." Blizard's injunction was evenly delivered, conversational. "I should be sorry to lose him at this stage. There! It is done!"

The surgeon straightened his back and rolled his shoulders. "Now, gentlemen, you see that the dura mater is sound and the pressure caused by the haematoma is relieved. The dressers will now remove any fragments of bone from the skull, after which they will pack the incision and replace the scalp. I will visit him again tomorrow, when I fully expect the object's pupils to equalise and respond to light."

As the group prepared to leave, Peggy caught Blizard's eye. He nodded, one eyebrow slightly raised. Peggy could have sworn she saw the glimmer of a smile. She flushed with pleasure and looked down to where Simmonds was lying and was reminded of the man who had brought him to the hospital. She wondered what he was doing at this particular moment.

Tom Pascoe awoke to a strange bed and a blinding headache. Slowly, reluctantly, he opened first one eye and then the other, and stared blankly at the ceiling. Immediately above his head was a pair of damp wool stockings and some equally damp breeches suspended from a rope, the smell suggesting it was unlikely that either had actually been washed in recent months. He turned his head towards a small window; several of its glass panes were missing and the gaps were stuffed with rags and scraps of brownish newspaper. Outside, a fine drizzle was falling.

A chair creaked. Tom raised his head and looked in the direction of the sound. A slim-built man, perhaps in his middle twenties, was sitting by the door watching him, his hands folded in his lap.

"Where am I?" said Tom, groping for his pistol.

"Which you is in Shadwell — and if it's your gun you're after, it's on the floor by your side. I reckoned it were less likely to blow your toes off there."

Tom nodded his thanks and let his head sink back onto the hard mattress. If he was still in Shadwell, he'd not been taken very far, a street or two at most. He looked back at the man. There was something familiar about his olive complexion and the large ears that seemed to dwarf his elf-like face.

"Have I not seen you before?" he asked.

"Aye, you might've done," said the man. Tom couldn't place his accent. Eastern European perhaps. "I were aboard the *Swansong*, a day since."

Now Tom remembered. "So you work for Master Boylin?"

"I am but a seller of old clothes, sir. I know nothing of the men who unlade the ships."

"Well, no matter," said Tom, gingerly prodding the back of his head with his fingertips. "I remember I was set upon but little else."

"Aye, you was fair knocked about," said the man. "If I make no mistake, they meant to do for you. Must've heard me and some others coming 'cause they cleared off pretty damn quick."

Tom checked for his pocketbook. It was still there.

"Did anyone see who they were?" he asked.

"That's no question for these parts. Not if you wants the truth, like."

Tom rolled onto his side. He understood the culture of silence, the wall of obduracy that met any question delving into the affairs of others. It was nothing personal: he was a stranger to the area, an outsider. He squinted out through the mud-spattered window. The light drizzle had turned to a steady downpour, creating a gurgling stream that was carrying away the detritus which had gathered in the alley since it last rained. A few hazy outlines scurried past, looking for cover. Suddenly, he remembered the ship he'd left the previous day.

"I must go," he said, struggling up on his elbow. "Be so good as to point me in the direction of the tideway and I'll be on my way."

"You'll not arrive unaided, sir," said the man. "I'll see you safely into a sculler and then you is on your own, if that suits."

Twenty minutes later the two men reached Pelican Stairs on Wapping Wall and made their way down the slime-covered steps onto the Thames foreshore.

"I don't know how I'm to repay your kindness, my friend," said Tom, picking his way through the mud, "but, pray, be so good as to tell me your name. If the occasion should arise, I should very much like to return the service."

"My name, sir, is Samuel Hart," said the man, inclining his head.

"Well, Samuel Hart," said Tom, "I thank you from the bottom of my heart and, if God so wills, we will meet again in happier circumstances."

He turned and gazed out over the river at the hundreds of small boats and ships littering the Pool. He was looking forward to feeling the *Swansong*'s deck below his feet when a small rowing boat, one of a dozen, caught his attention, perhaps a hundred yards away. He looked at it for a moment, its detail shrouded by the mist of rain. The figure in the stern sheets seemed familiar.

"That skiff . . ." Tom pointed.

"What skiff is that, your honour?" said Hart, shielding his eyes and following Tom's finger.

"'Tis naught," said Tom, as the boat disappeared amongst the scores of other craft, "I thought I recognised someone. I make no doubt I was mistaken."

"I regret I saw nothing," said Hart. "Shall I call a wherry for you?"

"Aye, thankee." Tom continued to stare down the reach. He was certain he'd not been mistaken. He wondered what had brought Boylin onto the Thames at this hour of the morning.

CHAPTER
FIVE

Something was amiss. Nothing Tom could put his finger on. Just a vague sense of unease that grew more pronounced the nearer he got to the *Swansong*. Fetching alongside the starboard companionway, Tom ran up the side.

At the top, his eye was met by a scene of devastation. He stopped and looked round in shocked silence. The scrubbed decks of yesterday were now a sickly trail of trampled molasses leading forward to the fo'c'sle. Down the middle of the deck, the hatch gratings and tarpaulin covers that should have been protecting the cargo from the elements had been torn away and lay in an untidy heap in the larboard scuppers. He looked aft and saw the door to his own cabin, sheltered beneath the break of the poop, now smashed and hanging at a drunken angle.

The rain had stopped and patches of blue appeared in the sky just as the first sparks of anger ignited inside him. His head throbbing, he climbed over the rail and picked his way through the debris, stopping by the main hatch to look down into the hold. It was too dark to see if anything had been disturbed and he moved on, his mind refusing to accept the evidence around him.

Ducking under the fo'c'sle break, he descended to the darkened main deck. Nothing seemed to have been touched here, or in the crew's quarters below. He wasn't surprised. There had been nothing left to steal — not since the crew had been discharged, and perhaps not before that either.

He climbed down the vertical ladder into the hold, his way lit by the glancing rays of the early morning sun filtering through the open hatches. On the orlop, several hogsheads had been smashed, their contents strewn about the ceiling boards.

Suddenly, he heard a dull thud.

He whirled round. The sound, as of something or someone falling against a bulkhead, had come from aft. He stood still, his ears straining to hear more, but there was nothing except the gentle whispers he knew so well — the creak of timber and the slapping of water against the hull.

Then he heard it again . . . the same dull thud.

He raced up the ladder and ran along the main deck, checking each of the officers' cabins as he went, ducking his head beneath the low beams. Reaching his own cabin at the end of the passageway, he drew his sea service pistol and thumbed back the hammer. Cautiously, he pushed open the door and stepped inside.

The floor was a carpet of smashed crockery, torn papers and items of broken furniture. To starboard, the door of his sleeping cabin had been kicked in, leaving a gaping hole in its lower panel. Below the great window at the stern of the ship, the long, velvet cushion covering the lockers had been ripped apart and the stuffing scattered about the deck. His mahogany desk lay on its side. He bent down and righted it, wiping the polished surface with the sleeve of his coat. It was as though an old friend had been wounded.

He lowered the hammer of his pistol. The noise must have been a barrel falling over. He stared out through the great window, to the majestic sweep of the Thames where Limehouse Reach ended and the Pool began, the rays of the morning sun sparkling on the surface of the water, the roar of the port no more than a distant rumble in his mind.

"Why, why, why?" he shouted at the empty cabin, pounding the upturned desk with his fist.

Another thud. This time from the pantry behind him. Tom raised his pistol and crept towards the narrow door on the larboard side of the cabin, his finger on the trigger. From the other side, came a faint scraping sound, as of a boot on the decking. He pulled back the hammer and lifted his hand to the door.

At that same moment Joseph Boylin was clutching at the skiff's gunwale as he prepared to disembark. He didn't much care for boats, and the smaller they were, the less he cared for them. Strange, he thought, given the frequency with which he used them. Gingerly, he reached for the tall mooring post at the foot of Shadwell Dock Stairs and hauled himself ashore.

"Get rid of the boat, Gabriel, and be quick about it," said Boylin. "I don't want nobody connecting it with us."

He watched Gabriel Newman climb ashore and shove the skiff out into the ebb tide. The night's work had taken longer than he'd planned. They should have finished well before daybreak, before the risk of detection increased. He turned at the sound of footsteps in the passage behind him. A man was walking towards them from the street. Boylin cursed his luck. There was no way of avoiding him. Today of all days he didn't want to be seen, didn't want anyone putting him at the riverside. Not after what had happened during the night. He wished he'd followed the others and gone ashore at Limehouse.

He wiped away the sweat from his forehead. The man was getting closer. Boylin bent his head and pulled his hat down over his eyes. The stranger appeared not to have seen them yet, seemed deep in thought. With luck, he'd pass before he noticed their presence. By then they'd be safe, lost in the crowds of Lower Shadwell.

Boylin risked a backward glance at the drifting skiff. It hadn't gone far enough. If the newcomer looked up now he'd see it and guess who'd cut it loose. He'd remember them, be able to identify them.

Boylin felt dizzy with fear. He peeped out from under the rim of his hat. The young man — the fellow couldn't be more than about eighteen — was staring in his direction. Boylin ducked his head and kept his hand in front of his face. The youth brushed past him. Boylin held his breath.

"Will it be Master Boylin?" The voice sliced through the publican's brain like a spear. "God be with you, now."

Boylin turned to face the youth, his hand reaching under his apron, his fingers clutching at the hilt of his knife.

Tom didn't see him at first. He stared into the pantry, his back pressed flat against the bulkhead to one side of the doorway, and waited for his eyes to become accustomed to the gloom. Gradually, he was able to make out a shape in the far corner of the cabin: an elderly man was sitting on the deck, his back propped against some shelving, an empty bottle of rum grasped to his bosom. Tom lowered the gun. He'd forgotten about the night watchman. And Denny, too. He'd forgotten his old cook. An irrational dread gripped him.

"Where's my cook?" Tom bent down and shook the old man's shoulder.

Startled, the watchman looked about him, his eyes red with sleep and drink.

"I said —" repeated Tom.

"I know what you said, young 'un." The old man's speech was hardly intelligible. "I reckon every ship in the fleet heard you."

"Well?"

"As I recall . . ." The watchman bent forward, his watery eyes seeming to focus on a point midway up Tom's chest. He blinked and tried again, his hand clinging onto the after bulkhead as he struggled to his feet. "As I recall, he turned in for the night. That were the last I seen of him."

"Where? Where did you see him?"

"Don't know." The man's eyes dropped to the empty bottle in his hand. He seemed surprised by its presence, held it up for closer inspection, and then let his arm drop. "Anygate, about the time we turned in, I hears somebody's topside. It weren't Denny, as I know of."

"What did you do?"

"Do?" whined the old man defensively. "I didn't do nothing. What d'you expect me to do?"

"You stayed here?" asked Tom in an incredulous tone. "You didn't go on deck and discover who was there or the nature of their business? What d'you think you're paid for, you scallywag?"

"I'm not a young man no more," said the watchman. "If I'd showed me face, they would have done for me, like."

Tom lunged forward, his face close to the elderly, rum-soaked waste of humanity. "Like what?"

The watchman raised an elbow above his head, the anger in Tom's voice seeming to act like a douse of cold water on the sagging skin of his face. Then his legs gave way and he sank to the deck, his back sliding down against the bulk-head, the empty rum bottle still grasped in his liver-spotted hand.

"It were terrible to hear him." Tom had to squat to catch the whispered sentence, the fury leaving him as quickly as it had arrived. Watching the old man rock back and forth, he understood his fear. It was not unknown for men to kill rather than let a witness live to give evidence against them.

"Who? Who was it terrible to hear?"

"Old Will Denny," said the watchman. "It were after I heard the men come up the side. It were then I heard him. There were a noise, like something being dragged past this 'ere door. I waited but all I hears is some shouting and then a splash. I can't be certain on it, like, but that's the way it sounded to me."

Tom left the old man and walked out into the sunlight, a mood of anger, frustration and fear enveloping him. Had the splash been the sound of Denny being thrown into the Thames? It made no sense. Why kill him? Denny could not have identified the men. Not in the darkness. Unless ... Tom remembered the skiff he'd seen a short while ago and the figure sitting in the stern. His concerns deepened.

With an effort, he thought again of the watchman he'd just left behind in the storeroom, clutching a bottle as others might clutch a talisman, a shield against the terrors of life. He regretted his outburst, his lack of self-control. Fear of what had happened to Denny, combined with exhaustion and a sense of helplessness, had all contributed. But that was no excuse for what he'd done, and didn't make it any easier for him to bear the guilt.

He fished a wad of tobacco from his coat pocket and bit off a chunk, feeling the pleasant, numbing sensation spread across his tongue. He wondered if his reaction was the inevitable consequence of a violent career, the years in which he'd seen enough death, destruction and human misery to last him all the days of his life. That was the nature of war. But was it possible that, even now, it continued to affect the way he behaved towards his fellow man? Tom tried to banish the thought from his mind. Of what use was it to contemplate the past unless it was to better prepare him for the future? He had known men who'd dwelt too long on the horrors of their profession and suffered in consequence. No, he had learned to sweep away all feelings of pity or emotion for those whose bodies and minds had been crushed in battle. He didn't believe it had affected him. Not then. But since?

Certainly his life had changed after he'd been put ashore by their Lordships of the Admiralty and been compelled for want of a living to take up command of a merchantman. Then, when a sail on a distant horizon had meant something to be avoided rather than chased, there had been time to ponder on the shipmates whose lives had been thrown aside, forgotten, disposed of. Perhaps he had not, after all, been as unmoved by his brutal past as he had thought.

He gazed reflectively into the limpid, grey-brown waters of the Thames. A light, south-westerly breeze ruffled the surface of the river. Instinctively he glanced up into the rigging, his hand gripping the mizzen shroud, gauging its tension. He let go at once. He knew what he'd touched.

It was blood.

Boylin's heart raced. He looked at the smiling young man's outstretched hand. For all the world it seemed to beckon him to the gallows. He struggled to breathe, as though the rope were already about his neck. He looked up. He knew the boy; had known his family back home in Ireland. The youth's eyes shifted to Newman and then back to Boylin, his smile fading.

Boylin's fingers closed round the handle of his knife, sweat running down his neck. He was trapped. God damn the boy, why was he here? Why him? For a brief moment he regretted what had to be done but the mood passed as quickly as it had come. The blade jumped free of its hidden place and was thrust upwards into the boy's gut as Boylin's lips drew back in a snarl of released emotion, the obstacle to his happiness removed. He saw the youth's eyes widen in astonishment, his mouth open in a silent scream, then watched him crumple to the ground, a soft rattle coming from within his twitching body.

Boylin dropped to one knee and touched the boy's shoulder, remorse overcoming him. The lad's head slumped to one side, the rattle ceased.

Someone was tugging at Boylin's elbow. He climbed unsteadily to his feet, and turned to see Newman staring up the alley. A man was standing not thirty yards away, at the junction with Lower Shadwell. He was looking up and down the main street, some baskets at his feet.

"Jesus, Mary and Joseph, will he have seen us?" said Boylin.

"Don't know," said Newman. "He might've done."

"Will you be knowing him at all?"

"No." A pause, then, "I'll not be certain. I might have seen him afore."

A fresh trickle of sweat coursed down Boylin's face. His nightmare wasn't over.

Sam Hart glanced down into the alley and hefted the baskets onto his shoulder. He should have been selling clothes an hour ago and would have been, had he not become involved in helping Tom Pascoe.

He clucked his tongue. He hadn't known the captain of the *Swansong*, except by sight and then only briefly. He hadn't even meant to be out at that time of the evening, the time of day when the mood changed and became altogether more threatening. He remembered turning off the Ratcliff Highway and hurrying down Fox's Lane towards the Thames, his progress accompanied by the voices of the unseen, echoing from the ramshackle walls of the houses; that, and the stench of rotting waste, rising mist-like in the half light.

At one point, he thought he'd seen a familiar face approaching, a woman in a dirty blue shawl, and his heart had leapt with hope, but she'd disappeared from his sight before he could be sure. He had thought of her then, his heart aching with the uncertainty of what might have happened. He'd forced himself to move on. One day he'd know the truth.

It was shortly after that he'd seen the man lying in the dirt and recognised him as the captain of the *Swansong*. It was probably the reason he'd chosen to help — the tenuous link with the past, a previous encounter, however short. He shook his head in disbelief. On such pretexts does the human mind decide to act. Sam smiled to himself. He realised he couldn't have ignored the captain's plight, even if he'd wanted to.

Now he looked down Lower Shadwell, where whirls of black smoke from the chimneys of the glue factories reduced the gaunt figures hurrying past him to an ill-defined grey. He began to move off, glancing down the alley to his right as he went. Two men were crouched over something. He couldn't see what. He turned away. It was none of his business.

And anyway, he was late.

CHAPTER
SIX

Tom sat in a worn but comfortable leather armchair in the first-floor chambers of Crown Office Row while he waited for the attorney to finish what he was doing. Outside, a soft breeze ruffled the leaves of the plane trees lining the borders of Temple Gardens, their swaying boughs partially obscuring his view of a sunlit Thames. Now and again a barge would drift by on the flood tide and he would hear the cry of the lighterman manoeuvring his heavy charge into the timber yards of Christchurch and Lambeth.

He sighed and looked round. The cramped and dusty oak-panelled room in which he was sitting was stacked high with bundles of papers tied with faded pink or discoloured white ribbon, jostling for space with wooden boxes of various sizes, as well as pens, inkwells and sundry other objects. In the middle of this crowded space was a cluster of desks, behind one of which sat a short, rotund man with a balding pate, whose eyes peered out from behind a pair of iron-rimmed spectacles.

John Formby, attorney-at-law, replaced the quill he had been using, and summoned Tom's attention. He was less than optimistic about the prospects of his client.

"You are to consider," said the lawyer, polishing the lens of his glasses with a bright red handkerchief, "that the unfortunate death of this man, Murphy, puts us in an invidious position. You are to consider, sir, that the coroner has the power to commit you to stand your trial. I have to say it is not a path I would relish travelling if I were in your shoes. Indeed, were you to ask my professional opinion, sir, I would say it is of the first importance that we nip this matter in the bud."

Tom stared at the attorney, aware for the first time that he was entering a world about which he knew little. He'd shot Murphy in self defence, yet ahead of him loomed the prospect of a criminal trial which might result in his own life becoming forfeit. He knew he should not have been surprised. The Shadwell magistrate had warned him to expect as much when he'd attended aboard the *Swansong* in the wake of the shooting.

"But I was quite forgetting." Formby pursed his moist lips. "We must first decide whether you are to be represented at all."

"Pray, what do you mean?" said Tom.

"Well, sir, in the first place it is unusual for counsel to appear at a criminal trial, let alone at a coroner's inquest. You must weigh in your mind the benefit of having your case put in the most advantageous way against the loss of goodwill that is likely to result from your representation by someone like me."

"What possible loss of goodwill can result from such representation?" asked Tom.

"I grant it must make little sense to you," replied Formby with the briefest of smiles. "Let me start by saying I do not know the coroner before whom you are to appear. What I say therefore is not to be taken as necessarily referring to this particular coroner, but as a general comment."

He paused, ran his tongue around the inside of his mouth and then continued, "Many judges sitting in this day and age are of the opinion, sir, that an innocent man has nothing to fear from the courts. If he is innocent, that fact will shine through and his innocence be established without difficulty. On the rare occasions the defendant might require help . . . why then, the judge is there to provide it. The judge, we are told, will see to it that no advantage belonging to the prisoner will be lost simply because he is not represented by counsel."

"I see," said Tom, who did not see at all. "Why then should I go to the expense, not to say the risk, of being represented?"

"My dear Captain Pascoe," said Formby, leaning back in his chair and resting the tips of his fingers in the form of a steeple. "In the first place you are to consider that you are not permitted to give evidence in your own defence. Your case, sir, will rest entirely on what you choose to say to the jury at the end of the inquest, and on what others say of you in their evidence-in-chief. In the second place, while the coroner will certainly ensure you receive the benefit of any point of law that lies to your advantage, he knows nothing of your case. How, then, can he defend you? What opportunity do you have for telling him anything about yourself or the circumstances of the case?"

"Have you not answered your own question?" said Tom. "My opportunity for putting my case will come when I address the jury."

"Alas, Captain, I have too often seen a defendant hang himself for want of a silent tongue. Too often, those who are not well versed in the law and its ways will fail to take advantage of the opportunities of cross-examination and then proceed to convict themselves through an address to the jury that is wholly devoid of thought or strategy."

"Then where lies the balance?" said Tom. "Am I to throw myself on the good offices of the court, or risk the loss of its goodwill?"

"Where, sir, the prosecution is very weak, I think there is a case for allowing the prisoner to defend himself but in this case . . ." Formby's voice trailed off.

Tom looked askance at the lawyer. The precariousness of his position was becoming clearer by the second. "You cannot be suggesting that I have something to fear from this inquest?"

"It is as well . . ." Formby hesitated. "It is as well that you be prepared for the worst, Captain Pascoe. I have seen no papers or statements relating to this inquest and nor do I expect to. But from what you have told me, it seems highly probable that the coroner will wish to hear from as many people as possible who were aboard your ship at the time of the shooting."

"Yes, I had considered as much myself," said Tom. "What of it?"

"Didn't you tell me, sir, you harboured a mutual dislike for the master lumper? What was his name? Boylin? And is it not the case that the lumper you shot was one of his men? Worse still, sir, is it not the case you were once Boylin's commanding officer and considered it your duty to have him flogged half to death?"

"That was the decision of a court martial."

"Perhaps," said Formby, "but is it not the case that Mr Boylin blames you, rather than the court martial? And if that is so, d'you not think it likely he will seek to do you some mischief? Has he not already threatened to do so? And who, pray, will you call to give evidence on your behalf? You cannot have forgotten your Mr Simmonds lies grievously hurt in hospital."

"I hadn't forgotten," said Tom, quietly.

Formby drummed his fingers on his desk and gazed out of the window as though considering the wisdom of what he was about to say. When he turned back to Tom he said, "You may as well know, Captain, that all of Boylin's men, including I might add, the two excisemen involved in this case, are suspected of being game — you are not familiar with the term? — It means, sir, they have compromised their right to be called honest men. They are rogues, sir, and would think nothing of robbing the scales of the blind goddess atop the Old Bailey for a penny farthing. Such men would have a great deal to lose, perhaps even their lives, if they were to refuse to do the bidding of the man in whose pockets they have made their home."

"I see," said Tom. "I wonder then, what are my chances?"

Formby shook his head and inserted a thumb into his waistcoat pocket, his expression sombre.

"Not good, sir. Not good at all."

Shortly before midday on the Tuesday following Tom Pascoe's conference with his attorney, Dr Robert Grimshaw, His Majesty's Coroner for the District of Shadwell, in the County of Middlesex, arrived at the Dog and Duck tavern in Limehouse to begin his weekly list of inquests. Deaths were depressingly frequent in this part of town.

Climbing the stairs to the first floor, Dr Grimshaw pushed his way through a noisy crowd of onlookers and walked to the far end of a large, low-beamed room that occupied much of the upper level of the public house. On his left, on a long bench, sat the jury. On his right, and also seated on a bench, were the witnesses who were to be called. At right angles to these two groups and facing the door through which he had just entered, was the coroner's desk at which his clerk was already seated.

Dr Grimshaw bustled up to the table and sat down. He was a ruddy-faced, portly man of about sixty, whose air of permanent distraction was apt to create an impression of unworldliness, an impression reinforced by the dishevelled state of his dress and the pince-nez perched on the end of his prominent nose. For the most part, His Majesty's Coroner was happy to allow this impression to remain. He regarded it, as did others who knew him well, as a kind of screen behind which he could lurk unseen until the time was right to show an altogether different facet of his personality.

At exactly five minutes past twelve, the coroner's clerk, a hawk-like man with a mood to match, rose from his chair and coughed.

"Oyez, oyez, oyez," he intoned. The general noise of chatter fell away. "All manner of persons who have anything to do at this court before the King's Coroner for this county, touching the death of Nathan Thomas Murphy, draw near and give your attendance." He paused and looked self-importantly round the room. "And if anyone can give evidence on behalf of our Sovereign Lord the King, when, how and by what means Nathan Thomas Murphy came to his death, let him come forth and he shall be heard."

The clerk sat down, and Grimshaw waited for the coughing, scraping of chairs and fidgeting to stop and the jury to pay attention. Outside, a steady downpour of summer rain set up a noisy drumbeat against the window panes. In the taproom on the floor below, the business of drinking went on unabated, the convivial sounds no more than a muffled drone, punctuated with occasional bursts of laughter and the clatter of pots.

"Members of the jury," said the coroner, "this case is an enquiry into the death of Mr . . . ah . . . Nathan Thomas Murphy . . ."

Dr Grimshaw's soporific tones droned on and Tom took the opportunity to look at the people with whom he shared his bench. Several he knew. The two excisemen who had been on board the *Swansong* were there, of course, as was Newman, the foreman-lumper. A fourth man, dressed entirely in black, sat slightly apart from the others and Tom guessed he was probably the physician called to give evidence of the cause of death. The remainder of the witnesses he recalled seeing in the hold of the *Swansong*, although what they could add to the proceedings he could not begin to imagine. He wished the injured Simmonds could have been here to give evidence on his behalf.

"If you please, sir."

Tom recognised his counsel's voice.

"Good gracious me, sir," said a startled Dr Grimshaw, "you are, if I am not sadly mistook, Mr Formby, of counsel?"

"I am indeed, sir, and I appear for Captain Thomas Pascoe at this inquest." Formby waved a sheaf of papers in his client's direction.

"Well, well, this is certainly unusual, Mr Formby. I trust your involvement will not add significantly to the length of this enquiry."

"Indeed, sir, I regret it most extremely." A small, apologetic shrug of the rounded shoulders. "I shall be as brief as I can."

"Very well, the quicker we start, the quicker we'll finish," said Dr Grimshaw, frowning. "Call the first witness, Mr Clerk, if you please."

One by one, the two excisemen, a cooper and two of the lumpers ambled, strolled or sidled up to a point immediately in front of the coroner's table. As each was sworn and gave his evidence, it seemed nothing could prevent Tom from being committed for trial. No, the deceased had offered no resistance to either the mate or the captain. No, there was no reason for the captain to shoot the deceased and yes, the witnesses had seen and heard everything.

"Call Mr Gabriel Newman."

Newman shambled to the allotted place, his narrow shoulders hunched forward, his hooded, deep-set eyes darting nervously about the room.

"Very good, Mr Newman," said the coroner after the foreman-lumper had taken the oath on a ragged copy of the Bible. "Perhaps you can tell the court what your duties were on the morning of Mr Murphy's death."

"I were the foreman-lumper, your honour." Newman swallowed. "I were in charge . . ."

Tom looked up, suddenly curious. Newman was stumbling on his words in a way which couldn't altogether be explained by his unease at his surroundings. He was afraid of someone or something. Newman finished speaking and waited for the next question.

"And what, pray, did you see during the course of the morning?"

"I were on deck when it happened," said Newman, scratching at his neck. "I saw everything. The captain shot Mr Murphy. He was after giving him no chance, your honour. No chance at all."

Tom looked at the faces of the jury. Had they, too, noticed Newman's unease? Suddenly, he was aware of a whispered exchange between the coroner's clerk and the usher. A moment later the clerk glanced at Tom, wrote something onto a sheet of paper, and slid it across to the coroner.

"Thank you, Mr Newman," said Dr Grimshaw, frowning at the paper in front of him. "Please stay where you are. I daresay Mr Formby would like to ask you a few questions."

"I'm obliged, sir." Formby struggled to his feet. "I shan't detain you for long, Mr Newman. Perhaps we could start with your evidence to the jury . . ."

This way and that, the cut and thrust of the cross-examination went on as Formby sought a way through the fog of obfuscation that had been Newman's evidence-in-chief. Discovered to be lying in one direction, the foreman-lumper would lie in another until that too was found out and he would change again. And it appeared to Tom as though nothing was clear but everything was taken at its face value.

"Sure I was below decks, but that was before, like. I were on the upper deck when the captain shot his gun, so I was."

"Then why did you say you were below deck?" said Formby, resting a plump hand on the back of his chair

"I thought your honour was asking me about the morning."

"Were you ordered to go below decks by the captain before the shooting?"

"Aye, so I was."

"And did you go?"

"Aye."

"Then how could you have been on deck at the time of the shooting?"

"Well now, I didn't go below decks."

And with each successive answer the jury looked ever more bewildered.

"I have, sir, no further questions of this witness," said Formby, slumping into his chair, a look of weary defeat in his eyes. Whatever hope there had been of avoiding a trial now seemed extinguished.

"Thank you, Mr Formby. I take it you have no objection to the release of this witness? Good. Thank you, Mr Newman, you may leave."

The coroner tapped the piece of paper that had been passed to him by his clerk. "I understand a new witness has come forward. I must say this is all very irregular, Mr Formby. I do hope we'll not have any more surprises and I may shortly be allowed to bring this inquest to a close. Did you, sir, know about this?"

"I regret I did not, sir," said Formby, turning to Tom and raising his eyebrows. Tom shook his head.

"Very well, call the witness, Mr . . . ah . . . Samuel Hart."

From among the tight mass of bodies at the back of the courtroom, Joseph Boylin watched the arrival of the new witness. He had a strange feeling he'd seen the man before — and recently.

"I am in the employ of Master Jonas Levi of Shadwell, a dealer in old clothing." Boylin was having difficulty in hearing what the man was saying, and pushed himself closer to the front of crowd. "It is his custom to require me to visit ships newly arrived in port and offer clothing for sale to those what wants to buy. It were for this purpose I were aboard the *Swansong* on this day."

The realisation hit Boylin like a tumbling sack of coal. He knew with a crushing certainty where he'd seen the witness before. He stared, all thoughts of Tom Pascoe and the rest swept from his mind, replaced by the vision of a narrow alley leading to the river, the body of a young man at his feet, a stranger standing not thirty yards away, baskets of old clothes on his shoulders, glancing down the alley towards him.

"I were abaft the main chains," Sam Hart continued. "On the upper deck, your honour. I could see what were going on, clear as day . . ."

Boylin turned dizzily towards the door leading to the street. He caught Newman's eye and beckoned him to follow as he made his way out.

Two hours later, Gabriel Newman was standing by the King James Stairs on Wapping Wall, his hands buried in his pockets, a knot in his stomach, his thoughts a jumble of excuses that refused to make sense. A gang of lumpers clambered ashore from a wherry and trudged past him, their eyes red-rimmed with exhaustion. He doubted they'd even seen him. Soon he was alone again.

He'd lost him. How he didn't know, although that hardly mattered any more. What mattered was how Boylin would react. The knot in his stomach grew tighter. It had seemed a simple enough task: Boylin had ordered him to follow the man who'd given evidence and find out where he lived. To begin with, it *had* been simple. They'd left the inquest at the Dog and Duck tavern and headed north. The streets were almost empty at that hour of the day and Newman had dropped back, fearful of being seen. Even when they reached the Ratcliff Highway and the numbers of people had increased, he'd had little difficulty in keeping the fellow in view. And so it would have gone on, had a passing whore not chosen that moment to distract him with an offer of her services. By the time he'd extricated himself, his quarry had disappeared. He'd searched, of course, but it was useless. The scrub could have gone down any one of half a dozen courts and alleyways.

Boylin was waiting for him when he returned to the Queen's Head.

"Will you be after telling me where the scrub lives?" said the publican.

Newman shrugged his shoulders.

"Answer me, now." Boylin jabbed an angry finger at Newman's chest. "Did you follow him, like I told you?"

"Aye, so I did."

"So where does he live?"

Another shrug of the shoulders.

"You lost him, you pox-ridden son of a whore." Boylin lashed out, striking the side of Newman's mouth with a clenched fist.

Newman cowered, blood seeping through the fingers he held to his face.

"I'll be knowing where he works." His voice was barely above a whisper.

"What did you say?" Boylin held his reddened face close to Newman's. "How d'you know? You lost him."

"He told the coroner, when he were giving evidence," said Newman, still cowering, a protective elbow pointing towards the publican. "He said he were working for Jonas Levi."

"So?"

"Sure, I'll be knowing where Jonas has his warehouse. You can ask him where the scrub lives."

Boylin stared at the lumper as though debating his next move.

"Tell the lads I want to see them," he said, waving a hand at the door of the cellar, a dangerous glint in his eye.

Jonas Levi was surprised to see the two men leaning against the wall of the ramshackle building that served as his warehouse. He didn't often get visitors and certainly not at this hour of the evening. He glanced up and down the street. There was no one else in view. He slowed his pace, the hem of his long black overcoat flapping as he walked, one hand clutching the wide brim of his hat, the other holding a walking stick.

The men looked up as he approached. Jonas held his breath and mentally prepared himself for the string of abuse he was sure would come. He was used to it; or at least as used to it as he was ever likely to get. The insults — or worse, the floggings and beard-pulling — were a daily occurrence, especially for those, like him, who held to the old ways of their people and dressed accordingly.

"Will it be Master Levi, now?" Jonas looked up at the sound of his name.

"Yes, my name is Jonas Levi." He bent forward in an arthritic bow. "How may I serve you, gentlemen?"

"It's a little word we'll be wanting, now."

Jonas eyed the man's pockmarked face with a caution born of hard experience. His senses taut as harp strings, he smelt trouble. A few years ago it wouldn't have been a problem, but now . . . How he regretted the stiffness in his joints, the slowness of his reactions. He shuffled round and began to retrace his steps. He'd return tomorrow. When the men had left.

He didn't get far.

Rough hands caught him under his elbows and carried him to the warehouse, his feet trailing in the dust. Inside, the street door slammed behind him and a hard shove sent him sprawling. His hat flew off and rolled away.

"I am a poor man." Jonas curled himself up into a ball, his arms over his head, his mouth filled with dirt. "What is it you want of me? Take everything. It is yours."

"Where's Hart?" The question startled him. He peered out from under his protective arm and stared at his questioner.

"Samuel Hart?" Jonas' knees were stinging where they'd broken his fall. He rubbed them. "I regret, good sirs, I've not seen him these two days since."

"Don't lie to me, old man. Where is he?" Jonas could smell the man's stale breath.

"He . . . he comes and he goes." Jonas trembled as the pock-marked face thrust closer. A hand caught the lapel of his coat and pulled him up into a sitting position, the grip so tight, it was choking him.

"I'll not be asking again." The voice had a hard, pitiless edge. "Will you be telling me where Hart lives or will I be flogging it out of you?"

A bead of perspiration trickled down Jonas' forehead. He didn't want to die. Not like this. "He has a room in Shadwell, off Old Gravel Lane. More than that, I don't know."

Jonas watched the man get to his feet. He closed his eyes, relief flooding through him. They were satisfied. They'd soon be gone.

He didn't feel any pain. The boot, when it struck the side of his head, was efficient in that respect.

CHAPTER
SEVEN

It was getting dark as Sam Hart turned off Lower Shadwell into Labour-in-Vain Street and headed towards the tumble-down warehouse where he worked. Jonas had told him to meet him there and warned him not to be late. More ships were due in the Lower Pool in a couple of hours' time and Sam was to take a selection of clothes aboard and sell them.

Nearing the building, he glanced up and saw that the door of the warehouse stood ajar. He slowed his pace — old Jonas never left the door open, something was wrong. Apprehension rising in his stomach, Sam ran the last few yards, his right hand reaching for the knife he always carried in the waist of his trousers. He wrenched at the door, yanking it back on its creaking hinges, letting what remained of the daylight to stream into the place.

Jonas was lying on the earthen floor, just inside the entrance, his knees drawn, foetus-like, up to his chest, his eyes closed. At first glance he might have been sleeping. Sam dropped to the floor beside him and stretched out his hand, gently touching the cold skin of Jonas' face. Below his head, a dark pool of blood had formed in the dirt.

Sam turned the body over. There was, as yet, no hint of the stiffness that was to come. On the right temple, above and to the front of his ear, was a deep gash as though the old man's head had been struck with a blunt object, the wound now matted with hair and drying blood.

Sam stood up, his mind numb with shock and grief. He walked to the door and looked up and down the street, unsure of what he expected to find. It was deserted, the stillness of the scene accentuated by the distant hammering from a shipyard. He went back inside, found a bolt of linen and laid it over the body.

Then he left the warehouse, closed the door behind him, and locked it. It was best that way. It didn't seem right to leave Jonas in a place where he could be seen. It wasn't decent. Even in death a man deserved some dignity. Retracing his steps, Sam called into the police office on Lower Shadwell and reported the killing, returning with a constable pushing a flat-bed handcart. He doubted anything would be done to investigate the death, beyond the posting of a few handbills in the area. Those responsible had long gone, leaving no clue as to their identity.

Sam had rarely felt so despondent or alone. He needed time to think, to be by himself, to try and make some sense of the old man's death. After the body had been taken away he walked up to the Ratcliff Highway and turned east, weaving his way through the late evening throng, his mind crowded with questions, the answers distant and elusive. Had Jonas died because of what he was — a Jew who clung to the old ways, to the traditional forms of dress that seemed to so enrage the Gentiles? He wouldn't have been the first to suffer for the sin of being different. Sam had often tried to find a tactful way of telling him of the dangers he faced by appearing the way he did in his long black caftan and broad-brimmed hat, sporting his beard and his ringlets. All of these spelt trouble on the streets of London. Sam suspected Jonas probably knew that, but had long ago made the decision not to compromise the values by which he lived.

But there was another aspect of the death that was puzzling. If the scuff marks leading from the street to the warehouse were anything to go by, Jonas had been dragged inside and almost certainly killed there. Sam had seen no blood in the roadway.

But why? Why had anyone thought it necessary to drag the old man into the warehouse? To steal from him? Nothing had been taken. To avoid detection? Few people ever walked that way.

In the far reaches of his mind he was dimly aware of a notion beginning to take shape. There was little to support it, yet it seemed to have a life of its own; it took root and grew. Sam's heart went cold as he considered the possibility that Jonas had died not for who he was, but because of his relationship to Sam. The thought shocked and revolted him by turns. Was it possible the murder was linked to the evidence he, Sam Hart, had given at the inquest? He had been warned to stay away. Everyone who'd been on board the *Swansong* that morning had been warned, and everyone knew the man from whom the order had come. Everyone except him.

69

Until a few days ago, Boylin's name had meant nothing to him. There was no reason why it should. He and the Irishman lived in separate worlds that had little or nothing in common. Irked by the warning to stay away from an inquest he'd not previously thought to attend, he'd made his own enquiries as to the source of the order and learned of Boylin and his violent reputation. It was then he realised he'd found the man he'd been looking for, the man responsible for the end of so much that had been good and happy in Sam's life. The decision to attend the inquest had followed as surely as night followed day. He didn't know what he hoped to achieve. It was enough that Boylin had ordered people to stay away. Perhaps his appearance would, in some small way, begin to repay the hurt the Irishman had inflicted.

Of the threatened consequences he had cared little — until now.

Deep in thought, Sam barely noticed the squat outline of a man standing in a doorway to his left, but some intuitive nudge compelled him to look back, his eyes retracing the arc through which they had just travelled. A breeze rocked a nearby lantern, momentarily spilling its light onto a pockmarked face, its mouth drawn back in a mirthless grin, its eyes mere pinpricks of reflected light. He'd seen the scrub before, knew him as Shamus O'Malley, a bully boy who would as soon settle an argument with his fists as walk away. He wondered what O'Malley was doing here, whether his presence was mere coincidence — or something more. The mirthless grin had seemed intended for him.

Sam crossed the road and turned down a deserted path that led to the river, the muffled thud of his footsteps strangely loud in the abrupt stillness. He slowed, adjusting his pace to the blackness of his new surroundings where the only light was that of an occasional star winking through a gap in the high clouds. Somewhere behind him a dog barked, a furious continuous sound of startled alarm. Sam stopped, aware of a sudden tension in the air.

He peered through the gloom, awake to every shadow, every darkened shape and object. He strained to hear above the sound of the dog's yelps though what he listened for he had no idea, only that he feared the unseen.

The noise of the animal grew quieter and then ceased, the ensuing silence enveloping him in its completeness. He thought of the man he'd seen in the Ratcliff Highway and wondered if he was being followed. On his own, the scrub presented few problems — Sam had faced bigger, fitter men than he and made them pay the price of their temerity — but he suspected there'd be others.

The outline of a man appeared out of the darkness, approaching from the opposite direction. Sam dropped back into a doorway, his hand sliding to the comforting touch of his knife. The stranger sidled by and disappeared. Cautiously, Sam stepped out onto the path and began walking quickly, his sense of isolation and vulnerability more sharply defined with each successive step.

He heard a gasp, not fifteen paces behind him. Then something heavy hit the ground. Sam spun round, his heart racing. He guessed what had happened; that the stranger had been mistaken for him and was paying for it with his life. Again he melted into a doorway, the bile of fear rising in his throat. He waited. From close by, a whispered sentence or two. A reply. And then all was quiet again.

He heard footsteps on the bare earth. Whoever it was, was moving quickly. The path was no more than three paces across and he knew his hiding place would not protect him if anyone were to glance in his direction. A shadow passed within arm's length and the sickly-sweet smell of sweat drifted towards him. He recognised the broad, stooped outline of Shamus O'Malley. He waited until the fellow had gone, then moved away from the door and peered round the corner of the building.

It was the smell of lime he noticed first. The sharp, sour smell that clings to the nostrils. Sam moved back. A heartbeat later he heard the wheezing sound of heavy breathing and a thickset figure shuffled towards him down the path. He knew instantly that it was Boylin; the same man he'd first seen at the back of the coroner's court. Except it *wasn't* the first time. He had the strangest feeling he'd seen Boylin's face on an earlier occasion.

But where? This was no time to think.

Sam drew his knife, running a finger over the point. Mentally, he rehearsed the movements. The outstretched hand that would cover the mouth and shut off the scream of fear, a single upward thrust of the blade between the ribs. Less than two seconds and the deed would be finished. The desire to end Boylin's life was physical in its intensity.

The sound of laboured breathing grew louder. Sam levered his shoulders away from the door, his knife readied.

He heard someone cough, a low, barely audible sound. He stumbled back into the shadows. It hadn't come from Boylin. It had been further away than that. Someone else was out there. Probably another of Boylin's men.

Sam thought quickly. He might still have time. There'd be no noise. Just a small grunt as the knife went in. Again he peered round the corner of the doorway. Boylin was almost on top of him. Another two seconds. No more than that. He looked beyond the approaching figure. It was too dark to see anything but if he was going to act he'd have to do it now. He moved forward.

Another cough.

Much closer.

Sam's throat tightened. He wiped away a trickle of sweat from his eyes. If he got this wrong, there'd be no second chance, no time to defend himself from whoever else was there.

Boylin was within reach. Sam ran his tongue over his lips and tasted the salt-filled sweat in his mouth. He raised his knife hand. Then a movement, close behind the approaching Boylin, flicked across the extremity of his vision.

He hesitated.

Boylin passed out of range.

A moment later a second shape slipped by.

Sam stared after them. He'd missed his chance.

The letter requiring Tom's attendance at the Marine Society Offices in Bishopsgate arrived on board the *Swansong* the following morning. It was short and to the point. Captain Thomas Pascoe was required to report, at his earliest convenience, for interview with Sir Michael Johnson of the West India Merchants and Planters Committee to explain recent events on board the barque, *Swansong*, and to give account of the loss of a substantial portion of her cargo.

Tom stood by the great stern window of his day-cabin, looking out over Limehouse Reach. He'd been expecting the summons. He slipped the letter into his coat pocket and turned towards the door. There was nothing to be gained from delaying the meeting with his employer.

An hour later, Tom was seated in a large, airy room on Bishopsgate facing the florid features of Sir Michael Johnson.

"I am heartily sorry on it, Captain Pascoe, but there it is." Tom was only half listening to the merchant who, probably out of embarrassment, was continuing to talk long after the need for it had ended.

"Captain Pascoe?" Tom was suddenly aware that Sir Michael had stopped talking and was waiting for a response.

"I beg pardon, sir," Tom was suitably penitent. "You were saying?"

"I was saying, Captain, that while the committee cannot condone the loss of your cargo for which you alone were responsible, it recognises the particular circumstances of your case. We are not, after all, insensible to the findings of the coroner that you were in no way culpable in the death of the lumper on board the *Swansong*. Nor are we blind to your desire to ensure the mate received immediate medical attention. As to the death of a member of your crew, that is another matter entirely and has no bearing on our decision."

"That's very civil of you, I'm sure. I . . ." began Tom, wondering if the merchant had any real idea of how close-run the inquest had been. He shuddered at the thought of what might have happened if Sam Hart had not given evidence and the court returned a verdict of lawful killing. He'd meant to find Sam after the case and thank him for what he'd done, but he'd gone.

"Quite," said the merchant. "However, I was about to say that what did concern us was your absence from your ship throughout the latter part of that day and the following night, in clear breach of the committee's written instructions. Whatever the circumstances alleged to be the cause of your absence, they do not, sir, excuse your failure to ensure the safe custody of your ship and its cargo. It is for this reason that your employment is to be terminated with immediate effect."

Tom felt as if he'd been punched in the stomach.

"I'm sorry —"

"No, no, Captain, let me finish." Sir Michael was in no mood for further interruptions. "Although our decision is irrevocable, the committee is, in all the circumstances, prepared to recommend your employment elsewhere."

Tom looked blank, unsure of where all this was leading. "You may not be aware," Sir Michael continued, "that the committee has, for some time, been considering, with His Majesty's government, the funding of a new body of police."

"Aye, I've heard talk," said Tom.

It was hardly a secret. One would have needed to be deaf not to hear the chatter in the streets and public houses of Wapping and Shadwell or, for that matter, across the river in Southwark and Rotherhithe. A proposal for a force of men whose sole function would be the prevention and detection of crime on the river was not something you could keep quiet.

"I am happy to tell you, Captain, that in the last week my colleagues have agreed to the idea. This very morning a notice calling for applicants for the new marine police institution was published. I have a copy here somewhere — ah yes, here it is. Now, Captain, what I am leading to is this. I and my colleagues are of the opinion that your skills as a seaman and naval officer would ideally suit you to the role of a supervising officer in this force. What do you say to that, sir?"

With an effort Tom looked up, conscious that he ought to be grateful to the merchant for the offer. "I am, sir, indebted to you," he managed. "It is of course an offer I shall consider most carefully."

"I'm exceedingly glad to hear of it." Sir Michael looked relieved. "In the meanwhile, allow me to present a letter of introduction to the two magistrates who will have charge of the institution."

"You are most kind, sir," said Tom mechanically. There seemed nothing left to say and, leaden-hearted, he rose to leave.

Leaving his meeting with Sir Michael, Tom hurried down Bishopsgate, towards Cornhill. He'd known, of course, that his absence from the ship and the subsequent loss of a substantial part of the cargo, would have its consequences. But he hadn't bargained for the loss of his command. If his employers had understood the full extent of his position, they'd not shown it. He was dismissed without the least hope of obtaining another command. A weight of depression enveloped him.

He felt in his pocket for the letter of introduction that Sir Michael had given him. He knew what it said. The merchant had read it to him before sealing it and handing it to him. Addressed to Mr Patrick Colquhoun and Mr John Harriot, the magistrates at the new police office in Wapping, it recommended his employment as a river surveyor in the new marine police. He knew he'd little option. It was that or nothing. He hung back, reluctant to commit himself. The sea had been his life. It was all he knew.

He walked on, his progress slowed now by the chattering lunchtime crowds spilling onto the sunlit street, mingling with the traders and cattle drovers already there. He crossed into Gracechurch Street and caught the scent of the river, carried up on a warm, southerly breeze. A slow smile spread across his wide face. The smell reminded him of the sea.

Mr John Harriot, recently appointed magistrate for the counties of Kent, Essex, Middlesex and Surrey, coughed and glanced over to where his colleague, Mr Patrick Colquhoun, was almost entirely hidden behind a copy of *The Times*. He waited to see if his attempt at catching the attention of the senior magistrate would have the desired effect and then coughed again. There was still no response.

"Strange he should have objected," he murmured.

"I'm sorry, my dear fellow, what was that you were saying?" Colquhoun looked out from behind the paper.

"I was just saying it was strange that he should have objected — one of the merchants at the meeting I was at yesterday. He objected to our proposals for a marine police institution."

"I hadn't realised anyone had," said Colquhoun. "What did he say?"

"Oh, complained about the cost. Said he thought the government ought to pay more towards the new organisation. Claimed they stood to gain most from a reduction in the volume of plundering."

"Where did he imagine the Administration would find the money to fund the new police?" said

Colquhoun, giving his newspaper a bad-tempered shake. "What's the wretched fellow think he's about? Doesn't he know there's a war on, not to mention this business in Ireland? Who was it, anyway?"

"Sir Sydney Devall."

"Don't know the fellow." Colquhoun paused. "Did he say anything else?"

"Nothing to speak of," said Harriot.

"Well, I suppose no damage was done," said Colquhoun, disappearing behind his newspaper again.

"In the meantime," said Harriot, filling his pipe, "we must parade the new force at first light tomorrow, even if —"

A knock on the door cut him short. A moment later the chief clerk had entered the room. "I regret this intrusion, your worships, but there's an applicant you might wish to see. He's got the usual letter from the merchants. Will I send him in?"

"If you please, Mr Yeardley," said Colquhoun, reluctantly deciding that whatever opportunity there might have been for reading was now gone.

"Good day, your worships." Tom Pascoe's muscular frame filled the doorway. "Sir Michael Johnson presents his compliments and wishes you would do him the kindness of reading this letter."

Sam Hart slumped into a window seat at the Prospect of Whitby in the drowsy heat of early afternoon. On the river, a dozen or more ships had spread their sails to the drying sun and stillness had overtaken the usual bustle of the port. He'd not been home since the incident in the alley off the Ratcliff Highway; had not wanted to give Boylin the satisfaction of catching him.

At least, not until he was ready.

His exhausted eyes swept the smoke-filled taproom, looking for the small, telltale signs of unrest that usually presaged trouble. He'd learned to spot the signals much as he'd learned to avoid the company of those he didn't know, and those outside the Faith. It wasn't often he was comfortable in the presence of Gentiles.

He leaned on his elbows. The attempt on his life — and he was convinced that was what it was — still puzzled him. Boylin had no motive for killing him except the inquest, and even that hardly warranted the effort that was being made to get him. Nor could Boylin's animosity be explained in terms of his concern for his own safety. Sam might wish the publican dead for the pain and suffering that he'd inflicted, but he had spoken to no one about what Boylin had done. The scrub had no inkling of the way Sam felt about him.

Yet there had to be a reason for the publican's actions.

Sam dredged through his memory. Time and again, the triggers pointed to his involvement in the inquest and each time he would shake his head. It made no real sense — even for someone like Boylin.

But there *was* something else. It niggled away at the back of his mind, something he'd heard. Slowly, incomplete words and phrases came to him, in themselves disjointed and meaningless.

"He saw them . . ."

". . . make sure he don't talk . . ."

". . . Shadwell Dock Stairs."

Sam tried to remember where and when he'd heard the words spoken. It was in the last few days, of that he was sure. Then he remembered. It had been in the alley off the Ratcliff Highway. On the night Boylin had come after him. He'd heard two men whispering. But what about?

Gradually an image was forming in his head: the Thames shrouded in the mist of early morning as though viewed through gauze; two men crouching in an alley, between them what looked to be a heap of rags. No, not rags . . . a body.

Sam stared out through the window of the Prospect, half-listening to the sound of a sea-shanty being chanted out on the tideway and the regular stamp-and-go of the crew of a brig weighing anchor. He cupped his beer mug in both hands. What possible connection could there be between the body by the Thames and Boylin? Why would that body result in Boylin wanting him dead?

The image came into focus. The figures he'd seen by the river that morning were familiar. He'd glimpsed them somewhere since — at the coroner's court. The first was one of the men who'd given evidence. But the second? Then he remembered the face at the back of the public gallery. It was Boylin. The pieces began to fall into place.

A gust of wind swept through the taproom and ruffled a piece of paper nailed to one of the oak pillars. The movement caught Sam's eye. It was headed

NOTICE in heavy ink, followed by some text that he couldn't read from this distance.

His mind returned to what he'd seen by the banks of the Thames. Was it possible he'd witnessed Boylin in the act of murder? Sam's fingers drummed the table. If so, that had to be the reason for the Irishman's interest in him. The publican was afraid of the evidence he, Sam Hart, could give.

The paper flapped again. Sam sighed, gave in to his curiosity, got to his feet and wandered across. A new organisation — a marine police institution — was being formed. He'd heard of the proposal, but it was the first time he'd seen anything in writing. He *was* in need of work. Had been since Jonas' death. Work and food. He hadn't had either for several days.

"Oy!" The voice came from close behind him. There was no mistaking the aggressive tone — or its intended target. Sam was used to the attention his olive complexion attracted. He glanced over his shoulder, and counted five men sitting further along the same bench as himself. The nearest was a large, muscular man with a broken nose and a squint in his left eye. He crooked his finger and beckoned.

Sam ignored him, turning away to scan the notice for a second time. Almost at once, he felt a hard shove in his back that sent him crashing into an oak pillar. He put a hand to his mouth and wiped away the blood. Around him, the buzz of conversation died.

"Have I, sir, done something to offend you?" said Sam, eyeing the man standing over him. He looked as if he could handle himself.

"Offend me? Get up and I'll tell 'ee how 'ee offend me, yer fucking Jesus killer."

Sam's temper flared. With an effort, he brought it under control and, turning away, got slowly to his feet. A fight would solve nothing.

"What's the matter? Ain't yer got no bottom, Jew-boy?" The man drew back his fist and swung wildly.

Sam turned to face the punch, deflecting it with a raised forearm. The others jumped to their feet and started towards him as another punch came in. He swayed out of range and then slid in with a pulverising blow to the man's face. Blood spurted from the broken nose and its owner sank, senseless, to the floor.

"You're welcome to the same, should you wish it," said Sam, rubbing his knuckles and looking at the remainder of the group. They didn't look the sort of men who might be persuaded by any appeal to reason. He knew he'd probably have to finish what had been started.

For a moment, no one moved. Then, with a bellow, one of the group lunged at him with a knife. Sam sidestepped and brought his hand down in a savage, chopping movement on the man's outstretched wrist. There was a howl of pain and the blade clattered to the floor. Sam drew his own weapon, crouched forward and waited.

The odds had improved. Only three men remained, doubt and fear in their eyes. Sam watched as, one by one, they backed towards the door, half carrying, half dragging their injured friends.

He caught sight of the notice nailed to the pillar, stopped, and read it for the third time.

CHAPTER
EIGHT

There were close to seventy-five men in the large, ground-floor room overlooking the Thames at 259 Wapping New Stairs, the atmosphere boisterous and noisy with the promise of employment. A door opened and two men entered. They walked to a raised platform at the far end of the room as the noise died out.

"Good morning." Mr Patrick Colquhoun nodded at the tightly packed assembly. "Most of you will already know me and all of you will have met my colleague, here, Mr John Harriot. The purpose of this meeting is to welcome you as new members of the marine police institution and acquaint you with its structure. More detailed instructions will be given to you later by the surveyors to whom you will be attached.

"You will shortly be posted to one of two departments. The first is the Judicial Department, where the tasks will be largely confined to the execution of warrants issued by this office. Seven of you will be posted there.

"The second is the Preventative Department, which will be divided into two sections. Forty-eight of you will be given the responsibility of guarding the ships of the West India Company, whose captains have paid for our protection. This group of constables will also be responsible for guarding the quays to which cargo is discharged, and they will be assisted by a further two hundred and twenty occasional constables who will be recruited as and when the need arises."

Colquhoun paused and looked round the room.

"The remaining section of the Preventative Department, consisting of sixty men, will patrol the river between London Bridge and the harbour master's house at Greenwich — about three and a half miles in length. I must warn you that the duties of this group will be the most hazardous, and there is no doubt that you will face the opprobrium of men long used to regarding the plunder of ships as their rightful perquisites."

"Mr Pascoe," Tom heard his name being called as the meeting finally came to an end. He looked up to see one of the justices' clerks waving at him. "Mr Harriot wishes to see you in his room, if you is at leisure, sir."

"We've had a small problem with one of the men I'd intended to allocate to you," said Harriot, when Tom joined him a few moments later. "He arrived drunk and has been dismissed, which means you'll have to wait until we find a replacement. We should have found someone for you by tomorrow morning, but in the meantime I've given you Robert Tisdale and Henry Kemp. They're both capable seamen from the East India Company."

The following day, Tuesday, July third, produced no replacement crewman for Tom, nor was there any sign of one on Wednesday when, at two o'clock that afternoon, he brought the police galley alongside Wapping New Stairs at the end of his six-hour tour of duty.

"Nothing untoward to tell you about," he said, handing over to his relieving surveyor. "You might like to keep an eye on the West Indiamen in Limehouse Reach. They've been losing a lot of sugar, but nobody seems to know how it's going."

Tom walked up the passageway and turned left towards the City. It would take him no more than five minutes to reach the two comfortable rooms he'd rented in a house on Burr Street — rooms for which he'd negotiated an annual rent of fifty pounds, including evening meals prepared by the landlord's wife.

He'd almost reached Hermitage Dock before he saw a familiar figure standing on the dock bridge staring out over the Thames.

"Why, it's Samuel Hart if I'm not sadly mistook," said Tom, surprised to see how thin and dishevelled the man had become. "Give you joy, sir."

"Joy, your honour," said Sam.

"I looked for you after the inquest." Tom was keen to explain his apparent lack of good manners. "I wanted to thank you for what you did, but you'd gone."

"Aye," said Sam, his voice flat. "The coroner had no further need of me."

"I owe you a debt of thanks, and not for the first time," said Tom. "If you is at leisure, will you not join me for a bite to eat and a jug of ale. We can talk while we dine. What do you say?"

"There is no need . . ." Sam hesitated. "But I confess I am a little hungry."

"Good," said Tom. "That's settled then."

Making their way to a small tavern off Wapping Street Tom ordered food and drink for them both.

"Pray, how was it you came to know of the inquest?" asked Tom, as soon as the waiter had left. "You were not, as I recall, one of Boylin's men."

"No." A shadow seemed to pass over his companion's features. "I worked for a seller of old clothes."

"I recall now," said Tom. "You said as much in your evidence. But you no longer work for him?"

"I regret it extremely," said Sam, "but my employer is dead. He was murdered on the day of the inquest."

"Ye Gods!" said a shocked Tom. "How did it happen?"

"I don't know." Sam appeared reluctant to talk and seemed relieved when the waiter returned with plates of food and the flagons of beer.

For a few minutes the two of them ate in silence. When they had finished, Tom tried again.

"Do you know why he was killed?

"It's possible he were killed for what he was, a Jew who held to the old ways."

"But you don't think so?" said Tom.

"No," said Sam, seeming to reflect for a moment. "I think there was another reason but what that was I don't know."

The two men faced one another in silence for a moment.

"Forgive me for asking," said Tom, at last, "but have you found work since his death?"

Sam gave a harsh laugh.

"Work? No, nor any prospect of it. Two days since, I went to the new police office in Wapping hoping they would accept me in some capacity. Alas, they did not."

"Did they say why?" said Tom.

"No, but then I am a Jew."

"Pray, what has that to do with it?"

"You don't know?" said Sam, bitterly. "You don't know that every Jew is considered a thief, whatever his circumstances?"

The foetid scent of unwashed humanity hung in the dry heat of a July morning as, two days later, Tom sat in the back of the courtroom and watched another defendant being brought in to toe the line in front of the magistrate's table.

"You are charged that on . . ."

Tom had seen it all several times in the week since he'd been appointed a river surveyor with the new police and been given his tipstaff and commission of authority. He thought of the dozen or so arrests he'd made, most of them resulting in no more than a talking-to by the magistrate, but one or two likely to pay for their impudence with a swift trial and a hanging outside the gates of Newgate.

"How do you plead? Guilty or not guilty?" barked the magistrate's clerk.

"It's me perquisites, your worship, so it is." The prisoner's whining voice was barely intelligible. "It's our right. Every man what works on the river is allowed his perquisites. I never stole nothing, your honour, so help me God."

It was always the same plea, the same defence — a belief in the absolute right of those who worked on the river to their "perquisites". Tom shook his head. He knew that, like as not, it was the only wage the man would see, the only means he had of feeding himself and his family.

"I find the case proved." Harriot's voice drifted past Tom's ear. "Fined five shillings. Seven days to pay. The property is escheat."

Tom looked across the courtroom and nodded, quietly satisfied. Sam Hart was standing by the door to the gaoler's room, next to Kemp and Tisdale. His crew was, at last, complete. Getting to this point had not been easy.

He recalled his interview with the superintending magistrate the same day he had taken Sam Hart for some lunch. Colquhoun had initially been reluctant to consider the prospect of a Jew being admitted to the institution, particularly, he said, given their well-known propensity to crime. He had eventually agreed to it, but it had taken a considerable amount of Tom's time and effort.

"Next case." The magistrate's clerk was looking at Tom. He jumped to his feet and hurried to the front of the court where two ruddy-faced young men were already waiting by the magistrate's table.

"Carry on, Mr Pascoe," said Harriot. "There's a plea of guilty in this case."

"I'm obliged, your worship. On Monday, July tenth, 1798, at about two o'clock in the morning, I was on patrol in the vicinity of . . ." Tom trotted out his evidence. It was routine and commonplace.

"Anything to say? No? Fined five shillings."

Tom headed for the door.

"Mr Pascoe!" Tom turned to see the chief clerk hurrying after him. "Mr Harriot presents his compliments, sir, and asks that, if you is at leisure, you might spare him a moment in his room."

Tom cursed under his breath. He'd planned to visit his old shipmate Simmonds at the hospital, but that would have to wait. He followed the magistrate into the back office.

"Sit you down, Mr Pascoe." Harriot frowned as he waved Tom to one of the two high-backed, leather armchairs in front of the desk. "I'll come straight to the point since I've but little time before the next case. I've received a confidential letter from Lord Portland, the Secretary of State for the Home Department. It seems the Administration is most concerned about a sudden and unexplained fall in the value of imported goods through this port."

Harriot paused while he reached for his pipe, lighting it with the aid of a wax taper.

"Seems," he said, sucking vigorously, "the fall is having its effect on revenue."

"Was there ever a case," smiled Tom, "when governments were not concerned with money?"

"I don't disagree with you," said Harriot. "But in this case Lord Portland has good case for concern. The cost of this war is, as you probably know, huge. Napoleon is sweeping all before him and we have needed to prop up the Austrians in an effort to keep them in the fight. Added to that, we have the cost of the rebellion in Ireland to consider, not to mention the threat of rebellion both here and in Scotland. All this at a time when the country has yet to recover from the recent war in America."

"I regret, sir, all I know of this is what I've seen in the papers and little of that makes any sense," said Tom.

"Forgive me, Mr Pascoe," said Harriot, with an apologetic sweep of the hand. "I'd quite forgotten you are only recently come ashore. The fact of the matter is that we are in a somewhat sorry state. The Irish have recently risen in open revolt and seem determined to slaughter one another with the utmost vigour. So far, the military is having little effect. Indeed, some say it is adding to the problem, but that's another matter.

"In the meantime, we face dissension north of the border. It seems the Scots are unhappy at what they regard as a curtailment of their freedom. Their perception is not helped by what is generally seen as an over-zealous judiciary and the suspension of habeas corpus. Much the same thing is happening in England, I fear.

"Dealing with all this costs money the country cannot afford. Any increase in the level of taxation — and Mr Pitt is threatening that — will almost certainly give rise to open rebellion. The fall in the revenue from this port is the final straw, and if it cannot be resolved, the Prime Minister will have little alternative but to impose the new tax and live with the consequences. His single, overriding aim, more pressing even than the urgency of domestic reform, is victory over the French."

Tom looked out through the window. The tide had fallen, exposing a broad stretch of mud sloping up to the walls of the police office. For nearly a minute he remained silent, contemplating the scene.

"I assume," he said at last, "the loss of goods is thought to be the result of depredations. There can be no other reason why the Secretary of State would wish to involve us."

"Aye," said Harriot. "That's about it. If we can find those responsible and put a stop to the plundering before Mr Pitt needs to raise his taxes, we may yet avoid a most calamitous uprising."

"Do we have any intelligence on who might be involved?"

"Very little, I'm afraid. What we do have suggests a highly organised operation controlled by a single gang, perhaps only one person."

"Pray, how do we know that?"

"The people at Customs House, sir. They say the fall in the volume of imports is mainly confined to sugar," said Harriot. "It's this targeting of specific goods which leads them to suspect the involvement of a single group of criminals."

"And you want me to see what can be done."

"Aye, Mr Pascoe, I do," said Harriot.

There was not so much as the hint of a breeze to bring relief to the heat of the afternoon as Tom made his way up Fox's Lane, conscious of a change in direction that his conversation with Harriot had signalled. For the first time since joining the marine police, he felt a thrill of anticipation at what he was being asked to do. Until this moment, he'd found it difficult to overcome the apathy with which he'd accepted his post. The routine of patrol, arrest and court appearance had been the reality of his daily existence since he'd joined the new institution, and had acted as a constant reminder of the life he had left behind. Now there was the promise of change.

He thought of the enormity of the task facing him and of the consequences of failure. There seemed little doubt the country would rise up in revolt if further taxes were imposed, however necessary the Administration felt them to be. Tom considered his options. There weren't many, and those he did have didn't look at all promising.

He looked up and saw the Three Foxes tavern. It was where he'd been given a beating the night the *Swansong* was plundered. He'd almost given up hope of finding those responsible. Certainly, he'd been unable to find anyone who'd seen anything. Even Sam Hart had been unable to help beyond the brief details he'd supplied on the morning after the incident.

Tom stared at the front door of the tavern. He had the oddest feeling he was overlooking some detail of the attack: something he had seen, heard, or perhaps smelt, on that night. He stopped and looked around as he searched his memory, but nothing came to him. Reluctantly, he walked on.

Turning into the Ratcliff Highway, he saw that a crowd had formed in the middle of the road, the source of its interest lost amongst the press of bodies. Tom strode on. Dancing bears, performing monkeys and the rest were not to his taste. He was about to pass by when he heard a cry of pain. He stopped and looked over the shoulders of the crowd. An old man lay in the roadway, hats scattered around him. Five youths were kicking his near unconscious body.

"Go to Chelsea . . ." shouted one of them, the rest of his advice drowned out by a bout of jeering from the crowd.

There was no conscious decision on Tom's part to become involved. Or at least not one he would have recognised as, with a bellow of rage, he launched himself at the crowd, his thrusting elbows forcing a passage through the scrum. Nearing the front, he caught sight of a flurry of movement on the far side of the circle and was surprised to see Sam Hart emerging from the crowd, his fists flying in all directions. The next moment they were both in among the braying youths.

"Behind you." Sam's voice was almost drowned by the excited yelps of the onlookers.

Tom spun round. One of the youths was closing with him, the sun glinting off the pointed steel blade in his hand. Tom sidestepped the incoming thrust. It wasn't enough. He felt the knife rip through the material of his coat, the point cutting into his flesh. Instinct took over. He lashed out, his fist connecting with a loud smack of flesh on bone. The youth's nose exploded in a bright ball of red gristle and his body crumpled to the ground. Breathing hard, Tom swivelled round at the sound of a footstep behind him, his right fist drawn back and ready to fly again. Just in time, he recognised Sam.

"If I'd known what a bonehead the scrub was," grumbled Tom, nursing an injured hand and looking about him, "I'd have hit him somewhere else. Have they all gone?"

"Aye, they've gone," said Sam, laughing. "Except that there cove what you whacked — and the hat-seller."

"The old man! I'd quite forgotten him!" Tom looked round at the gaunt figure in the roadway, now sitting up with his shoulders hunched forward, the papery skin of his shrunken face hidden behind a long white beard tinged with yellow.

"Are you hurt, sir?" Tom helped him to his feet and watched him pile his meagre assortment of hats on his head.

"I am well enough, sir." The old man looked at Tom with bright, coal-black eyes, his heavily accented English only just comprehensible. "I thank you for your protection."

He turned and shuffled away, his black, ankle-length coat incongruous in the heat of the afternoon, a collection of tins and brightly coloured rags suspended from a string round his waist.

"The mark of poverty," said Tom, quietly.

"I don't know about that, your honour, but you and he should both be at the apothecary's," said Sam, nodding at a dark patch of blood oozing from under Tom's blouse.

"You're probably right," said Tom, gingerly pressing against the wall of his stomach, "yet I suspect it would've been the devil's own job persuading the old man of such a course. As for myself, it is only a flesh wound, but since I was on my way to the hospital I may choose to see the apothecary if he is at leisure."

Sam pursed his lips and shook his head in mock despair.

"Why do you suppose he was being flogged?" mused Tom.

Sam shot him a glance.

"The old man?" he asked, quietly. "For no other reason than he was a Jew."

"You know him?" asked Tom.

"Know him, no, but I've seen him walk these streets for many a year. His name is Moses Solomon. You saw the hats he wore and the coloured rags around his waist, and the tin cans? They are all the stock of his trade as a hat-seller and ragman. It's a common enough occupation for a Jew, especially an Ashkenazi, like me and the old man there."

"But the beating. Is that a common occurrence for a Jew?"

"Aye, it is for men like him who hold to the old ways and have not the strength to resist attacks. For them, the barbarous jeers and cuffs of their fellow beings are daily fare. It was the same for my old employer, Jonas Levi, although I tried to warn him many a time."

"And you? What about you?" asked Tom. "From what I saw a few minutes past, there can't be many who'd best you. Where did you learn to handle yourself so?"

"The Jew's Punch." said Sam, his eyes twinkling. "My tutor was Mr Mendoza."

"Daniel Mendoza? The prizefighter?"

"Aye, the very same."

"So it's him I should thank for my deliverance," laughed Tom. Then, suddenly sombre, he added, "But I'm ashamed of my fellow countrymen that they should behave thus."

"Aye, it is bad, but not as bad as in other parts of Europe," said Sam. "My mother and father originally came from Poland, where I was born. We and the other Jews who lived in our village were forced to leave when I was no more than a lad because of the treatment we suffered at the hands of our neighbours."

"You came here straight from Poland?"

"No," said Sam, shaking his head. "After we left the village we travelled to Prussia, hoping to reach Berlin. It was a long way and the winter snow was deep and difficult to cross. But eventually we reached the city where we believed we would be made welcome. We had been told that many Jews lived there and would help us find shelter and work. But when we arrived at the gates of the city we were ordered to another gate — the Rosenthaler Tor — the one reserved for cattle and for us Jews."

"But you were allowed to enter the City?"

"Aye, we were allowed to enter but only after we were interrogated," said Sam, smiling sadly. "We found shelter in the Jewish ghetto of the city and soon my father was again following his employment as a peddler selling beads. I often walked with him and witnessed the abuse and the beatings heaped upon him by the strangers who passed us in the street. He was not a strong man and could not defend himself. One day, when we had been there for about three months, he told us that we had been refused permanent residency in Prussia and would have to leave. The authorities said there were too many of us Jews coming from Poland and they could allow no more to remain. They said we were *Betteljuden* — Jews who moved from place to place seeking charity wherever they went. At first we did not know how we would survive, but then we began to hear tales of England where a Jew might live and work free of the humiliation that was his daily fare in Europe. That was how we came to travel here."

"And your father found work here?" asked Tom.

"Not at first," said Sam. "He sought help from the *parnasim* of the synagogue in Gun Yard and they gave us charity which allowed my father to buy some beads to sell. My mother often says that by comparison with the rest of Europe, England is a haven of safety and tranquillity for those of our faith."

"I fear that must prove small consolation to men like our friend the hat-seller," said Tom.

Sam nodded, watching the last of the crowd drift away.

"Chelsea!" said Tom.

Sam looked startled. "I beg pardon, your honour?"

"One of those scrubs said 'Go to Chelsea'. What do you suppose he meant? Does the old man come from Chelsea?"

"No sir, he's a local man," said Sam, ruefully. "The words are used as an insult against us Jews. I'll tell you the story one day."

His injury more uncomfortable than serious, Tom left Sam and continued his way to the London Hospital. He was shocked by what his new crewman had told him about the place of Jews in society; had not realised such prejudices existed. He'd seen Jews walking the streets of London, of course. It would have been impossible not to have noticed the broad-brimmed hats and long black caftans that most of them wore, or to have avoided their persistent attempts to sell their lemons and beads and the rest.

But prejudice and ill-treatment? He could only suppose his years at sea had shielded him from the excesses of his countrymen in their treatment of these people.

Reaching the hospital, he crossed the yard to the receiving room. It was full. He decided he'd come back after he'd seen Simmonds, and turned to leave.

"Why, Captain, you are quite done for."

Tom's heart missed a beat. He looked round to see Peggy Tompkins standing by the door of one of the consulting rooms, another woman beside her.

"It's nothing serious, Miss Tompkins," he managed. "I'll be right enough."

"You'll do me the honour, sir, of letting me be the best judge of that," said Peggy. She waved a hand in the direction of her companion, a short, stoutish woman of about fifty, with thick, protruding lips and close-set eyes. "This is my colleague, Miss Squibb."

"Charmed, Miss Squibb." Tom barely had time to bow before Peggy took him firmly by the elbow and led him into the empty consulting room.

"What happened?" she asked when the two of them were alone.

"Some unpardonable scrubs — I beg pardon, Miss Tompkins — some lads making sport of an old man," said Tom. "A friend and I thought it high time they were taught their manners."

"And you were stabbed?"

"A flesh wound," said Tom, suddenly embarrassed. "One of the fellows fancied his chances. I'll live."

"Take off your jacket and your shirt if you please. Captain, then sit down." She indicated a stool in the corner.

Tom hesitated, decided it was best not to resist, and did as he was told. She followed him over and bent her head close to the wound, her lips pursed in concentration. He stole a glance at her, noting the delicate sweep of her neck, her creamy skin, and the way the tip of her nose tilted. A wisp of her raven-black hair had escaped from the confines of her mobcap and he was reminded of the first time he'd noticed her.

"Have you never seen a girl before, Captain?" The hint of a smile played on her lips.

Tom coughed and looked away, his cheeks on fire.

"There's nothing damaged that I can see," said Peggy a few moments later, "although, to be sure, you've suffered a pretty cut and will doubtless be feeling the result for a day or two. Shall I arrange for you to see the apothecary?"

"No, I'll not trouble him," said Tom. "If you will dress the hurt for me, it will more than suffice. And perhaps tomorrow I may return for the bandages to be changed?"

"Tomorrow might be a trifle soon, Captain," she said, avoiding his eyes. "But you may come at the same hour on Wednesday and somebody will see to the new dressing."

"Thankee," said Tom, when Peggy had at last finished dressing his wound. "But I was quite forgetting I was on my way to see Mr Simmonds. How does he do? Well, I hope?"

"Mr Simmonds was discharged a week since," said Peggy, pushing the fallen lock of hair back into place. "The principal surgeon, Mr Blizard, found that your friend's hurt was not as serious as first thought. But if you wish to see him, we expect him back on Monday so that he may receive his certificate."

"Certificate?" said Tom, perplexed.

"Aye," said Peggy. "All patients are expected to return to the hospital after they're discharged. They're required to give thanks to God and to the Board of

Governors for their recovery. When they do so, they're given a certificate."

"Do many return?"

"Yes, they do, and with good reason. If they fail to do so, they forfeit their certificate, and without a certificate they'll not again be treated by this hospital."

"I'd no idea," said Tom.

"Now, if you'll excuse me, Captain," said Peggy, turning to go, "I must leave you and see to other patients."

CHAPTER
NINE

It was early evening by the time Tom settled into the stern sheets of the police galley at the start of another tour of duty. The soft pink of the dying day glinted off the surface of the Thames; dancing patterns of light reflected on the furled sails of nearby ships.

"Cast off fore and aft," said Tom. "We'll head up to the Bridge."

He glanced at Sam as the galley pulled away from the stairs, and caught a glimpse of a preoccupied frown on his friend's face. He'd seen that same look before, when Sam appeared to withdraw into himself. He'd once tried to coax the reason out of him but Sam had been reticent, even resentful, and Tom had thought better of raising the matter again.

A movement close to the Southwark shore distracted him. His eyes flitted over the maze of vessels, searching the lengthening shadows thrown across the water by the forest of masts, but he could see nothing out of the ordinary. Not at first. Then a sack appeared at one of the forward gun ports of a brig moored off Griffin's Wharf, and dropped into a skiff lying alongside.

The boat's single occupant heaved the sack into the stern sheets and returned to his place amidships. It was a common enough sight and one to which few would have given a second glance. Close by, another dozen brigs and snows were surrounded by a cluster of small boats, scuttling about like so many ants, but something drew Tom's attention to this one particular skiff and its occupant.

He studied the man, noting the quick, furtive turns of his head as he looked up and down the reach, and the apparent casualness with which he lounged on the thwart. Tom hesitated, weighing the effort needed to cross the busy river against the possibility of detecting an offence.

"Give way together! Handsomely now!" Tom felt a rush of adrenaline as the twenty-seven-foot galley curved round in a tight arc picking up speed as she went, her sleek lines slicing through the ebbing tide, her bow-wave creaming the water. He raised himself a few inches off his seat and peered through the flying spume. Fifty yards still separated him from the skiff, but already their approach had been noticed. The man was pointing frantically at the approaching galley, and others were now running from the deck of the brig and lowering themselves into the waiting skiff.

Tom wiped the spray from his eyes and stared beyond the skiff to the distant foreshore where a layer of black clay was just visible above the falling tide. It would be difficult but not impossible for the men to put ashore there and escape into the back lanes of Southwark. He looked back at the rocking skiff as the last of the men from the brig dropped into her and her oars were slipped into place.

"They're going for the shore . . ." he said, trying not to shout. Then, "No, they're turning."

Incredulous, Tom watched the bows of the skiff point down river. He turned at the sound of a warning shout and was in time to see a barquentine close on his starboard beam clubbing down on the tide, her t'gallants flapping lazily in light wind. Tom cursed his own stupidity and hauled on the starboard guy, his body thrown sideways as the rowing galley heeled in a tight turn to pass under the ship's stern, losing precious seconds in the process.

Seconds later the galley had cleared the barque's stern and was picking up speed. Soon they were flying again, the galley's bow-waves tossed high, her three-man crew wide-eyed, straining at their oars; their faces glistening with sweat; their quarry now fifty, perhaps sixty, yards ahead of them. Martha's Dock, Pearson's Wharf and Mr Butler's Wharf all came and went. On the north bank, the grey, forbidding battlements of the Tower of London slipped quietly astern, there place taken by an untidy jumble of buildings hugging the shoreline of the parish of St Katherine where thick black smoke belched from a score of chimneys. Tom looked over his shoulder. The barquentine, was still very close.

"They're turning," shouted Tom, staring at the fleeing skiff. "They're heading for — Christ, they haven't seen her. They haven't seen that barquentine! They'll —"

There was a splintering crash as the skiff collided with the big ship. Her bows reared up out of the water and sheets of spray spewed outwards as her gunwales scraped down the length of the barquentine's hull, her crew tossed around the bottom-boards like pebbles in a shaken jar.

Tom swung the galley into the tide and, waving the barquentine on her way, fetched alongside the damaged skiff, his eye drawn to a thin, bedraggled figure in the stern sheets. The man's face was partially hidden by long strands of greasy hair. Tom felt sure he knew him.

"You there!" he said. "Look at me, sir!"

Slowly, the man raised his head, his blanched features a mask of fear.

There was no doubting the crumpled form of Gabriel Newman.

Rowing against the tide, it was dark before Tom arrived back at the police office with Gabriel Newman and the other men he'd arrested on suspicion of theft.

"The case appears to be perfectly straightforward, Mr Pascoe," said the magistrate, after listening to Tom's account of what had happened. "I really can't see why you feel it necessary to introduce the element of King's Evidence. What possible advantage could there be?"

"If we charge these men with larceny, they'll certainly go down," said Tom, irritated by the questioning of his judgement, "but we'll get nothing else out of them."

"What do you mean?" Harriot looked up sharply.

"One of the prisoners is a man called Gabriel Newman," said Tom, pinching the bridge of his nose in exasperation. "He's a close associate of Joseph Boylin."

"Boylin? I know the name from somewhere," said Harriot.

"He runs the Queen's Head in Shadwell and is said to have strong republican sympathies," said Tom. "His premises are used as a passing-house for most of the lumpers and coal heavers working Limehouse Reach and the Lower Pool. As such, he controls much of the port area and decides who works and who doesn't. I've heard he rules his patch with an iron fist, and there are those who say he's either directly implicated in the widespread plunder of the port, or he knows who is. Either way, Gabriel Newman could offer us a way into his world."

"Yes, I remember now. Mr Colquhoun has mentioned him." Harriot leaned back in his chair, his interlaced fingers resting on his substantial stomach. "But do we have any evidence to show that he's involved in plundering the port?"

"Last Tuesday I checked the records of the Shadwell police office for details of property reported stolen on the river these six months since," said Tom. "I compared the figures against the records kept by the Tackle House porters. Amongst other things, these records provide the names of the master lumpers who hired tools to unlade specific vessels. In a significant number of cases, the ships from which cargo had been plundered were unladed by Boylin, the plunder taking place within three to four weeks of the start of the unlading process."

"Mmm," grunted Harriot, polishing the top of his cane with the palm of his hand. "Not the strongest evidence I've ever heard . . ."

"It is nevertheless a substantial pointer as to who might be responsible," said Tom, breathing deeply. The search for facts that could and would be tested in a court of law was trying his patience. "If the prisoner Newman can be persuaded to talk, we might well obtain the necessary evidence."

"We might, sir," said Harriot, staring at the surface of his desk as though trying to remember something. Suddenly, he looked up. "I recall now having heard you mention the name Boylin to me on a previous occasion. As I remember, you knew the fellow from your days at sea. Didn't you have occasion to court-martial him?"

"Yes, I did."

"And wasn't Boylin later involved in the unlading of your own ship, the *Swansong*?" said Harriot watching his subordinate through a cloud of tobacco smoke.

"Aye." Tom's irritation was rising again. The questions had the feel of an interrogation.

"That was the cause of further trouble between you, if I'm not mistook."

"Do you mean to suggest, sir, that personal interests have got in the way of my professional judgement?"

"Well, sir, have they?"

Tom's eyes narrowed. He'd already recognised the potential for a conflict of interest, but that didn't mean he was about to admit it.

"I know, sir, where my duty lies."

"Good," said Harriot, eyeing him carefully. "There is a great deal riding on this matter and, frankly I've no time to waste appointing someone else to look into it."

For a moment or two the magistrate sucked on his pipe.

"Let's suppose you're right about Boylin and he is the man we're after. How, precisely, d'you see Newman helping to catch him?"

"As I said, sir, Newman is a close associate of Boylin," replied Tom. "Indeed, my enquiries show the two men have known each other from boyhood. In spite of this, the relationship between them is not warm and Newman is rumoured to be in constant fear of Boylin. I believe it was fear that prompted Newman to give perjured evidence against me at my inquest. It was almost certainly done on Boylin's orders."

"Good God, sir," cried Harriot. "Is Newman involved in that case as well?"

"In the normal course of events," said Tom, brushing aside the interruption, "I would've said we had absolutely no hope of persuading Newman to tell us what he knows about Boylin. But now we may have a chance."

"Because he faces the prospect of being hanged?"

"Precisely, sir. The value of the stolen property is more than enough to hang him. Newman already knows this and his neck will be itching as we speak. What I propose is that we ask him to turn King's Evidence against Boylin in return for a Royal Pardon."

"I see." Harriot took his pipe from his mouth and examined the bowl with more than usual interest. "It could work. Of course, the trial judge will need to be satisfied that Newman's role in the original offence was a minor one and Newman will have to give evidence against at least two of the others. If those conditions are met, he might get a pardon."

Tom waited.

"Very well," said Harriot. "On that basis, speak to him, but don't make any promises we can't keep. Granting a pardon isn't up to us, more's the pity . . . Yes, what is it?"

A light knock on the door and the chief clerk entered the room.

"Begging your pardon, your worship, but if Mr Pascoe is at leisure, he might wish to go to Limehouse Reach. There's a floater what he might be interested in seeing."

"By your leave, sir?" said Tom, getting to his feet. "I'll take my crew with me."

"Certainly, Mr Pascoe. I think we've finished here."

An hour later, Tom stood on the foreshore of the Isle of Dogs, a lantern in his hand, looking down at a bloated, black-mottled cadaver lying on its back, its grinning, mud-filled mouth drawn tight over protruding teeth, the skin of its arms and legs peeling away. The bile rose in Tom's throat. He'd seen enough to know its identity.

"Are you certain he's your cook?" Tom's fellow surveyor, Joshua Judge, glanced enquiringly at him.

Tom looked back at the devastated features that had, in life, been William Denny, late of the *Swansong* and now barely recognisable. Nearly five weeks in the Thames had seen to that. It was only the clothing that enabled him to be sure of the identity of the man who'd served him, first in the Navy and then, in more recent times, aboard the *Swansong*.

"Aye, it's Denny. He was a good man," said Tom, shaking his head. "He didn't deserve to die like this."

"Does he have a family that'll claim the body?" Judge seemed keen to be away.

"He spoke of a brother, but as to his whereabouts . . . I'll make enquiries of the Navy Board. It's a long shot but they may know something." Tom shrugged, his eyes still fixed on the corpse. "Are there any injuries? Anything that would suggest a struggle?"

Judge looked uncomfortable. "I confess I've not looked. He's not a pretty sight."

Tom squatted down, his forehead furrowed in concentration, his mind cleared of all emotion. The sadness he'd felt when he first saw Denny's lifeless form was now banished to the nether regions of his mind. This decomposing mess was no longer his old shipmate, not even a human being. For the moment the corpse was reduced to an object, a thing of interest only in so far as it might help his investigation. Beyond that, he dared not go.

He studied the remains, searching the lifeless form with care, noting the missing shoes, the peeling black skin and the grey flesh beneath, the abrasions on what was left of the chin and nose. None of these concerned him. He'd seen the way carcasses sank in the early stages of death, before the putrefying gases floated them to the surface again, face down, the head and feet lower than the torso, the bodies dragged back and forth by the tide. It was the reason so many lost their shoes or suffered abrasions to the chin and forehead. And within ten days or so, the skin would turn to black and begin to peel off and the eyes lose their colour, replaced with opaque balls of grey. Suddenly, Tom stiffened.

"Hart? D'you hear there?" Tom peered over his shoulder. "Bear a hand and fetch me a cloth. Anything will do, but dip it in the water first, will you?"

"One damp cloth coming up, sir."

Tom held the lantern closer and dabbed at the mottled skin of the forehead until he found what he suspected would be there.

"Can you see? Hidden just under the hairline." Tom pointed. "The skin is parted and reveals the skull."

"Aye, so I do," said Sam doubtfully. "But that could've happened after he went overboard. He could've struck the keel of a ship or some such."

"You might be right," said Tom, getting to his feet. "Remind me to ask the physician doing the post mortem, what he thinks. It might be something or it might not."

He turned back to Judge. "You'll be taking the body in, of course."

"This man discovered it." Judge beckoned to one of the onlookers. "He'll wish to claim his reward from the coroner. I'll tell him to take it to the office at Wapping.

113

I thought you might prefer that. The post mortem can be done there and you'll be given the findings directly."

"No," said Tom, with greater force than he'd intended. "I want you to take him in yourself. I suspect he was murdered, and I want the body preserved for whatever evidence it can still yield. Your man can claim his reward later."

He turned to go, but stopped and looked back at the body lying in the mud. Something was missing. He bent down and let his eyes move over Denny's remains for a final time. It would come to him. Of that he was sure. Very slowly he raised a hand in salute.

"Adieu, my friend," he murmured. "Until we meet again in Fiddler's Green."

CHAPTER
TEN

Gabriel Newman stared at the wooden floor as the morning sunlight streamed in through the bars of his cell window. Wretchedness gripped him — had done so for at least the last half-hour. There was no escaping Tom Pascoe's incessant questioning. From beyond the thick stone walls of the prison he could hear the clamour of passing traffic, a constant reminder of the freedom that was no longer his.

"Sure, I'm a dead man if I talks," he said, sitting on the edge of his cot, his forehead resting in the heel of one hand, the other tracing patterns on his knee.

"And you're a dead man if you don't," said Tom, crouching in front of him. Then his voice softened. "Your only chance is to turn King's Evidence, old cock. Think on it. What's Boylin ever done for you?"

Newman didn't answer at first, then, slowly, his eyes swivelled to meet Tom's.

"You'll not be knowing him like I do," he said, his voice devoid of emotion. "Sure, he's a dangerous cully you'll not be wanting to cross. Besides, he'll be knowing I've snitched and then I'm as good as dead."

"He'll never get the chance if you tell me what I need to know," said Tom. "You and I both know Boylin's up to his neck in villainy. I just need a few details to fill in the gaps, and for that I might be able to save your neck from being stretched."

Newman winced. "What sort of details?"

Tom expelled a lungful of air and sat down on the cot.

"What happened to the old man on the *Swansong*?"

"They say he were thrown overboard," said Newman, carefully picking the dirt from under a fingernail. "Sure, everyone knows that."

"Who threw him overboard?"

"How will I be knowing?" Newman shrugged.

"You're lying to me, Gabriel." Tom leaned in close to Newman's ashen face. "You know exactly what happened that night."

"I can't be telling you, Master Pascoe. My life's worthless, else."

"Please yourself," said Tom, getting to his feet. "I've tried to help you; now, as far as I'm concerned, you can swing."

"Wait." Newman raised a hand, his fingers outstretched.

"Aye?" said Tom, turning back from the door of the cell.

"What is it will be happening to me . . . If I tell you what I know, like?"

"Depends what you tell me," said Tom. "But if it's good, a King's Pardon."

"And I'll not swing?"

"I told you, a King's Pardon. So no, you won't swing."

Newman struggled with his fears, his eyes fixed on his lap, his fingers folding and unfolding in unceasing movement.

"There *is* something I can be telling you . . ."

"Yes?"

"On Thursdays, Master Boylin is after having a sporting night at the Queen's Head. Most times, a gentleman comes down from London and they talk, privately like."

"What about?"

"I'll not be knowing that, your honour. All I've heard is Master Boylin is mighty happy to see him."

"What does he look like, this gentleman? What's his name?"

"I don't know that neither," Newman replied. "I never sees him. I just hear folk talk, that's all."

"Christ, Newman, you think that's enough to save your neck?" shouted Tom. "You'll have to do a deal better than that."

"Master Hart's in danger." The words came tumbling out, mumbled, indistinct.

"Sam Hart? What d'you mean?" Tom grabbed the Irishman's shirt and pulled him to his feet. "What sort of danger?"

"It's . . . it's on account of what he saw," said Newman, his hands clasped, the pupils of his eyes dilated with fear. "He's in mortal danger."

"You mean someone wants to kill him?" said Tom.

"Aye."

"What's he supposed to have seen?"

Newman turned his head away. He'd said too much. He felt the walls of his cell closing in on him. If he told Pascoe the truth — that he'd been present when a young man had been murdered and that Sam had seen them — he'd certainly hang. And yet, if he didn't, he'd still hang.

"A man was turned off," he blurted. "Master Hart saw it done."

"Master Hart has never mentioned anything about this to me," said Tom.

Newman shrugged. "Perhaps he'll not be knowing what he saw."

"So you're telling me someone wants to kill Master Hart because he witnessed a murder. Is that right?"

"Aye, it were that and . . ." Newman stopped, appalled by his indiscretion.

"And what?"

"Naught. It'll not be any of me business," said Newman, avoiding Tom's eye.

"Tell me, you death's-head-on-a-mop-stick, before I kill you myself." Tom bent forward, his fingers closing round Newman's throat. "Is it because of the inquest?"

"No, it'll not be on account of that." Newman struggled for breath. "He's found out about Master Hart."

Tom let go.

"Who has? And what's he found out?"

"Ask Master Hart, your honour. He knows." Newman's eyes blinked rapidly.

"When will it happen, this attempt on Master Hart's life?"

"I know no more than I've told you, your honour," whispered Newman.

"Then I can't help you," said Tom, stepping to the door of the cell. "If you won't tell me what you know, that's a matter for you."

Newman watched the door close and heard the key turn in the lock.

"Will I be after having a pardon now?" he called out.

In the distance, he heard a long, derisory laugh and the sound of retreating footsteps. Then silence.

Sam Hart watched the tip of his oar with exaggerated interest as he raised it clear of the water and leaned forward for another pull. He'd upset Tom. That much was obvious. But his business was his business, and he had no wish to discuss the threats made on his life or the reasons for them, even with Tom.

"Don't think I'm not grateful, but —"

"I simply want to know," interrupted Tom, "what Newman meant when he told me Boylin had found out about you? What's he found out?"

"He thinks I saw him murder a man," said Sam, watching a barge drift by, a stream of air bubbles following in its wake. "But I saw nothing beyond what looked like some rags in the roadway and Boylin crouching over them. I've tried to find out who the victim was, but no one's talking."

"No, it wasn't that," said Tom. "Newman mentioned the killing and then said there was another reason Boylin was after you. He wouldn't tell me what it was."

Sam shrugged his shoulders. Was it possible that Boylin now knew of his hatred of him and the reason for it? Was he afraid of what Sam might do to him? That, at least, would explain the threats and Boylin's attempts on his life. He looked up. Tom was watching him, waiting for an answer. But he wasn't ready to talk, to explain what had happened. It was too soon. The pain was still too raw.

Rain spattered on the window panes as Peggy Tompkins walked down the length of George Ward, checking that everything was in order: the blankets smoothed, soiled bandages picked up off the floor, the lunch plates cleared away. She skirted round a group of students gathered round one of the beds, listening to the principal surgeon.

"It is of the utmost importance," William Blizard was saying, "that an incision of adequate length should be made rapidly and with one sweep of the knife." He ran a finger around the patient's upper thigh in a swift circular movement. "Pain, gentlemen, is lessened by opium — I trust you're listening to all this, Mr Gerrard — and by preliminary compression of the nerves supplying the part. Are we all clear on that?"

The principal surgeon looked up as Nurse Tompkins passed. She thought she saw the flicker of a smile cross his thin lips but she couldn't be sure. Reaching the far end of the ward, she turned, just as a raucous voice from beyond the ward door shattered the calm.

"Why, bugger me if it ain't Captain Pascoe!" There was no doubting Charity Squibb's staccato boom.

120

"You've come to see Miss Tompkins, ain't you, Captain?"

Peggy's cheeks turned to fire as all eyes swivelled to the door of the ward and then to her. Even Mr Blizard had stopped talking. A moment later, the door banged open and Charity stood in the opening, her body swaying from side to side, a grin on her fat lips, a bottle of gin in her right hand.

"He's 'ere, Miss Tompkins." Charity's bellow would have done credit to a bos'un's mate at the height of a battle. "Your Captain Pascoe's 'ere . . . you know, the feller what you've been talking about."

Peggy hurried over and caught hold of Charity's elbow, propelling her back through the door from whence she'd come. It was a second or two before she saw Tom.

"Why, Captain Pascoe," she managed. "Give you joy, sir."

"Joy, Miss Tompkins." He looked as uncomfortable as she felt.

"Why, of course," said Peggy. "I'd quite forgotten. You have returned for a change to your dressings. And some days overdue, are you not?"

"Aye, I regret I was otherwise engaged. Is it of inconvenience to you?"

"Of all things, it is not," said Peggy, glowering at the still grinning Charity. She motioned Tom to follow and led the way across the lobby to Harrison Ward.

"Where are all the patients?" asked Tom, surveying the empty room into which they had come.

"It's been like this for some time," said Peggy. "Nearly half the hospital is closed for lack of financial contributions. Our benefactors have been obliged to contribute more to the war effort and consequently have less to give to us."

"And the sick? What happens to them?"

"They must wait until a bed becomes available," said Peggy in a matter-of-fact tone. "Now, Captain, if you would be good enough to remove your coat and blouse, we'll see what we can do for you."

She worked in silence, removing the old dressing and cleaning the wound, aware of the pleasure she felt in Tom's presence, at the sound of his voice, and the feel of his skin. Only once before had she felt this way about a man, but that was over. She would never see him again. She pushed the memory from her mind.

"Have you always been here? At this hospital, I mean?" Tom's voice broke in on her thoughts.

"Not always." Peggy glanced up at him. Outside the rain had stopped and a patch of blue sky had appeared, low down on the horizon. "I left home to accept a position as a governess in London. It was from there I was offered the post of a servant at this hospital."

"Oh?" said Tom, enquiringly.

"It . . . it wasn't entirely my choice that I should change my occupation thus," said Peggy. She looked away, afraid he would see the unsettling effect he was having on her. She got up quickly and walked over to a cupboard by the door, presently returning with a bundle of freshly laundered bandages. After a moment or two she summoned the courage to go on. "My young charges were a delight to care for, but alas it was not to be."

She looked up at the sound of voices in the lobby. A new patient was being carried into George Ward. She thought of going to Miss Squibb's assistance, then changed her mind. Her fellow nurse could deal with the admission.

"You must miss the children," said Tom.

"Yes, I do," said Peggy, biting her lip. "They were wonderful."

"Forgive me, Miss Tompkins," he said. "I did not mean to pry."

"'Tis nothing," she said, stooping to gather up the soiled bandages.

"Miss Tompkins . . ." Peggy caught the note of hesitation in his voice. "Would you do me the honour of allowing me to speak with you again, when you are next at leisure?"

She paused for the briefest of moments.

"I regret I am not at leisure. That is, not until a week hence, if that suits."

"Of all things, it suits," said Tom, beaming. "We might go to a pleasure garden or to the city. Wherever you wish."

Peggy busied herself for a minute, keeping her back turned towards him. There was a great deal she'd not told him about herself, about the real reason for her journey to this place, about what had happened to cause her to resign her position as governess — and of the man responsible. Her mind travelled back to the last time she'd seen him. Was it possible that she still loved him, even after what had happened? The thought frightened her, as though thinking of him might somehow affect the way she had begun to feel about Tom. With an effort, she again pushed the thought to one side and looked back at her patient.

"I would like that," she said.

The babble of conversation was deafening in the crowded, smoke-filled taproom of the Queen's Head that Thursday evening. Not that the noise appeared to trouble the larger than usual number of dogs who sat yelping between their masters' legs or being cradled in their arms.

In a corner of the room, partially hidden by a wooden latticed screen, Tom sat at a table, his eyes scouring the room, stopping occasionally to examine some detail before moving on again. The place he'd chosen was comparatively dark, or at least dark enough to prevent him being seen by any but the determinedly curious. He'd disposed of his distinctive naval coat, changing it for one of drab brown, and borrowed a wool hat which now covered his long, yellow hair.

He hoped Newman was right about the gentleman who, he claimed, came to Boylin's sporting nights. The information had been weak, but then so was most of the intelligence he regularly received from the dozen or so informants he was cultivating in and around the port — a snippet here, a whispered rumour there or a half-baked interpretation of what had been witnessed.

Much too often he was forced to take a calculated risk and hope his snouts were right.

"Gentlemen, gentlemen, if you please." Boylin stood on a chair and waved his arms in a vain attempt to silence the assembly. Tom swung round and watched him through the lattice. "All those as has a fancy is welcome upstairs for an evening as would warm your hearts."

The blare of voices rose to a hellish din. Dogs were scooped up by their owners and taken towards a door at the foot of the stairs. Tom waited until the taproom was all but empty and then followed the sounds of tramping feet, up a steep staircase.

At the top, he entered a large, low-ceilinged room at the centre of which was a circular, wooden-framed structure about six feet in diameter and about four feet in height. Above this and suspended from a soot-blackened ceiling was a series of fish-oil lanterns. A crude bar stood to the left of the door and behind this was stacked a number of spirit barrels, their once gleaming gilt hoops now filthy and blackened, their sides blistered by the heat of nearby candles. The rest of the area was bare save for a few tables and some benches.

The room filled rapidly. The first comers occupied what little space there was around the circular structure, forcing the later arrivals to drag benches or tables and stand on them so as to gain a better view. Further back, men nursed their dogs in their arms or struggled to control the more restless brutes on the end of brass-studded leather leads. By the door, an elderly man waited, cap in hand, receiving payment from each man that entered. Tom handed over his coins and made his way to the side of the room. From here, he commanded an uninterrupted view, both of the door through which he'd come and the circular pit. Of Boylin, there was no sign.

Soon, the room could take no more occupants and the old man moved to the windows through which the late evening sun was streaming, and put up the shutters. In the ensuing gloom, the lanterns above the pit were lit to shine down onto the white-painted floor, their stuttering light spilling onto the rough faces of those who pressed against the ring.

Then, as if at some unseen signal, the crowd fell silent and heads turned towards a second doorway that Tom had not previously seen, its presence hidden by a curtain. A moment later, this was flung back and Boylin came into the room, his scarred and shrivelled features leering at the expectant onlookers. Behind him came a short, pinch-faced youth of perhaps eighteen, carrying two rusty cages, each filled with a mass of heaving brown fur. Tom recognised him as the youth he'd seen outside the hospital, the one who'd followed him into Fox's Lane.

The two men pushed their way through the jostling swarm and climbed into the centre of the pit where the cages were set down and the wire doors opened. Immediately the boy plunged his ungloved hand into the squirming mass and began pulling at the tails of snarling, snapping rats, depositing them onto the floor of the walled pit.

126

Tom pressed himself behind a pillar and surveyed the scene for a minute or so before turning to the rest of the crowd.

A gentleman, Newman had said. But he'd been unable or unwilling to give any description. In a sense it didn't matter. Tom was confident he'd know the fellow when he saw him, would recognise the signs of awkwardness he'd seen so often in the behaviour of those who had no wish to be recognised.

"Gentlemen, you are welcome to my house." Boylin cleared his throat, the back of his extended fingers touching lightly against his lips, his lank, grey-streaked hair framing his wasted features. "Tonight, for your pleasure, we have no less than four hundred of these handsome creatures as will be pitted against all comers as is prepared to chance their fortune. The first contest will be a fight to the death between, on the one hand, no fewer than fifty of the largest and most ferocious creatures to be found anywhere in London and, on the other, Lucy, the undisputed champion fancy of Wapping. But first things first, gentlemen. Come now, fill your tankards with the finest beer this side of St Paul's."

The tankards filled, a murmur of approval rose from the assembled crowd as a huge bear of a man elbowed his way to the front, carrying a scrawny terrier that struggled to be let loose, her nose pointing directly at the pit, her ears pressed forward.

Behind her, the other dogs that had, until this moment, been largely docile and quiet, now set up a din of howling and barking as the musk of the excited

Lucy reached their quivering nostrils. At once, the fifty or so rats scurried to the side of the pit and, in a frantic attempt to escape, climbed one on the other, forming a pyramid of perhaps two feet in height, their noses pointing up the wall.

"Come, good sirs, you that have dogs, make them shut up." Boylin appeared keen that the business of making money should begin without delay. "Now, what am I wagered Lucy will turn off this prodigious quantity of creatures in five minutes and not a moment longer? Come now! Let's see the colour of your money. Don't be shy, gentlemen."

Amidst the commotion of whining, yelping, struggling dogs, money swiftly changed hands and was given to the old man with the cap, he acting as the stakeholder for the bets that were laid.

The clamour rose to a roar from the packed room as Lucy's owner held her close to his face and whispered to her. The hound struggled to be free, her barking now a constant, high-pitched yelp of unfettered excitement. The man looked to where Boylin's assistant stood by the unmoving pyramid of furry animals.

"Blow on them, Jacob."

From the other side of the room, Tom saw the door to the stairs open a crack and a pair of eyes appear. A short pause and the door opened wider, revealing a thin-faced man of about fifty with a long, sharp nose and cold, expressionless eyes. In contrast to his grey, almost pallid features, he wore a brightly patterned velvet coat over a white silk waistcoat and matching stock and ruffles. For a moment, he remained where he was, his hand stroking a tuft of black hair growing from a mole on his chin.

Tom felt a thrill run down his spine. There was nothing in the man's expensive dress that set him apart from at least another half-dozen gentlemen in the room. Yet something about his behaviour drew Tom's attention as surely as a moth to light.

"Lay away there, Jacob." Tom glanced back to the pit where Lucy's owner was waving furiously in the direction of the rodents, his face flushed with excitement. "Blow on them, for all love."

Jacob obediently blew into the living pile and the rats scattered, scurrying headlong into the centre of the pit. The next moment the terrier was down and rushing at the rodents, her teeth sinking into the neck of first one and then another of the terrified creatures, shaking their bodies from side to side. A cornered animal leapt at its tormentor, sinking its teeth into the dog's muzzle and hanging from the frenzied brute's nose until battered free by the dog's owner.

By the door to the stairs, the stranger flapped a silk handkerchief in front of his nose as though to wave away some unpleasant smell, while his eyes moved round the room, searching for something — or someone.

In the pit, the sordid spectacle of the ratting went on. Blood-flecked saliva frothed around the dog's snapping jaws while dead and dying balls of brown fur were strewn about the floor. The crowd roared its approval, driving the maddened Lucy to ever more frantic efforts until she was finally plucked, still snapping, still snarling, from the blood-soaked pit.

Tom looked back at the stranger. He was still by the door. Suddenly his eyes widened a fraction and his head inclined in the briefest of nods. Tom swivelled round and searched the crowd. Boylin was on the far side of the room, his attention apparently absorbed by what was going on in the pit. Tom studied him for a moment. His focus on the pit was a little too studied, his concentration a little too intense.

Tom's eyes swung back to the stranger. The swaying crowd had obscured his view. He moved to his right, just as an anguished scream tore through the stamping, cheering, drink-fuelled mob. He spun round. In the centre of the pit, he could see the boy, Jacob, standing stock-still, his right arm held out in front of him, a look of horror on his white face. From his hand, a creature the size of a small rabbit dangled, its long, yellow teeth clamped firmly about the boy's thumb, its own neck partially severed, an eye torn from its socket.

Wine-dark blood oozed from the boy's wound and fell in ever faster drops to the floor while the crowd shouted and waved in a mad fury of advice that stopped short of actual help. The boy reached up with his free hand and caught hold of the animal's tail to pull it free until renewed howls of advice stopped him. His let his hand fall back, tears filling his eyes, his mouth tightly closed. Another commotion and the bear-like man whose dog had been the first to fight, clambered into the pit. Grabbing the squealing rat by its throat, he inserted a poker into its mouth and levered it open.

"Best you cut along and see the apothecary with that there hand, young Jacob," said the man, flinging the unfortunate animal to the floor and beating it with the length of iron.

"What? And lose my thumb?" The look of horror on the boy's face drew a groan of sympathy from the crowd. "I'll take my chances, if it's all the same to you."

Tom glanced round for the stranger. He'd gone. So had Boylin. He cursed his stupidity. To his left, the door to the stairs banged closed. He leapt forward and opened it. A coat tail was disappearing through the door at the bottom of the stairs. He hesitated, trying to decide if he should follow. The coat hadn't belonged to the gentleman but it might have been Boylin's. He looked at the second door, the one through which Boylin and his assistant had arrived. The curtain across the opening twitched.

He thought rapidly. The information from Newman had been vague — hints but no real evidence to implicate either Boylin or the stranger in any offence. Even if there had been, he had no authority to act. His powers did not extend this far from the Thames. If anything went wrong . . .

The crowd bellowed its approval at the start of another one-sided orgy of killing as Tom passed through the curtain. On the far side was a short corridor at the end of which was another flight of stairs leading to the ground floor.

Running down the stairs, he entered a small, square room, furnished with a table and some chairs. On a mantelpiece to his right was a lantern, its feeble glow throwing most of the room into deep shadow. Aside from these, the place appeared to be empty. Tom stared into the shadows. On the other side of the room he was able to make out a door and, next to it, a window. It was, he thought, just possible that Boylin and his visitor had left. There had been time enough. Then he caught a faint whiff of lime. His body stiffened, and he closed his hand round the butt of his pistol.

"Will it be Captain Pascoe?" Tom jumped at the sound of Boylin's voice coming out of the darkness. "Is it the magistrate's authority you'll be having to search my house, now?"

"Where is he, Boylin?" growled Tom. "The man you were with."

"I'll not be answering any questions from you, mister," said Boylin, a tremor in his voice. "You've no right to be here. Now, get out before —"

"I asked you a question, Boylin." Tom caught the publican by his coat collar and lifted him up against the wall. "I want an answer."

Behind him, a stair-tread creaked. Tom spun round. Three men had entered the room and were closing with him. Tom pushed Boylin aside and drew his sea service pistol.

"Far enough, I think."

The men stopped, their eyes flicking between the gun and Boylin as though unsure of what to do.

"You've not heard the last of this, mister," said Boylin, waving the men back. "You'll not be coming into an innocent man's house and be getting away with it. You'll pay for this."

"I'm still waiting for your answer, Boylin." Tom swung the barrel round and pointed it at Boylin's chest.

"Jesus, Mary and Joseph." Boylin's jaw dropped as he stared down the muzzle. "I'll not be knowing his name and that's the truth. He came on account of the ratting."

"Why don't I believe you?" said Tom, prodding the publican's chest with a finger of his free hand. "Where is he now?"

"He's gone, Captain." Boylin spread his arms wide, his gaze shifting from the gun to look imploringly at Tom.

Tom turned towards the door. One of the men stood in his way, a thick pair of arms folded across his chest.

Tom moved fast. With pulverising force, he punched the heavy gun-barrel into the underside of the man's jaw, smashing his teeth and sending him crashing, senseless, to the floor.

Outside, a horse's hoof stamped on the hard surface of the alley and a coach door slammed. Tom leapt past the prone figure on the floor, yanked at the door and ran out into the alley. A black coach was disappearing round the corner of the building, swirling dust obscuring the bright paintwork of the coat of arms on its lacquered door.

★ ★ ★

The following day, the sun had not yet made its appearance over the Isle of Dogs when Tom arrived at the police office. Harriot wanted to see him. He wasn't surprised. It wasn't unusual for the magistrate to be at his desk at this hour. He walked up the stairs and knocked on his door.

"Come in, come in, Mr Pascoe," said Harriot, throwing down a sheet of paper he'd been holding. "Damn politicians! Seem to think I've nothing better to do than answer their bloody-fool questions. Sit yourself down. Coffee?"

"Thankee, sir." Tom smiled at the magistrate's outburst; his reputation for plain speaking was well known. He poured himself a coffee and waited for his superior to begin.

"I wanted to catch you before you went afloat," said Harriot. "How did you get on with our friend Newman? We were talking, I think, about a Royal Pardon for him in exchange for some information about Boylin."

"Yes," said Tom, settling himself into a chair. "Unfortunately he wouldn't tell us anything about the scrub."

"That's a pity. Did you get *anything* out of him?" Harriot pushed a pair of spectacles up onto his forehead and rubbed his eyes.

"He did mention a couple of things."

"And they were?" Harriot stifled a yawn and waited for Tom to continue.

"He thought I might be interested in a gentleman who occasionally calls at the Queen's Head for a private meeting with Boylin. He claimed to know nothing beyond that but I thought it was worth a visit. I was there last night and I'm fairly sure I saw the gentleman Newman was referring to."

"Forgive me, Mr Pascoe, but where is this story leading to?"

"Just this. If, as we suspect, Boylin is shifting a large quantity of plunder out of the port, he'll need some help to get rid of it. He can't just turn up at the front door of some coffee house with a couple of tons of sugar and expect to sell it. He'll need a copeman to handle it for him."

"And you believe this gentleman that you saw last night may be the copeman, the receiver?" Harriot leaned forward in his chair, suddenly awake.

"Aye."

"Did you, by any chance, recognise him?"

"I'd know him if I saw him again. But if you mean, could I name him, then I regret not. I think we're going to need Newman's help in that direction despite the fact he says he knows nothing."

"Yes, well . . ." Harriot reached for his pipe and lit it, his eyes half-closed against the rising smoke. He puffed quietly for a minute or two, his face turned to the rain-streaked window from where the early morning light was spilling onto the polished floorboards. Finally, he said, "What was the second thing Newman told you?"

"Apparently, Boylin's got it in for Sam Hart," said Tom. "Wants him killed."

"Why?"

"Not sure. The talk is that it might have been a killing that Sam is supposed to have seen, but we've not managed to find a victim or even anyone who is prepared to talk to us. Hart says that all he saw was a bundle of rags on the ground."

"I see." A note of concern crept into Harriot's voice. "And that's the only reason for the threat?"

"No, there's another, but both Newman and Hart have refused to tell me what," said Tom. "Whatever it is, I think it probably lies at the root of Hart's difficulties, or at least the major part of them. I have a feeling it might also explain why Hart gave evidence at the inquest I was involved in."

"So Hart knows of the threat?"

"Yes, he knows. Apparently it's common knowledge on the riverside. He says he's not concerned, but I'm not at all sure I believe him."

"No, nor me. I'd like to be kept apprised of any developments in that direction. From what you tell me, Boylin is more than capable of carrying out any threat he makes." Harriot leaned across the desk and picked up the paper he'd been reading earlier. "On another subject, didn't you once tell me Boylin was suspected of involvement in the United Irishmen cause?"

"Aye, I think I might have mentioned it," said Tom.

"I thought so," said Harriot. "Well, it seems His Grace, the Duke of Portland, has received broadly similar information. The authorities in Dublin Castle have responded to his request for intelligence about Boylin, confirming that they know of him. Indeed, they suspect him of the killing of a militiaman and say he was on the fringes of the republican movement, but was considered too unpredictable even for them. I've told Lord Portland that you suspect him of being involved in the plundering of the port and, further, that if anybody can solve the case you can. Have you any thoughts about where we might go from here?"

Tom gazed thoughtfully at the magistrate's craggy features. "I regret, sir, we are still some way from being able to prove Boylin's involvement in all this, but there *is* something we could do in the meanwhile. It's a long shot but it might work."

"Spit it out, man. We haven't got all morning." Harriot gritted his teeth and gripped his thigh. Looking up, he caught Tom watching him. "Don't worry about me, sir. Made the mistake of standing in the way of a musket ball when I was in India. Fortunes of war and all that."

"Amen to that, sir," grinned Tom, fingering the scar on the side of his face. "But as I was saying, there is something we might do. It involves locating the sugar stolen from the *Swansong*. If we can do that and link it to Boylin, then I think we will have a stick with which to beat him."

"Do you know where the *Swansong*'s cargo is?" Harriot's eyebrows shot up.

"Not exactly," Tom replied, "but according to one of Sam Hart's informants, it was taken ashore on one of the lower reaches. He didn't, I regret, know which one. After that it disappeared."

"Not much of a future there, then," said Harriot, rolling his eyes. "Not only do we not know where it is, but even if we did, it would've been sold by now."

"I don't think so," said Tom. "The case generated a lot of interest in the newspapers, and I wouldn't mind wagering that whoever's got the goods is having a sorry time shifting it. I don't think anyone will touch it for months."

"Supposing you're right, Mr Pascoe, you still don't know where it is."

"Except for one thing."

Harriot looked up expectantly. "And what might that be, pray?"

"You've never met Boylin, have you, sir? If you had, you'd have noticed his heavily scarred face. I've little doubt the damage was caused by slaked lime."

"I don't quite understand what this has to do with your missing sugar, Mr Pascoe."

"As I say, the *Swansong*'s cargo was apparently taken ashore on one of the lower reaches, which effectively rules out anywhere above Blackwall Point. If that's the case, it means the sugar will have been carried a distance of between two and four miles from the ship, depending on exactly where it was landed. It doesn't make any sense carrying it that far unless Boylin was taking it to a place he knew well, a place so isolated that the chance of detection was almost nil. If, as I believe, Boylin is still working with lime, that points to the pits south of Bow a short ride up the River Lea. Apart from the odd hoy, nothing much moves in those parts. It's a perfect hiding place."

"It seems an enormous risk for him to have taken," said Harriot, removing his pipe from his mouth and blowing a cloud of smoke into the air. "Why d'you suppose he didn't give it straight to his receiver, whoever he is?"

"For the reasons I've already suggested," explained Tom. "The receiver was probably frightened off by the interest of the press and didn't want to get involved. As soon as he knew that, Boylin would've had no option but to hide the sugar until things blew over, And the only place he knew well enough and which suited his purpose, was the lime pits around Bow."

"But there are closer lime pits than that," said Harriot. "What about those north of Limehouse?"

"Too busy," said Tom. "Too many people wandering about."

"Hmm," said the magistrate. "What d'you propose, then, Mr Pascoe?"

"First thing is to find out if my theory's right," said Tom, getting to his feet. "I'm going up to the Lea to see what I can find. I'll be able to tell you more once that's been done."

"Very well," said the magistrate. "But be careful. You know as well as I do how dangerous the lower reaches can be."

"We have little choice in the matter," said Tom. "I'll take Hart with me."

CHAPTER
ELEVEN

Peggy looked at the clock above the door of George Ward. Five minutes past four and still no sign of the relief nurse. She wondered if Captain Pascoe would wait for her. Perhaps he would think she'd changed her mind. She thought of asking Miss Squibb to run down to the main entrance with a message, but realised that Charity Squibb could no more leave the ward than she could. She glanced at the clock again, went to the door and looked out, then returned to her table in the centre of the ward. She stood there for several moments, drumming her fingers.

A week had passed since she'd last seen Tom Pascoe and she was surprised by how difficult she'd found the waiting. Hardly a moment passed without her thinking of him, trying to imagine where he was and what he was doing. She'd often see him in her mind's eye, his tall, muscular figure striding towards her along an unnamed street, his face creased in a smile. At other times the image would fade and she'd see only a part of him, the thickets of fine hair below the knuckles of his hand, the scar on the side of his face, the ripple of muscle in his forearms. Why she should feel this way about a man she hardly knew, she could not tell. It was enough that such pleasures existed.

She forced herself to look round the ward, checking that the floor had been swept, the surgical dressings collected, the patients fed, the water box filled. It was the same old routine, day after day, but she hadn't minded.

Until now.

Now the morning prayers with which each day began had lost their meaning. The daily search for bed bugs was a nuisance. The surgeon's and apothecary's rounds were a test of her endurance.

The door of the ward opened and Peggy turned to see the relief nurse coming towards her, the woman's thick, fleshy hands swinging across her chest as she walked. Peggy smiled a welcome, her tension forgotten, her mind already on the afternoon to come. She caught sight of Miss Squibb grinning broadly, and remembered that her colleague was to accompany her as a chaperone. She felt a stab of disappointment. The thought of having the captain to herself was infinitely more pleasurable.

Quickly, she hurried to the room she shared with Miss Squibb, removing her apron and mobcap as soon as she was out of sight of the ward and letting her long, black hair tumble to her shoulders. She picked up a brush from the table next to her bed and applied it to her thick tresses until they shone, her head bent forward against the quick, sure movements of her arm. That done, she went over to her bed and, from beneath it, pulled out a wooden box. This she opened and took out two silk ribbons of the brightest red, which she placed on the bed. She returned to the box and carefully removed her best — her only — bonnet, a gift from her mother when Peggy had left home. With infinite care she tied the ribbons in her hair and put on the bonnet, fastening it below her chin with its own length of blue silk. For the first time in many a month, she felt beautiful.

By the time she and Charity had reached the gates of the hospital, Tom was already waiting for them, his face freshly shaved, his old blue and white uniform replaced by a brown coat and brown breeches. She noticed he'd added a snow-white lace stock at his throat and lace ruffles at his wrists. He smiled and bowed as they approached.

"Give you joy, Miss Tompkins, Miss Squibb."

"Joy, Captain Pascoe," said Peggy, her heart skipping a beat

She turned her head to indicate Charity, her hand lightly brushing the ribbons in her hair. "Miss Squibb will accompany us if you have no objection."

"No, Miss Tompkins, of all things I have no objection and may I say how well you look in your bonnet." He gestured towards a hackney carriage. "We travel to Temple Stairs by carriage and from there take a boat to Vauxhall Gardens. What do you say, ladies? Or would you prefer Ranelagh Gardens?"

"Why, sir, how wonderful," said Peggy, accepting Tom's hand as he helped her into the carriage. "Let it be Vauxhall. I've heard the waterworks are quite the thing. And the music too."

She didn't say a great deal over the course of the next ten or fifteen minutes. The excitement of meeting Tom had given way to a certain reserve, occasioned by the returning awareness of how little she had told him about herself or her past life. If she hoped for a blossoming of their friendship, she knew she would have to tell him sooner or later. She wondered how he would react, what his response would be.

The filthy, ramshackle buildings of Whitechapel gradually gave way to the taller, grander buildings of Aldgate, the brothels replaced by synagogues, the drinking houses by rag-and-bone shops. At the top of Aldgate, the carriage bore left into Fenchurch Street, where broad sidewalks and lines of wooden posts separated pedestrians from the dangers of flying hooves and fast-turning wheels. Here, the houses were freshly painted and the shops well stocked. Even the leaves of the plane trees were greener and fresher than those on the shrivelled stumps in Whitechapel.

Absorbed in her thoughts, it took Peggy a minute or two to recognise her surroundings. Her pulse quickened as she peered through the carriage window and saw the familiar landscape — the houses she used to pass on her daily walks and the shops she had visited. She barely had time to take it all in before the tree-lined avenue she knew so well came into view and, with it, a flood of memories. She thought of the man she had once loved, and wondered what had become of him. With an effort of will, she tore her eyes away from the avenue and stared at the floor of the carriage, aware that she was trembling. It was not as if she still cared

143

for him. The affair was over. Yet the shock of seeing the place again and the reawakening of memories she had hoped were buried forever were real enough

The moment passed and a lightness returned to her mood. She looked across to where Tom was talking to Miss Squibb and smiled with pleasure. Within the past few days she had begun to hope that his arrival in her life might herald a change in the pattern of her existence; allow her to put behind her the experiences of her past. She didn't want anything to stand in the way of that.

She'd tell him everything — some day.

The massive dome of St Paul's came and went and the carriage picked up speed, dropping down Ludgate Hill into Fleet Street where, a few yards short of Temple Gate, it turned left towards the river.

"Perhaps, Miss Squibb, you might prefer a seat in the bows," said Tom when they reached Temple Stairs, and whistled up a passing wherry. "You'll be able to see so much more from there."

Peggy smiled at the contrivance as she herself was guided to the stern sheets of the skiff to sit alongside Tom. She looked affectionately at Charity. The older woman had her faults, still drank to excess, and still demanded money from the patients. But Peggy had begun to see another, kinder side to her character that did much to balance her initial opinion of her colleague.

She draped her arm over the gunwale, her fingers trailing in the water as the boat drew away from the stairs and began its long, sweeping turn to the west. It felt to Peggy then that she had stepped into another world, one where the foetid odours of Whitechapel were replaced by the damp smells of rope and tar and fish; a world where the cries of tradesmen and cattle drovers gave way to the strange language of the watermen. Gone was the rush and bustle of the streets, replaced by the rhythmic pace of the tideway, the soft gurgle of the waters and the splash of oars. And though she knew nothing of the Thames, it seemed to her that here, on the upper side of London Bridge, away from the hurly-burly of the Pool, the pace of life was slower, more tranquil.

It was an hour before they reached Vauxhall Stairs and alighted, stiff-limbed, onto a wooden pontoon jutting out into the river. Charity was the first up the steps to the bank and along the path to the gardens, leaving Peggy and Tom to follow at a slower pace.

"Miss Tompkins . . ." said Tom, as soon as they were alone.

"Yes, Captain," said Peggy.

"Miss Tompkins . . . there is something I should tell you." He paused and seemed to struggle with what he had to say. "I . . . I regret I've been compelled to change my employment. I no longer command a ship."

"Why, Tom — I may call you Tom? — will you seek another command?"

"No, the circumstances of my dismissal mean I'll not again go to sea unless my country demands it of me," said Tom. "I've accepted a post with a new organisation, a marine police institution. And yes, of course you may call me Tom."

"So Tom it is," she said, looking up at him. "Are you content? With this turn of events, I mean?"

For a moment Tom said nothing, watching the light of the dying sun filter down through the leaves of the poplar trees and cast its dancing light on the richly decorated pavilions on either side of the central path.

"Are you?" Peggy repeated her question.

Tom glanced at her, unsettled by her directness, wondering if there had been something in what he'd said that had allowed her a glimpse of the unhappiness he felt at the loss of his seagoing life.

"Content?" he said, looking away from her. "Yes, I'm content with my lot, though it's true I might have wished certain matters had happened otherwise."

They walked on down the broad grass path of the pleasure gardens, worn thin by the tread of many feet. Tables laden with the food of a score of nations were set out for sale on either side of the path while, around them, richly attired promenaders sauntered beneath a thousand glass lanterns suspended between the trees. The sound of chatter mingled with the distant echo of an orchestra playing a piece by Handel.

"And that is a matter of some concern to you?" said Peggy,

"Why, yes," he said. "I deeply regret the loss of my command, and the circumstances of it." He paused, aware that he'd spoken to no one about the events of the past six to eight weeks. There'd been no one in whom he'd wanted to confide; not Simmonds, nor even

146

Sam Hart, and certainly not those who stood in present seniority to him. He thought of the chain of events which had brought him to this point, wondering if their cumulative and corrosive effect had not had a greater impact than he'd previously thought possible. And if that were so, what of the war which had so dominated his recent life?

He'd never before given the matter any consideration, had always considered human suffering and the vicissitudes of human existence to be part of the rich pattern of life; a pattern over which he had no control. For him, nothing was to be gained by dwelling on the events of the past and he had long ago learned to dismiss them from his mind. And yet the death of his old cook and the bludgeoning of Simmonds *had* affected him, had caught him with his defences down and shaken his confidence in the fabric of a society he'd believed in and fought for.

"Do you suspect anyone in particular of being responsible for the plunder of your ship?" said Peggy.

"Yes," said Tom, slowly. "But I must tread with care if I'm to avoid the accusation of self-interest."

"How is that?"

"I have charge of another, unrelated investigation that should have enabled me to avoid becoming involved in the *Swansong* case. Unfortunately, the more I look into this new case, the more it seems to lead me back to the events concerning my old command."

"I see," said Peggy. "And is this other investigation important?"

"Aye, it is," said Tom, suddenly reminded of what Harriot had told him of the consequences of failure; the risk of rebellion by a people weary of the cost of war. He looked down into Peggy's upturned face. "I have but little time in which to discover the truth . . . But enough of this. Let us stop and take some refreshment and talk of other things."

Peggy smiled. "Of all things I would like that," she said.

It was ten o'clock on Friday morning before Newman and his fellow prisoners were called from their cell below the Sessions House at Old Bailey. Tom watched them climb unsteadily up the central steps, through the floor of the courtroom and into the dock. One by one they came to a halt, their heads bowed, their shoulders slumped as though resigned to their fate, their faces lit by a shaft of sunlight reflected in the long, rectangular mirror suspended above their heads.

Tom saw Newman turn towards him with a frightened, pleading look in his eyes. He shook his head. There was nothing he could do for the man. Not now. It was a matter for the Court whether Newman received a Royal Pardon or not. He sucked a mouthful of air through clenched teeth and contemplated the man he'd tried to cultivate as his window onto Boylin's world. He'd coaxed, promised, cajoled, and finally threatened Newman with the chains off Blackwall Point, to make him talk. Yet despite the contrary assurances he had given Harriot, he was far from certain that what Newman had told him was either accurate or complete. Like all villains, Newman was, in his view, a compulsive liar who, even under the threat of imminent death, seemed pathologically incapable of telling the truth.

He wished he could be equally dismissive of the threat to Sam's life. He glanced at his friend seated on the bench below the public gallery and thought of his restlessness, of his haunted expression that seemed increasingly in evidence. More and more, Sam appeared to him like a man stooped low under a heavy burden, wholly beyond the help of his friends.

"All persons having any business before my lord, the King's justice . . ." The droning voice of the court usher interrupted Tom's train of thought. A scraping of chairs, the squeak of a door, and in swept the majesty of the law, resplendent in his red robes, black sash and full-bottomed wig.

The trial did not last long. In the witness box, Tom kept rigidly to the facts — he'd given evidence too often to depart from the bare details — and at the end of his evidence-in-chief he waited to be cross-examined. But none came. Only the bewildered faces of the defendants, mute with fear, incapable of rational thought, stared back at him. He looked down into the well of the court where half a dozen barristers sat idle, their eyes avoiding the judge. No one stirred.

He knew then the inevitable outcome. The trial before this one had lasted sixty minutes from beginning to end, time to examine five witnesses, perpetrate clever jokes, banter the prisoner, charge the jury and find the case proved.

"Prisoners at the bar —" the trial judge, the Common Sergeant of London, glared at the men in the dock "— you now have the opportunity to enter your defence. You are not required to take the oath and no one will question you on what you say . . ."

When it came, it was pitiful: the stumbling, wheedling, pleading, incriminating statements of the prisoners that swept away what little hope remained for them. If the jurymen were listening, they gave no sign of it, but sat stony faced and unmoved on the far side of the courtroom. Tom looked at the corpulent figure of the trial judge, his hands clasped over his stomach, his eyes closed, the Sword of Truth on the wall above him poised as if to fall on his head.

Someone coughed. The judge's eyes snapped open, as though a spring had been released. He looked around, caught sight of the indictment in front of him, shuffled his papers and turned to the jury.

"Members of the jury." The voice was slow, measured, sepulchral. "This is a case in which the prisoners at the bar stand in fear of their lives. If, in the contemplation of all the evidence, you should feel compelled to return a verdict of guilty to this indictment, I must warn you that no judge could, in the discharge of his lawful duty, give these men the least hope of mercy this side of the grave."

The Common Sergeant paused and sniffed at a posy of herbs on the table in front of him before continuing. "You should know that if you convict while there is any rational doubt in your minds as to their guilt, you may commit that foulest of all enormities, murder under colour of the law . . ."

The jury did not retire. A low groan rose from the public gallery as each of the prisoners heard the guilty verdict. Even the stony eyes of Justice who had witnessed this scene a thousand times before, appeared to look down from her plinth with pity. In the dock, Newman staggered. He clutched at the iron grill atop the wooden surround and stared at Tom in shock and disbelief.

Tom looked away. There was nothing anyone could do now.

The day had been a long and hard one for Peggy and she was not done yet. Night had fallen by the time she hurried out of the main door of the hospital and across the deserted courtyard where an unseasonably cold wind was gusting out of the north. She wrapped her cloak closely around her and bent into the squall. Behind her, two porters carried a stretcher on which lay the body of a patient.

Making its way to the iron railings bordering the Whitechapel road, the little party turned right along a stone path that led directly to the dead house, an isolated building at the eastern end of the hospital grounds. The task wouldn't take long. Her job was to ensure that the porters took the body where they were supposed to and didn't try to sell it to one of the surgical students. Peggy felt in the pocket of her dress for the heavy iron key to the mortuary and shuddered. She'd never got used to the presence of death, or the pungent smell that lingered on her clothing for days after each visit.

She lifted the lantern she was carrying as the black shape of the house loomed out of the darkness. A fresh gust of wind brought with it the first whiff of decomposing flesh. Peggy covered her mouth with her free hand. She could already picture the marble shelves running down the inside of the building and the naked bodies of perhaps half a dozen people lying side by side, waiting for burial.

On the far side of the iron railings, a twig snapped. Peggy jumped and stared into the darkness. Someone was there. She was sure of it. She moved closer to the two porters, her heart thumping. A shadow moved.

"Miss Tompkins?" Peggy leapt back at the sound of her name. She lifted the lantern higher.

"Who is it who calls me, sir?"

A pair of hands appeared in the circle of light and gripped the railings.

"It is I, Miss Tompkins."

Peggy moved closer to the iron fence and held out the lamp. She couldn't make out the face.

"I own, sir, your voice is familiar but —"

"It's Joseph, Miss Tompkins. We were friends, once, were we not?"

"Joseph?" Peggy's heart somersaulted with shock as she remembered the man she had once cared for. She moved closer, her pulse quickening. She'd not seen him since the day it had happened. She'd never forgiven him for what he'd done, and yet . . .

She could see him now, in her mind's eye, as clearly as if it were daylight — his long, wavy hair that refused to lie down, the deep blue of his eyes, the curve of his mouth whenever he smiled. She remembered him in the hallway of her master's house that day when they'd first met; he standing by the library door talking to the master, she climbing the stairs from the kitchens on her way to the nursery. He had turned and looked at her with his laughing eyes as she hurried on, bringing the heat of a blush to her cheeks.

He'd come to the house often after that, and while they rarely had the opportunity to speak, she'd found herself looking forward more and more to the prospect of seeing him. The friendship had blossomed, and over the weeks that followed she would agree to meet him. More often than not he would contrive to give their chaperone the slip and they would walk, unaccompanied, to the bookshops in the shadow of St Paul's or down to the Thames, west of London Bridge. Sometimes they would stop at one of the dozens of coffee shops in and around the City and she'd listen entranced to his stories of growing up in Ireland; of the hardships and the pleasures; of the beauty of the distant Wicklow Mountains and the wild flowers that grew in the hedgerows near his home. Yet, even then, she'd seen his moods change and his eyes harden, and he would grow distant from her as though his mind were far away in some secret place to which she could not go. Those moods both attracted and repelled her. She feared him and she loved him, and it was her heart that ruled the day.

Even when it happened, there was a part of her that wanted to continue their relationship. The details often came back to her and she would experience afresh that revulsion for him, mixed with a longing for his presence she could not explain. And then she would think of little else but what might have been, of the life she might have led . . .

"Sure, I've been looking for you these three years since." His voice had changed, was more guttural than she remembered, but it was still Joseph's voice. "Will you be telling me why you left, now?"

A face pressed itself to the railings, dimly visible in the glow of her lantern. She stared, thought at first the light was playing tricks, that she was mistaken in what she saw. She held the lantern closer to the railings. The light fell on a face she hardly recognised, its marble-like skin pulled taut over one cheek, a thousand, wispy wine-red veins traversing the desert of his ravaged skull, a canvas patch over one eye. Her hand flew to her mouth to suppress the scream that rose in her throat.

"You'll not be finding me attractive no more, Miss Tompkins?" A hard edge crept into Joseph Boylin's voice. "Will you not be wanting us to be friends now?"

Peggy's hand slipped from her mouth, her jaw hung open.

"Forgive me, sir, I had not expected to see you. But I give you joy at our meeting."

"Joy, Miss Tompkins." The bitterness dropped from Boylin's voice as quickly as it had come. "Perhaps we might talk?"

154

"I regret, sir, I am not presently at leisure to speak with you," said Peggy, indicating the stretcher and the waiting porters. "If . . . if you are content, we can perhaps talk at some other time . . .?"

Even as she said it, Peggy knew she'd made a mistake, knew what she had loved was now only a distant memory, coloured by time. To see him again was to risk everything she hoped for in her life.

CHAPTER
TWELVE

Gabriel Newman woke to the sound of keys rattling in the door of the condemned cell and a gruff voice calling his name. Obediently, he followed the turnkey back along the same passage he had taken hours before, his mind numb with fear, unable to think of anything beyond the inevitability of his coming demise.

He was to hang. Again and again that single thought coursed through his befuddled brain, each time more painful than the last, like a score of daggers plunging into his heart. He wished he could have his life again. How different it all would be. He'd tell Master Pascoe everything he wanted to know. Not for him the pointless sacrifice of his life. What a fool he'd been! He'd not again throw away the chance of a pardon — of life itself. He'd not be afraid of Boylin if it meant he could live. He stumbled up the stairs and stood again in the dock, this time alone.

A chair creaked, and he looked up to see the Common Sergeant put down his quill pen and regard him quizzically. Dimly, he wondered what further perils awaited him. The judge was speaking. Newman tried to concentrate but the words sounded fuzzy, indistinct. He couldn't take them in, his mind was a blank. He wished the judge would stop, go back and repeat what he'd said. What did he mean? Had he said what Newman thought he'd said? He looked at the turnkeys. And then wished he hadn't. Their expressionless faces took from him the flickering flame of hope that he desperately wanted to believe in.

". . . the Secretary of State for the Home Department has, sir, graciously consented to the proposal of this court for the grant, in this case, of a Royal Pardon. You are therefore, sir, free to go."

Newman stared at the judge and then at the turnkeys. He was free to go? Just like that? He stood, unmoving, staring at the bewigged figure in red. One of the turnkeys pulled roughly at his sleeve. Newman was holding up the next case. He was no longer wanted.

He ran from the building and turned down Old Bailey, towards Ludgate Hill, his euphoria threatening to explode within him. It was as though he had cheated Death and denied the Devil his plaything. Into Ludgate Hill, past St Paul's and through to Watling Street he ran, ignoring the stares of the few still on the streets of the City. Soon it was Tower Hill and, in the distance, the great battlements of the Norman Tower, rising into the night sky. Nothing could compare to the joy he felt, the thrill of his spirit now dispossessed of its anxiety. Ten minutes more and he'd crossed the old wooden bridge at Hermitage Dock, the air full of the deviant perfumes of the river.

He was almost upon it before he saw the solitary lantern hanging over the door of the tavern. He stopped. He'd have a drink. There was no rush. He'd spend a few minutes considering his next move, what he'd say to Boylin. He'd be safe here for an hour or two.

He ran up the steps into the taproom, its walls yellow with tobacco stain, the light of a dozen candles flickering in the draught of the open door. He stood for a moment, his bloodshot eyes scouring the tightly packed drinkers for anyone he might know, who might cause him difficulty with Boylin. He ordered a drink from the pot-boy and walked to a bench overlooking the limpid waters of the Thames. He sat down and closed his eyes, drowsy with relief.

"Newman."

The voice was very close to his ear. His eyes snapped open. He knew who it was.

"Will you be coming with me, now?" Boylin stood with his hands on his hips, his lips drawn back in a scowl. He jerked a thumb in the direction of the door.

Newman stood up. There was no point in arguing. He'd already seen Shamus O'Malley standing by the door, with two others he didn't know. He knew they would need little encouragement to reduce him to a bloody pulp. He followed the publican to the door, wondering how Boylin had learned of his release. As far as he knew, there'd been no one in court who might have carried the news. Not that it mattered now. If Boylin knew the real reason behind his freedom, there would be only one outcome. The publican had his own way of dealing with those who crossed him.

"Where've you been, you villain?" Boylin shrieked, when, ten minutes later, they'd reached the privacy of the cellar at the Queen's Head.

Newman wiped the palms of his hands against his slops while he took in the familiar surroundings of the cellar, made alien by the night — the low-beamed ceiling, the crumbling stone walls, the door at the foot of the stairs, one of its hinges missing. He saw the silent, menacing circle of men, their faces in shadow, only the lower half of their bodies lit by the wavering glow of a tallow candle. Newman wondered what he was expected to say. Boylin was merely playing with him, knew perfectly well where he'd been and what he'd been doing.

He flinched as the publican approached. Soon the blows would fall. He'd seen it too often to believe otherwise, had experienced the smashed knuckles and bloodied lips that were the hallmark of Boylin's existence. He smelt the stale reek of beer on his breath, the lime and the sweat on his unwashed clothes.

"Ain't you got nothing to say?" The shrill rasp carried its own menace.

"I don't know what you can be meaning." Newman hoped he sounded convincing.

"You don't know what I can be meaning, you scallywag?" Boylin's voice rose an octave.

"I —" began Newman.

"Don't be interrupting me when I'm a talking, you addlepated bog-brother." Boylin's fist sank into Newman's stomach. "Where've you been these twelve days since? Will that be clear enough?"

"Sure, we was collared," gasped Newman, winded by the punch. "It were Pascoe. He were after coming out of nowhere and he nabbed us."

"Pascoe? That villain?" Boylin's eyes bulged in disbelief. "What's happened to the others?"

"They's in Newgate —" Newman stopped.

"I can see that, you fucking apology for an Irishman." Boylin's neck turned a deep scarlet. "But when's they coming out? You're out, why aren't they?"

Newman's head came up with a jerk. Boylin didn't know. At least, not yet. Boylin didn't know about him turning King's Evidence or the Royal Pardon or that the others had been condemned. He was fishing for answers.

"They'll not be coming home," said Newman. "It's a scragging for them. I were acquitted. Judge said there weren't no evidence against me."

Boylin stumbled backwards.

"Will you be thinking me stupid?" he screamed, drawing back his boot and smashing it against Newman's knee.

Newman pitched forward, a sharp pain shooting through his pelvis and along his spine. Another kick, this time to his ribs. A stabbing, agonising spasm ripped through him. The others joined in. He'd not the strength to protect himself, even to cover his head. The kicking went on until he thought he could take no more. Abruptly, it stopped.

From far away, the sound of men talking, laughing, enjoying themselves. It came from above his head, from the taproom. It might just as well have been another

160

world. Blood oozed down the side of his face and onto his neck. He lay still, unable to move, the searing pain like hammer blows to his brain.

"Don't piss me about," said Boylin, his index finger jabbing the air. "I want the bleedin' truth. How is it you's acquitted and the others measured for their eternity boxes? I reckon you turned Evidence. That's what I reckon."

Newman's stomach somersaulted. To confess was to ensure his own death. Boylin would see to that, revel in the extinguishing of a life, the exercise of absolute power. Yet to say nothing would have the same effect. He struggled for an answer that would satisfy Boylin, that would stop the beating.

"Dear Holy Mother of God, I swear I said nothing,"

"D'you expect me to believe that, you poxy bastard?" Boylin's neck grew redder. He stepped towards Newman, a bag in his hand. "You cross Joseph Boylin and you pay for it, d'you hear?"

Newman recognised the pungent smell of lime.

"No, Jesus, Mary and Joseph, no." Newman tried to speak. His tongue had swollen, slurring his words. He fixed his terrified eyes on the smoking bag, anticipating the agony to come. "Why would I want to talk to the bastard English?"

He waited, knowing this was what Boylin enjoyed — inflicting pain, watching the fear in another man's eyes. He wouldn't stop now. Not until he, Newman, was dead. He wiped the blood from his eyes and raised his head, peeping at the publican from under half-closed eyelids. It would, he thought, end as it had for the old man on the *Swansong*.

He trembled at the memory. It was always with him. An unwilling spectator watching Boylin smash the old man's skull against the rail of the barque before pitching him into the Thames. And then Newman had done what he had so often done before when confronted with Boylin's violence. He had melted back out of sight, fearful of what he'd seen, of what he knew.

The seconds ticked by and still Boylin remained where he was. Newman stole another look. The publican was leaning against an upturned barrel, his chest rising and falling, his mouth gulping for air, like a fish out of water, the bag of lime swinging in his hand.

"Where's that Jew-boy, Hart?" The question startled Newman. He looked up at Boylin's wreck of a face, at the pitiless, single eye that seemed to mock the notion of humanity.

"I've not seen him these three days since." Newman looked away, unsure as to why he'd lied. It could hardly have mattered to have told the truth — that he'd seen Hart at the Old Bailey earlier in the day.

Except that the old certainties of his life had begun to change.

It was nearly midnight of the following day when Tom left the police office and stepped down into Wapping Street. There was no moon, and whatever lighting he might have expected from the occasional lamp over a shop doorway had long since been snuffed out for the night. But still the street was thronged with people, a steady hum of voices filling the darkness as he headed for Burr Street and home.

He grimaced at the thought of a wasted day, most of it spent at the Marine Society offices in Bishopsgate trying to persuade an obdurate young clerk to let him have sight of the *Swansong*'s manifest.

"I regret, sir, that won't be possible," the truculent, pimple-faced youth had informed him. "Not without the written authority of the merchant concerned or the master of the vessel."

"I am — was — the master of the vessel." Tom had taken an instant dislike to the boy.

"But you ain't now," came the triumphant reply. "No written authority, no manifest."

Tom clenched his teeth at the memory.

"Master Pascoe?" Tom's hand flew to the hilt of his cutlass. "Can I be having a word with you, your honour?"

"Who are you?" said Tom, peering into the darkness and cursing his lack of vigilance. "Identify yourself."

"Pray, a word with you, sir, if you please," repeated the voice of a young man. "It's important."

"Then speak and look lively about it," said Tom, giving up on his attempt to see who it was.

"Not here, I beg. Some private place, but not here."

"Very well, the police office then. It's but a few yards and we'll not be disturbed," said Tom. "Walk in front of me, where I can see you."

Reaching the main door of the office, Tom pushed it open and let the light from the hall candle fall on the youth's face, the same youth he'd seen in the moments before his flogging in Fox's Lane and the one who'd subsequently carried the caged rats at the Queen's Head. He waited for him to speak.

"I see you know me, your honour."

"I've seen you before," said Tom. "Nothing more. What do you want to speak to me about?"

"You asked for my name, your honour. I couldn't give it to you at once since I was afeared of being overheard," said the boy. "But it's Jacob, Jacob Newman. If I'm not mistook, you know my brother, Gabriel."

Tom's eyes widened. "I do indeed. I'd no idea Gabriel had a brother. What can I do for you?"

"Sir, I beg you not to speak to anyone of our meeting. My life would be worthless if it were ever known I had spoken to you. And not only my life but my brother's also."

Tom nodded, lit a fresh candle and led the way along the corridor to the empty courtroom, where the smell of unwashed bodies still lingered in the air. Closing the door, he leaned against it and waved Jacob to a seat on one of the benches.

For a while the young man sat mute, staring at the faltering candle light. Once or twice he looked up, an agitated expression on his face.

"I . . . I scarce know where to begin," he said at last. "The truth is I've lived in mortal fear of me life ever since the night it happened. I speak now 'cos Gabriel told me how you got him his pardon. I'll not forget that, your honour. Gabriel says no man alive is as straight as you. Reckons you've got bottom and is

164

afeared of no man, not even Master Boylin." He raised his head a fraction and then looked down at his lap. His head still bowed, he said, "For sure that man would knock a cove on the head for a word out of place and think naught of it. He's done it afore and I dare say he'll do it again."

"What did you want to tell me?" said Tom.

"He turned off the old man. The one from the *Swansong*, your honour." Jacob's words came out in a rush. "Murdered him and threw his body into the tideway."

Tom stiffened. He wondered if the boy knew that the old man of whom he spoke was William Denny, the ship's cook and Tom's shipmate from his earliest days in the Navy. Before he could say anything, Jacob spoke again.

"It's been troubling me something terrible, your honour. Ever since I saw him do it, I've scarce slept a wink."

"You were there?" said Tom, surprised. "On the *Swansong*? You saw what happened to the old man?"

"Aye, so I was."

"Why are you telling me now?" said Tom. "Has something happened?"

"Master Boylin gave me brother Gabriel a flogging a day since. I'll not be knowing for why but I thought to myself the time's come to tell what I know about that evil man. Somebody's got to stop him afore he does for us all."

The boy's dark eyes seemed to plead for approval. Tom waved him on.

"I were in the Queen's Head on the night Master Boylin did for the old man. Much earlier that evening, I saw Gabriel come into the house, but afore I could speak to him, Master Boylin hails him and they went down the cellar. When they came out again, Gabriel was straight out the door, his face pale as the grave, like I've not seen before. Then Master Boylin calls me and tells me to cut along to the accident hospital in Whitechapel and watch out for a big man what was wearing the coat of the King's Navy. That man was you, your honour, though I didn't know it at the time. When I saw you I was to follow you and tell the men what was waiting for you which way you was a'coming."

"Yes, I remember you," said Tom. He hesitated, another memory stirring in the far confines of his mind. "The men who were waiting — was one of them Boylin?"

"Aye, so he was," said Jacob. "How did you know?"

Tom gave a tight little smile. "Let's just say, I know a limey man when I smell him. But I interrupted you. Pray continue."

"There ain't much to tell, your honour, except Master Boylin don't seem to like you a heap. He wants to put you to bed with a spade, like."

"Then what stopped him? D'you know?"

"Oh, I knows right enough. One of the men hears someone coming and he calls to the others to run. Master Boylin weren't happy at all but he shifts his bob like the rest of them."

"Do you know any of the other men by name?" asked Tom.

166

Jacob hesitated. "No, your honour."

Tom recognised the pause for what it was. He decided to ignore it and move on. He guessed the boy was probably protecting his brother.

"What happened after that?"

"I went back to the Queen's Head," said Jacob. "I'd no sooner sat down for me pot of Hammond's when Master Boylin comes in, all flushed like. Tells me to meet him by the stairs at Limehouse Hole at midnight."

"And you went?"

"Aye, I did as I was bid. When I got there, I saw about six lads waiting. Most of them I knows from the Queen's Head. Not their names, like." Jacob's voice faltered as he met Tom's eye. "Just their faces."

"What happened then?" said Tom, deciding to get the men's names later.

"A little later, Master Boylin arrives and says we're to go out to a barque what was anchored in Limehouse Reach, on account of he wanted to learn the captain a lesson. There was some skiffs at the bottom of the stairs and we took 'em."

"Go on," said Tom, moving away from the door.

"We came to a West Indiaman, just off Cuckold Point; a three-masted, ship-rigged barque. She was your *Swansong*, your honour. All in darkness, she were. We climbed up the side and when we reached the upper deck we listened, but it were all silent as the grave. Master Boylin orders some of the lads to search the lower decks for any of the crew. He told the others to go into the hold and wait for him. Master Boylin bid me to follow him and we went through to the great cabin. There was no one in there, but Master Boylin told me I had to break everything on account of the captain was a villain who deserved no better. He helps me and soon the job's done. Then he tells me to look in the other cabins for anything what was valuable. The door of one of them was barred so I broke it down and saw an old man inside. He were crouching in the corner."

Again the boy looked at Tom, a quick, darting movement of the eyes.

"I called Master Boylin and when he came, he asked the old man if he were the watchman and the old man says he were the cook. So Master Boylin asks him where the gold were kept. When the old man told him there weren't no gold as he knew of, Master Boylin cuffed him, like, and he cried out something terrible, your honour."

Tom's jaw muscles flexed and the pulse at his temple throbbed.

"Master Boylin told me to fetch him on deck. I was much afeared. I'd seen him in a bad mood afore and it weren't a pretty sight. But I'd no choice. Not if I wanted to live.

"When we gets on deck, the old man, Denny his name was, were asked again where the gold were kept but he wouldn't say nothing. All of a sudden, Master Boylin catches hold of him and strikes his head on the rail. There's blood everywhere. Denny let out a loud groan and Master Boylin told him to shut up, but he wouldn't. So he grabs Denny by the handkerchief he's wearing round his neck and twists it. The old timer were making choking noises like he couldn't breathe and his eyes bulged as if they were about to drop out. He struggles with Master Boylin and tears at his face and ears with his fingers. I sees blood on Master Boylin's face. All of a sudden the old man goes limp. I reckon if he weren't dead then, he weren't far off. The next thing I knows he's been upped and tipped over the side and Master Boylin's left holding the handkerchief."

Tom was sweating. He remembered the fresh scratches he'd seen on Boylin's face on the day of the inquest. He'd wondered what had caused them and now he knew. And he remembered something else, something that had been troubling him since that morning on the foreshore of the Isle of Dogs, when he'd seen the lifeless body of his cook. The red and white handkerchief William Denny always wore around his neck had been missing. He drew a sleeve across his forehead. Not for the first time, he wondered at the wisdom of going on with this investigation, whether he had the moral courage to remain impartial in the face of all he now knew.

"Did anyone else see what happened?"

The boy hesitated again. "Not as I know of. Leastways, I didn't see nobody.

Tom looked at the boy. He was holding something back.

"Does your brother know of your presence here?" said Tom.

"He knows nothing of this," said Jacob, his eyes widening. "You'll not be telling him I've been talking, will you?"

Tom considered him for a minute. "What else d'you know of Master Boylin's activities?"

"He's a big man in these parts. That much I know," said Jacob. "There'll not be many times when he's not out and about."

"What does he do when he's out and about?"

"Don't know, your honour. No one knows. He's often gone from the Queen's Head, even during the day. We's all afeared of asking him."

"What about you? Apart from the *Swansong* has he ever told you to commit depredations?"

Jacob looked up quickly and met Tom's eye as though unsure of what lay behind the question. Tom sensed the boy's concern.

"If I'm to help you," he said, "I must know all there is to know about Master Boylin. If you've ever been with him or he's ever asked you to steal, there's much you can tell me that'll help catch him. Do you understand?"

"Aye, thankee, your honour, I do," said Jacob. "It's just that . . . well . . ."

"I understand," said Tom, his outstretched hand resting on Jacob's shoulder. "You don't want to be spending the next fourteen years in a penal colony, still less swinging on the end of a rope outside Newgate. All I can say is that I'm after Boylin, not you. Nothing'll happen to you if I've anything to say."

Jacob bowed his head, his hair falling over his eyes. When he spoke, there was a quiet determination in his voice. "I went out most nights. It were the only way me brother and me could get work to live. Master Boylin only gave work to those who did what he wanted. There weren't no money, else. When there was work, I'd be on the colliers in Southwark. Gabriel would be unlading the West Indiamen down Limehouse way."

"How much would you and the rest of the gang reckon to steal — when you weren't working on the colliers?"

"Maybe a ton," said the boy. "It depended on how many of us there were. We always worked nights. Others, like Gabriel, worked days."

"And Boylin didn't go with you?"

"No," said Jacob. "He came with us to the *Swansong* but that were the first time I knows of."

Tom stroked the underside of his chin and pondered the information he was being given. The theft of only a ton of sugar or coffee, or anything else, was hardly likely to cause concern in the highest circles of government, even if it was repeated on a nightly basis.

"Was all the plundering done in the same way?" he asked. "I mean, did you always board the ships or did you also take from the lighters?"

"We went onto the ships," said Jacob. "I knows there are others that plunder the lighters but that ain't Master Boylin's game — leastways, not that I knows of."

Tom leaned forward, his hands resting on the bench in front of him, thinking. This wasn't making any sense. Either the lad, Jacob, was mistaken in his belief that Boylin did not, in normal circumstances, touch the lighters or he, Tom, was mistaken in his suspicion of Boylin. He turned and looked through the nearest window. Outside, rain pattered against the glass and ran down the casement, the reflective glimmering of the candle sparkling in each tiny bead of water. Was it possible he'd been wrong to focus his investigation on Boylin?

Once again he was forced to consider the possibility that he was allowing his personal prejudices to get in the way of his professional objectivity. He traced a line through the condensation on the glass. The more he thought about it, the less likely it seemed that Boylin was the one involved in the plundering of the port. And yet, everything he knew about the Irishman persuaded him to the contrary view. His long-held suspicion, now confirmed, that the sacking of the *Swansong* and the murder of his cook was Boylin's doing, merely served to reinforce his belief in the Irishman's penchant for criminality. There had to be some other way in which the scrub was stealing and disposing of large quantities of property.

"What about the people he works with?" he said, turning back into the room and facing the boy. "D'you know anything about the gentleman who comes to see him at the Queen's Head, from time to time?"

"No, nothing," said Jacob. "I see him, for sure. Always comes on sporting nights. But he and Master Boylin don't talk where others might hear. They go downstairs to the back parlour. Sometimes, after the gentleman leaves, Master Boylin carries on like a rat with a dog on his tail. Other times, he's all smiles."

"D'you know what the gentleman is called?" said Tom.

"No, it don't do to ask no questions."

"And Master Boylin?" said Tom. "What do you think of him?"

"I want to see him swing in chains like what he deserves," said Jacob fiercely. "His head on Temple Bar is too good for him. My brother Gabriel's a good man, same as many of us what's come to this place from Ireland. We wasn't always savages and drunkards like what you English think on us. We was honest God-fearing folk, but the likes of Master Boylin dragged us down and forced us to work for pay as wouldn't keep a dog alive for a week, never mind a man and his family. Often times he don't pay us at all and we's forced to commit depredations to live. Prison's too good for the likes of him, your honour."

"For him to hang, I'll need you to give evidence," said Tom. "Without it we have nothing. Will you do that?"

"Aye," said Jacob, looking steadily at Tom. "I'll do whatever it takes to see him in Hell."

CHAPTER
THIRTEEN

Neither Tom Pascoe nor Sam Hart was under any illusion about the dangers involved as they left the police office and headed east towards the hamlet of Ratcliff and the desolate marshlands that lay beyond. Few cared to pass that way, and those that did asked no questions about what they saw. It wasn't wise to look too closely at the bands of a hundred men or more travelling west from the sea towards London. Or what they carried on their mule trains. Tom's hand brushed the butt of his pistol. He'd worry about that when and if the situation arose. For the time being he had other things on his mind.

Going out to the River Lea on the borders of Essex had seemed to make sense when he'd mentioned the idea to Harriot earlier in the week. Then it had seemed self-evident that Boylin should have chosen that remote spot to hide the sugar taken from the *Swansong*. Yet now, with the immediacy of the operation upon him, Tom was beginning to have second thoughts. Even if the sugar was there, its presence would fall a long way short of proving Boylin's involvement in its original theft, still less his role in the widespread plundering of the port.

Twenty minutes later, he and Sam had reached the far side of Ratcliff where they joined a lane which led north before turning right across the marsh, its rough surface dotted with patches of white lime fallen from passing carts. Ahead of them in the distance was the high bank bordering the River Lea, while over to the right was the church of St Anne, its belfry rising above the hovels of Limehouse. The sight reminded him of how he'd always searched for his first glimpse of that belfry, and the White Ensign fluttering from its masthead, as his ship rounded the Isle of Dogs into Limehouse Reach. It had, for him and for countless others, signalled the end of a journey — and the nearness of the brothels and drinking houses of Wapping.

After a while they turned off the rutted track and struck out across the marsh itself, their boots sinking deep into the soft bog as they headed for the embankment. Reaching it, they climbed to its summit and were able to look down on the Lea, from whose shimmering, grey-white surface a thin, mist-like vapour was rising. On the far side, the Plaistow Levels stretched away to the horizon, with nothing to ease the monotony of the landscape save the occasional building and a tethered animal or two. To their right, a mile or so away, a cluster of East Indiamen rode at anchor off Blackwall Point, their massive hulls seeming puny in the distance.

Tom turned to look in the opposite direction. No more than a quarter of a mile upstream, two large luggers lay moored alongside a wharf, their square sails brailed up, their hulls low in the water. He felt a surge of excitement. They were what he'd hoped to find. He dropped to one knee and signalled Sam to do the same while he surveyed the scene.

The wharf itself was an untidy jumble of abandoned carts, wheelbarrows, lengths of timber, empty sacks, picks and shovels, all in varying states of disrepair. About twenty yards from the water's edge and close to the foot of the embankment were three huts, each facing the river. Two of these appeared to be no more than storage buildings but the centre one was larger, with windows on either side of a central door and, at the rear, a brick-built chimney stack from which a column of grey smoke now curled.

"Sir . . ." Sam nodded his head in the direction of the middle hut.

A door had opened and a man of around sixty emerged, wandered to the water's edge and looked up and down as though expecting a new arrival. He stood there for a minute or so and then returned to the hut, closing the door behind him.

Tom nodded and glanced up at the fading light of the day. It would be dark in an hour.

"Get some rest, Sam," said Tom, rolling onto his back, his fingers laced behind his head. "We might need it."

He closed his eyes and thought of Peggy.

"Wake up, your honour." Tom felt a sharp dig in his ribs. "We got company."

176

Tom peered through the darkness in the direction Sam was pointing and could just make out the shape of a yawl moored astern of the two luggers, its mainsail still hoisted, its boom raised, spilling the wind.

"Did you see it arrive?" said Tom, a hopeful note in his voice.

"No, I regret not," said Sam. "I were asleep, same as you. But I'll warrant the crew's in yonder hut. Maybe four or five of them from the noise they're making."

"Best we take a look," said Tom.

The two of them clambered down the rise, aware that the stakes had been raised. Getting caught was no longer just a question of compromising the investigation. Now, with five or so men to contend with, it was their lives at risk. Fifty yards short of the wharf, Tom was able to make out the faint outline of a group of men sitting in a half circle, outside the middle of the three huts.

"What d'you suppose they're up to?" said Sam.

"I don't know, but it's possible they're here to crew those luggers," whispered Tom, stripping off his coat and handing it to his friend. "Anygate, we've not a moment to lose. You wait here while I have a look around. There's no point in us both getting caught."

"With respect, sir, you must be bleedin' joking," spluttered Sam. "They'll catch you for sure."

"I'll not do anything foolish, Hart. I promise," said Tom, grimly determined. "But it's got to be done."

"Sir, listen to me," pleaded Sam. "You don't know these people like what I do. If they catch you they'll turn you off as quick as look at you. It'll be your throat cut and no mistake. At least let me come with you. Even the odds a bit."

"No, stay here. I'll not be long. Give me the lantern, will you? I may need it."

Tom opened the gate of the storm lantern and inspected the wick, before looping the handle over his arm. Then he drew his sea service pistol and crept silently into the night.

Boylin was optimistic. Things were going well. True, he'd not yet persuaded his usual receiver to take the sugar off his hands but he was confident he soon would. He wiped his face with the palm of his hand and stared out across the Lea. There were some who'd suggested the lack of a buyer was the result of all the trouble over the deaths of the two men on the *Swansong* and the near death of the ship's mate. Boylin disagreed. The river was a dangerous place and men died all the time — some murdered, some drowned and some because they were plain careless — and seldom was there any fuss.

Except in this case. And if it wasn't the deaths that had caused the delay, what was it?

His back began to itch. He already knew the reason. He'd tried to tell himself that Pascoe's arrival in the port had made no difference, that life could go on as before. But the evidence to the contrary was all around him. Those who, in the past, had thought little of plundering a ship, now looked over their shoulders and feared the consequences of capture.

Boylin glanced at the men sitting with him at the wharf side; a quick, nervous look. It was too dark to see their faces or for them to see his. He was oddly relieved. They wouldn't see the fright he knew was in his eye, the deep dread that was always there when he thought of Pascoe.

His thoughts drifted. There had been a time when his life had been different.

A small boy, a thin scrag of a child was playing in the meadow below a mud hovel . . . It was winter, the ground hard as iron, a bitter wind cutting through the rags he wore. He was hungry, but still he played, happy in his own company, free to come and go as he pleased. He was used to the pangs of hunger and the sight of his skeletal frame. It was how he had always lived.

He looked up and saw a man approaching across the frozen fields, the stranger's steps unsteady and unfamiliar. Only when the man drew near did the boy recognise his father, thinner than he remembered, his face a sickly hue. The boy had not seen him in many months; gone, his mother had said, to find work in Dublin — wherever that was. Now he was back.

For weeks, the boy listened to the hacking cough in the corner of the room where his father lay. No one spoke to him, explained to him what was happening. It was as if he didn't exist. He was sent out into the meadow to play by himself.

One day, his mother wept and instinctively the child knew he would see his father no more.

That was when life began to change for him.

Men would visit his house, the house where he and his mother lived. And afterwards there would be a little to eat and a small fire in the hearth. It was then that the young boy began to see the look on his neighbours' faces when they passed in the lanes round the village, and for the first time in his life, he knew shame . . .

Boylin stared into the blackness of the night, listening to the tall reeds close to the banks of the Lea rustling in the summer breeze. The boy he had once been no longer played in the meadows below the mud hovel. In place of innocence came a determination to wipe away the shame he felt. He smiled bitterly. The neighbours in the village had soon learned to stop looking down on him and his mother.

"Who's this Pascoe cully I've been hearing on?" Boylin turned at the sound of the wharfinger's voice. "Ain't it time someone knocked him on the head, like?"

Boylin's breathing became more rapid and his shoulders heaved.

"Sure it will be something for me to think about," he said, his voice heavy with sarcasm. "Will you be telling me when you see him?"

"Well, he ain't been out here and that's for sure," said the wharfinger. "I'd have seen him else. You can rest assured, if I sees him snooping round, he'll get more than he bargained for."

Tom approached the first of the three huts, his progress hidden by the brambles and hawthorn that grew at the foot of the embankment, ducking out of sight as the moon came out from behind a cloud. Then, creeping forward he peered in through the dust-covered window of the first hut. The place was full of sacks, ropes and assorted oddments — but no sugar. He turned away and looked at the remaining two buildings. The far one appeared to be another store-room while the middle hut was almost certainly the wharfinger's house. Getting a closer look at either of them risked his exposure.

Suddenly he was aware of men's voices coming from the front of the huts, the words too muffled for him to understand. He'd have to get closer. He hesitated and weighed up the risk. He could go back to the embankment and come in at a different angle but that would take time. And time was in short supply. He made up his mind.

Stooping low, he sprinted across the open space between the buildings, stopped and waited to catch his breath. The murmur of voices went on unabated. Now all he had to do was get to within earshot of the group. He checked his escape route. Behind him lay about fifteen yards of open scrub. If anything happened, he'd never make it to the cover of the brambles before someone took a pot-shot at him. He pushed the thought away and edged round the side of the middle hut. The voices of the men were clearer. A few more feet and —

The twig snapped with a deafening crack.

He'd known it was there, had felt it as he brought his boot down. He stiffened. The voices stopped.

"What were that?"

"How do I bleedin' know? Get off your arse and look."

Tom crept to the back of the hut and pressed himself against the wall. He caught the sound of footsteps approaching. His hand dropped to his pistol, thumbing back the hammer. It was going to be close. He wondered if the man was armed. Either way, he'd have less than half a second to decide whether to shoot or not. There'd be no second chance. If he missed, it would be the other cully's turn.

"There's naught 'ere."

The guttural voice made Tom jump. He raised the pistol, holding it at arm's length, and waited. In the silence he could hear his heart beating as he stared into the night. Another footstep. He couldn't make out if it was getting closer or moving away. The footstep was followed by another, then another. They were retreating. A moment later the burble of conversation began again.

Tom let out a lungful of air and lowered his pistol, his sense of relief tempered by the knowledge that he still needed to hear what the men were saying.

He looked up at the sky. Half-a-dozen stars had appeared. The sky was clearing and a gentle breeze rustled the trees down by the river. A moment later, the moon's pale disc emerged from behind a cloud and shed its light over the wharf. Tom inched forward and cautiously poked his head round the edge of the hut.

The group was perhaps six strong. At the far end of the semi-circle was the man he'd seen earlier, the one he and Sam had supposed to be the wharfinger. Next to him was a thick-set fellow, his face in shadow. Of the others, only their backs were visible. Tom noticed one was wearing a high, cone-shaped hat.

"No one visits these parts as I don't know them." Tom saw the wharfinger gesticulating. "The sugar in them luggers is as safe as the Bank of England and no mistake."

Tom leaned forward, straining to hear the words. The cone-shaped hat moved, its owner's voice drowned by the sound of coughing. More words, too indistinct to hear. Tom moved back a pace or two, He'd heard enough. There was sugar in the luggers. But whose? From the *Swansong?* Or from somewhere else? He would have to look.

He glanced across the wide expanse of the wharf, bathed in the ghostly tint of moonlight. It was impossible to reach the vessels by that route and remain unseen. He looked over his shoulder at the high embankment where clumps of bramble and hawthorn at the base offered some shelter.

That way would give a more realistic chance of success. From there he could make his way upstream and then swim down to the boats. He took a last look at the half-circle of men, willing them to stay put until he'd finished what he had to do.

Ten minutes later Tom lay on his stomach, studying the fifty-yard stretch of river between him and the wharf. The rain of the last few days had raised the water level close to the top of the bank. He'd have to rely on a few reeds growing close to the bank for cover. Silently, he slipped into the river.

It didn't take Tom long to reach the wharf. Catching hold of the timber supports, he levered himself out of the water and peeped over the edge. The dark shadow of the embankment lay across the distant huts, hiding them and the men, from his view. He looked behind him. From across the Plaistow Levels a swirling blanket of mist was racing towards him, tumbling over the sodden marshes faster than a man could run. It reached the river and swept on, hiding the moon and the stars, and all else, from sight.

Tom scrambled up the slime-covered supports and crawled to the side of the nearest lugger. A canvas sheet covered the hold. Drawing a knife from his belt, he cut the rope holding the canvas in place and folded back a corner. He could see nothing beneath it. He reached out, groping for the shape of a barrel he hoped would be there.

It wasn't.

Frantically, he stretched further into the darkness, his fingers brushing against something solid. It was a barrel! Relieved, he found a second, then a third. He pushed the canvas cover further back and squinted at the nearest cask, searching for its identification markings, but it was too dark to see. He would need the light from the lantern he'd brought with him, but that was out of the question. Even with the mist as thick as it was, the light would be visible from the huts and, anyway, the mist could go as quickly as it had arrived. His stomach lurched. He knew he had little option but to get under the sheeting and hope the light wouldn't be seen.

He cocked his head and listened. He could hear the drone of conversation from in front of the huts. Picking up the lantern he slithered under the canvas and crawled along the top of the closely packed barrels. There had to be a loading space at one end or the other, a space that would allow him to take a good look at the casks.

Reaching the stern, he felt around with his fingers and found what he was looking for: a gap of about two feet between the last of the barrels and the after bulkhead. He dropped down onto the ceiling planks and lit the storm lantern, shielding the flare of light with the adjustable shade. He opened it a fraction and let some light spill onto the nearest cask. There was no mark. He tried again with a second and then a third cask. Still nothing. Tom bit his lip as he considered the possibility that the marks had been removed. He still hadn't looked at the underside and nor did he wish to. He'd been on the lugger too long already and turning the casks onto their sides would take time and risk a noise he could ill afford.

He stopped, aware of the sudden quiet: the distant murmur of voices had stopped. He closed the lantern, scrambled back to the opening and lifted the canvas a fraction. The mist was clearing. He could see the lower half of the lugger's mainmast. Across the quay, traces of the mist still lingered, reducing visibility to a few yards.

Tom fought down his rising panic. If he couldn't see, then neither could the men at the hut. But why had they stopped talking? He listened for the sound of approaching footsteps and heard only the faint lapping of the water against the hull of the boat and the faint rustle of the breeze through the trees.

A large part of him wanted to leave, to get away while he still could. But he still hadn't found the markings. He had to go back. The silence was unnerving. He hesitated, his heart pounding. Then he ducked back below the sheeting.

Reaching the stern, he opened the lantern for the second time, pulled the nearest barrel towards him and tipped it onto the ceiling boards. It slipped from his hand and dropped with a thud. Tom's pulse surged. He stopped and listened, wiping a trickle of sweat from his eyes, his imagination running riot. The men were creeping up on him. They had to be. He was trapped. Why else the silence? Then his eye caught sight of some painted marks on the underside of the barrel. He looked more closely. Two letters and two numbers, contained within the shape of a heart, each number separated by a horizontal line. Quickly, he checked a few more barrels. All had the same letters, only the upper of the two numbers was different on each occasion.

"Found it," he breathed, replacing the casks and preparing to leave.

Suddenly, the boat rocked.

Tom froze. Footsteps moved along the narrow deck above his head, the tread slow and deliberate. Then silence. Quietly, he climbed onto the barrel tops and started to crawl towards the opening in the canvas sheeting. Another ten feet or so and he'd be there.

"I heard something." The voice made Tom start. He reached for his pistol.

"Have it your way. But there ain't no one here."

Then another voice from further away, perhaps on the quay.

"I tell you, I heard something for sure."

The boat rocked again as the footsteps moved towards the opening in the canvas sheet.

Tom curled his index finger round the trigger and waited for the inevitable.

On the embankment high above the wharf, Sam Hart sat on the damp grass, chewing on his bottom lip, his nerves frayed with the uncertainty of waiting. Tom had been gone for longer than expected. If he didn't show up soon, he, Sam, would have to go looking for him. The mist was lifting but was still too thick for him to see further than a few yards.

A man's voice cut through the silence. A short, excited yelp from somewhere near the wharf. Sam leapt to his feet and stared into the swirling sea of white. He hesitated, unsure what the shout had meant. He'd been ordered to stay put. For a moment longer, he tossed the decision around in his head, then, crouching low, he sped down the hill.

Suddenly, the outline of a lugger came into view. Sam stopped and dropped to one knee. He could make out two figures moving around on the deck. He drew his knife and crept closer, a clump of reeds between himself and the men, concealing his presence. They seemed to be looking for something or somebody. Sam looked along the length of the boat. A section of the canvas sheeting covering the cargo appeared to have been turned back. The wind caught it and it flapped noisily. One of the men pointed at it and said something.

Sam tensed. If Tom was under that canvas, he was in real danger. He thought quickly. He'd not get both men; not before the alarm was raised. The man nearest the flapping canvas moved forward. Another second or two and it would be too late.

Sam got to his feet and stumbled along the towpath, his head lolling to one side, his tongue protruding from his mouth in what he hoped was a convincing portrayal of an imbecile.

"Food. Food for the love of God." Sam's voice was slurred. "Will you spare some food for a poor man?"

Startled, the two men spun round and drew their pistols.

"What is it we'll be having here?" The nearest of the two men was the first to recover. He stepped off the boat, caught Sam by the throat and turned to his companion, his tone mocking. "Sure, it's a little Jew-boy and he'll be wanting food."

"And food he shall have," said the second man, scooping up a handful of dirt and rubbing it into Sam's face. "That's for snooping round where you'll not be wanted."

"Food! Water!" Sam spat out the dirt, his tone pleading. "Will you let a poor man eat?"

"The cully wants more food. It's greedy, he is." The man stroked Sam's cheek with the barrel of his gun.

"Haven't we just given him all a man could ask for? And didn't the ungrateful scrub spit it out?"

Sam was ready for the punch, when it came. He saw it form in the man's eye, watched the fist clench into a ball and the elbow reach back ready for the strike. He'd not trained under Daniel Mendoza to miss the opportunities such signs provided. The urge to break the man's jaw welled up inside him. But that wouldn't have helped Tom. Not yet. He rode the punch, doubled up in a pretence of pain, and fell to the ground, his eyes searching the lugger for any sign that Tom might still be there.

He caught sight of a movement. Only a small one. So small, in fact, he couldn't be sure he hadn't imagined it. The canvas sheeting appeared to bulge and then subside. It was over in a second.

"Thankee, kind sirs." Sam struggled to his feet and touched his forehead, his eyes turned to the ground. "I'll not trouble you further."

"Where d'you think you'll be going, now, my little Jewish friend?" A kick sent him sprawling again.

Again he climbed to his feet. This was the moment. The explosive force of the punch smashed into the face of the nearest tormentor, pulping the gristle that had been his nose and loosening what was left of his teeth. Sam didn't wait to see the result. He slewed his body round, elbows bent and fists clenched, and prepared to spring at the second man.

Then he stopped, his mouth open.

In front of him stood the bedraggled figure of Tom Pascoe nursing his right elbow. At his feet lay the unconscious body of the second man.

"Where the —?"

"Close your mouth, Sam," grinned Tom. "There's a fly trying to get in."

Sam obediently closed his mouth. Then, "Did you hurt your elbow, sir?"

"Aye. Caught it on the scrub's chin. Silly bugger left it in my way." Tom nodded towards the huts, shrouded in what was left of the sea mist. "Best we get out of here before they come looking for their friends. And Sam . . ."

"Aye, sir?"

"Thankee."

"Not something I want to repeat," said Tom when they had finally regained the top of the embankment. He looked back along the route they had taken, half expecting to see the men from the huts pursuing them, but there was nobody.

"Amen to that," said Sam. "Did you find anything?"

"I found the sugar and I also found the markings," said Tom, stripping off his sodden blouse and wringing it out.

"What markings are they?"

"All merchants mark their cargos with some form of identification," said Tom. "We had our own system on the West India ships. If you'll hand me my coat, I'll show you."

190

Tom slipped gratefully into his dry coat and retrieved a notebook and pencil from one of the pockets. Then he jotted down some figures and letters within the shape of a heart. "The letters are the initials of the owner. They are always followed by two numbers separated by a horizontal line. The bottom number shows the total number of barrels in the consignment while the top number is the individual number of the barrel. All the numbers and letters normally appear within some kind of shape — a heart, as in this case, or a circle or a box. I'm fairly sure everything in those luggers came from the *Swansong*. The initials are right and so is the heart shape. I just need to make sure about the serial numbers."

"How will you do that?" asked Sam.

"Oh, that's not difficult," chuckled Tom. "The *Swansong*'s manifest should tell me all I need to know."

"Didn't you tell me," said Sam, as though only half listening, "the *Swansong* was plundered the night I found you? The night of your beating?"

"Aye, so I did."

"Those barrels were never taken off the *Swansong*," said Sam. "Leastways, not by any villains."

"What d'you mean?" said Tom, staring at his friend.

"The noise would've woken the dead, sir," said Sam. "When them rogues plunder a barky like yours, they take their own little sacks — blackstraps, they call them — and put the sugar or coffee in them. They don't take the whole barrel. Those hogsheads must've been taken from somewhere else. Maybe off the lighters while they waited their turn at the Legal Quays. You know as well as I do, those lighters can stay out on the tideway for three, sometimes four weeks before there's space for them at the quays."

"Christ, you're right." Tom smacked his forehead with the flat of his hand. "*That's* how they do it. Seize fully laden lighters, run them down on the ebb tide and strip them clean at the first quiet spot they reach. No one would stop them, not the revenue nor one of our own patrols. Why should they? There's nothing suspicious about a couple of lighters going about their business. Only . . ."

"Only what, your honour?" said Sam.

"Something's not quite right," said Tom. "There's only two luggers down there at the wharf, holding perhaps fifty hogsheads each."

"So? How many do you want?" said Sam, a faint smile on his elf-like face.

"Those luggers must have been here since shortly after the *Swansong* began its unlading," said Tom. "That's seven, nearly eight weeks ago. Boylin is supposed to be tearing the bottom out of this port. He can't be doing that if he only shifts two luggers worth of sugar every seven or eight weeks. All of which means that if Boylin is the man we want, he has to be doing his plundering in some other way."

"There ain't another way as I knows of," said Sam.

"There has to be, Sam," said Tom, remembering his conversation with young Jacob, "and we have to find it. That, and why Boylin thought it necessary to go aboard the *Swansong* in the first place."

Tom gazed out over the dark mass of the Plaistow Levels and listened to the sigh of the wind. He'd come out to this distant place with no greater expectation than the possibility of finding the *Swansong*'s cargo. But now this exchange with Sam had raised more questions than answers. It was no longer the cut-and-dried solution he'd hoped for. If Boylin was only shifting small amounts of stolen goods, he could not possibly be the man responsible for the plundering of the port. If, on the other hand, he *was* responsible, then the thefts were being carried out in a way he'd yet to discover.

"What d'you want to do? Arrest them?" said Sam, jutting his chin in the direction of the hut.

"What for?" said Tom, bitterly.

"I had larceny in mind," said Sam.

"Aye, I grant you we've just seen some men in close proximity to sugar we believe to have been stolen," said Tom. "But we've got three problems. In the first place, we don't know for certain the sugar is stolen. In the second place, even if we could be sure it was from the *Swansong*, too much time has now passed between the act of larceny and the finding of these men in possession. We could never prove their involvement in the initial taking. And in the third place, I don't fancy our chances against five men. Even if we arrested them, we'd still have to get them back to civilisation."

"So what are you going to do?" asked Sam, a note of disappointment creeping into his voice.

Tom held up his hand at the sound of a commotion drifting up from the wharf.

"Sounds as if they've found those two cullies," he said. "Time we were going. As to what I'm going to do after that . . ."

Tom paused and looked at his friend.

"I just don't know, Sam. I just don't know."

CHAPTER
FOURTEEN

Boylin pushed open the door of the Queen's Head and shambled through the deserted taproom as the first glimmer of dawn appeared in the sky. Entering the back parlour, he reached for a pipe from the mantelpiece and lit it before settling down in front of the empty fire grate. Sleep was out of the question. What had happened had frightened him. Two of his men flogged to within an inch of their lives less than thirty yards from where he'd been sitting. And as if that were not bad enough, flogged in total silence. Not he nor any of the men he'd been with had seen or heard anything.

He shivered and leaned forward in his chair, his hands cupping the bowl of his pipe. Who they were and why they'd come, he had no idea — unless it was to steal the sugar. He pondered the possibility. Plunder he could understand. It made sense to him. And someone *had* disturbed the canvas sheeting and some of the barrels.

Yet nothing had been taken.

That's what made no sense. Clearly the men who'd come and gone in the night knew what they were about; could have taken what they wanted and disappeared. It was as if they'd expected to find the

195

sugar, had known it was there and were merely confirming its presence. Boylin's face paled as the implications took hold. If those who had come knew of the existence of the sugar, someone must have talked. But who? And to whom? The revenue, or someone else with an eye to a quick profit? Whoever they were, it was clear he needed to get rid of the stuff. And soon. Yet the only man capable of taking this quantity of sugar had already made it clear he wanted nothing to do with it.

"You'll be taking it this time, mister," muttered Boylin, under his breath. He took out his pocket watch. It was still early. He thought for a minute and then headed back out into a wet, blustery morning.

An hour later, he turned into Mincing Lane, a broad, cobblestoned avenue lined with leafy planes behind which stood a terrace of opulent houses. Boylin felt a stab of envy. He'd been here on many occasions in the past and each time been aware of his own sense of inadequacy, of a deference he felt to the wealth residing behind these walls.

Halfway along the lane he came to a halt outside one of the houses and looked up at the darkened windows. Then he pushed open the wrought-iron gate and mounted the few steps to the front door. He rang the bell.

The entrance hall into which he was ushered was a large, high-ceilinged space with a floor of black and white marble, off from which led several doors. To the right of the main entrance, a broad flight of stairs rose to the first-floor landing along which ran a balustrade of polished mahogany. Boylin glanced up, more from

196

habit than any expectation that he'd see her. He knew she'd long since gone from this place.

He permitted himself the briefest of smiles as he remembered their meeting through the railings of the London Hospital. Soon they would be together again — he and the beautiful Miss Tompkins . . . He turned at the sound of a discreet cough. The liveried servant who had let him in was waiting for him by the library door. Reluctantly, he walked in.

The minutes ticked by and Boylin's mood of apprehension increased. He stood by a long oak table, gazing at the book-lined walls, and the large fireplace at the far end of the room. Coming here had not been a good idea. He'd given no real consideration to what he would do if his proposals were rejected — as was likely. He tugged nervously at an earlobe. It was one thing to know a man's business, quite another to blackmail him. Suddenly he wished he were back in his own world where the rules were so much simpler. He turned at the sound of a cold, unwelcoming voice.

"I bid you good morning, Mr Boylin." Sir Sydney Devall, merchant of the West India Merchants and Planters Committee, entered the library and gave a perfunctory bow in the direction of his unexpected visitor. "Pray, what brings you to this part of London at this early hour?"

"Business, your honour, business," said Boylin, his mouth gulping for air. He guessed, from his host's slightly dishevelled appearance, that he'd disturbed his sleep.

"Business? On a Sunday, and at this godforsaken hour?" Devall's voice took on a harsher note. "You know very well the terms on which I do business, Mr Boylin. We meet at the Queen's Head. That has been our arrangement for some time, has it not? And certainly I do not conduct business on a Sunday."

"It's begging your pardon I am, your honour. I meant no offence, but matters is pressing and I couldn't be waiting to see you."

"This really will not do, Mr Boylin. You do handsomely out of our relationship and this is the way you thank me." The cold eyes bored into Boylin's soul. "But now you're here, what have you in mind?"

"You'll be recalling our little talk more than two months since, your honour? When I was after telling you I had some sand as might be of interest to you . . . ?"

"Sand? Ah, you mean sugar. I do recall it, Mr Boylin. What of it?"

"You wouldn't believe how many fine gentlemen there's been as wanted to buy it, and at a handsome price, your honour, but I told them it was yours, your honour. Yours when you wanted it, like."

"Are you a dolt, sir?" said Devall, his eyes narrowing. "A fool? Or perhaps you take me for one. Why, there's not a merchant in London who'd touch that stuff. Not after all the commotion your people caused on that barquentine. The *Swansong* wasn't it? Two men killed and the second in command of the ship beaten almost to death, as I recall. The story was in the papers for days."

"I knows nothing —"

"Yes, yes." Devall waved an impatient hand at Boylin. "You've already told me you had nothing to do with any of it, although I doubt there's a magistrate in London would be convinced by your protestations. I told you on the night you first approached me that I wanted nothing to do with the sugar. Why should I have changed my mind in the meanwhile?"

"Why, your honour . . ." Boylin struggled to control his anger. "Do I need to remind your honour of our arrangements?"

Devall's ruddy complexion grew suddenly pale. He turned away from his visitor and crossed the polished parquetry to one of the full-length windows overlooking the garden, the fingers of one hand playing with a tuft of black hair sprouting from a mole on his chin. For a long moment he stared out at a threatening sky. A gust of wind rattled the window frames and thrashed the long boughs of a nearby beech.

"I find . . ." he said.

"Yes, your honour?" Boylin rubbed the sides of his breeches with the palms of his sweating hands.

"I find," repeated the merchant, his voice quieter than before, less confident of its authority, "that on reflection, I may have a buyer for this commodity. Perhaps you would be good enough to leave your sample bag and we shall meet again. Shall we say ten o'clock on Monday? My usual table at Jerusalem's? We can talk further."

A few minutes later Sir Sydney Devall watched as his visitor was escorted from the library. The merchant disliked being threatened, especially by the likes of Joseph Boylin. He glanced at the sample bag of sugar on the side table and then at the departing figure of the publican, a thoughtful look in his eye.

"I warrant you'll regret your threats, Boylin," he murmured.

Monday morning had dawned chilly despite the appearance of the sun over the Isle of Dogs some thirty minutes earlier. Tom stood on the pontoon at the base of Wapping New Stairs, watching the breeze ruffle the smooth surface of the tideway. Here and there, seagulls swooped screaming over the water or settled in the rigging of ships, preening themselves high above the ceaseless activity of the port. He was thinking about his recent interview with young Jacob Newman; had hardly slept for thinking about it.

The boy's evidence would provide a major turning point in his pursuit of Boylin. An eye-witness to murder, as well as the theft of the *Swansong*'s sugar. It didn't come much better than that. He would see the boy again, get a written statement from him, and tidy up a few outstanding points.

He turned to face the crew. Hart, Kemp and Tisdale stood in line, a wooden arms chest on the floor of the pontoon in front of them.

"Your appointments if you please, Hart."

Sam stepped forward, opened the chest, and stepped back for Tom to examine the contents.

200

"Carry on!" said Tom, peering in.

"Thankee, sir," said Sam. "One boat-gun, together with powder and shot, four pistols together with powder and four balls apiece, four sticks, four hangers — beg pardon your honour, four cutlasses — and one axe, all present and accounted for."

"Good." Tom glanced at his men. "This morning we have a total of thirty-two West Indiamen in the Upper Pool, ten of whom have paid for our protection. As usual, I shall be visiting each of the ten and will speak to the constable on board. But before that, I want to have a look up round the Bridge."

"Something special we should be looking for, your honour?" Sam asked, kneeling down to fasten the lid of the arms box.

"Nothing specific," said Tom. "But I'm concerned about the number of strangers who've appeared in the area these few weeks since."

"I've noticed them myself." Sam looked up. "I've heard they's Irish, coming on account of the fighting over there. Is that true, sir?"

"Seems that way," said Tom. "According to the newspapers, almost the whole island has risen in revolt. Thousands, so they say, have fled the trouble and come here. What concerns me is that they expect to find work, and you know as well as I do how hard that is to come by."

"I feel for them, sir," said Sam, "but what's it to do with us? We can't help them."

"No, we can't help them," said Tom. "But if they don't get work they'll be easy prey for troublemakers and then it *does* become our concern. Now, if we're all done, it's time we were afloat."

He followed his crew down the stairs to the waiting galley. Out on the reach, a dozen or so barges drifted up on the flood tide, their hulls low in the water, their lightermen hunched over long sweep-oars. Further upriver, the coal-encrusted hull of a collier lay broadside to the current as she backed and filled her way to the coal wharfs of Southwark. Tom watched for a while before dragging his thoughts back to the questions he'd need to put to young Jacob, when next he saw him. The list was a long one.

"All ready, sir." Sam's voice penetrated his thoughts. "The arms box is stowed aft, all proper, like."

"Thankee, Hart. Stand by to cast off." He sat himself down on the box, and glancing up and down the river, checked the position of such vessels as were underway. Then, "D'you hear there? Cast off fore and aft. Away starboard."

The fast-flowing current caught the galley's bow and drew her rapidly away from the river bank. A pause, then, "Give way together."

Twenty yards short of the nearest lighter, Tom pulled hard down on the starboard guy and the heavy galley swept round in a great arc to bring the tide under her stern, her course set for London Bridge.

"Steady all," said Tom.

The galley floated up past the Tower, towards the white-fronted Custom House and the fish market at Billingsgate, the slanting rays of the rising sun flashing

202

and sparkling on the surface of the water, clothing everything in its burnished light.

There was nothing on that run. At least there was nothing that Tom had been able to see, his attention largely taken up in avoiding the heavy press of vessels that filled the Upper Pool. It was difficult enough avoiding a collision without the added complication of keeping an eye out for the unusual or the suspicious. But he'd come to realise how important it was to the routine of his task, this ability to sift out normality and dismiss it to some hidden part of the mind; to leave the conscious being free to scrutinise incidents most men would have failed to notice in the first place.

"Easy all." Tom altered course to avoid a couple of laden barges making for Young's Quay, his eyes automatically scanning the two lightermen before moving on to a sailing hoy just behind.

It was strange, he thought, how a man's occupation altered his perceptions and his priorities. As a seaman his whole being had been alive to every pitch and roll of his ship, every change in the weather, every sound in the rigging. Now he found that the way a man moved or looked about him, the weight of the goods he carried, his studied air of indifference, or even his presence at a particular time and place, were all likely to draw his attention. It was almost as though he'd learned to smell a man's guilt just as he could once have detected rotten wood in the hull of his ship or a change in the song of the wind.

Fifty yards downstream of London Bridge, he swung the galley towards the Middlesex shore and prepared to go about. Already he could see the downward sweep of water forcing its way between the arches, deceptive in its deadly beauty, the long, smooth wave dipping towards its midpoint, ready to pull down all but the strongest oarsmen.

"Near enough I think," said Tom, heaving on the larboard guy and watching the bows come round. He caught the smell of coal dust and looked over at the half-dozen colliers moored down-river of Battle Bridge Stairs. He smiled as memories flooded back.

"Happy thoughts, your honour?" said Sam.

"Not as I would call happy. I was just recalling the times I spent aboard one of them hulks. Years ago mind."

"I didn't know you was on colliers," said Sam, surprised. "I thought you was in the Navy."

"So I was, Hart, so I was," said Tom, contemplating the ill-kept brigs, a pall of coal dust hanging over each. He wondered if the life of the crews was any different to the one he'd endured all those years ago — the brutality, the hunger, the cold and the tedium. "The colliers were another part of my life, when I first went to sea. I was just a lad, then."

"How d'you come to join the King's Navy?" asked Sam, tugging back on his oar.

"I decided it was what I wanted to do, and volunteered. Was rated able."

Sam's eyes widened in disbelief. "Volunteered? For the lower deck, sir? You weren't pressed, like?"

"Aye, the lower-deck it was." Tom laughed, the dip in his mood quickly disappearing. "And no, I wasn't pressed. Collier crews were protected in those days. Different now, of course, but then the Navy couldn't touch us."

"You were lucky," said Sam. "It's awful hard on the men what's pressed, don't you agree, your honour?"

"I do," said Tom. "None of us was insensible to the sufferings of those who were pressed, but the Navy needs more men for the defence of the country than it can get by other means."

He stopped, aware that his explanation was never going to convince a land man that a more efficient and humane means of recruitment could not be found, that the subject had been endlessly talked about, with every alternative dismissed as more brutal or unfair or inefficient than the one it hoped to replace. He doubted Sam would believe him if he said there was not a captain afloat who'd not far rather have a willing land man on his ship than a pressed and sullen seaman, however good the latter was at his trade. It was —

A sudden, anguished scream tore through his brain. He jerked his head round, his eyes searching the untidy mass of shipping over by the Southwark shore.

"Over there, sir," Sam's measured tones acted like a balm to his jangled nerves. "Yon brig! Off Butler's Wharf! See? On the upper deck."

"Aye, I see it now," said Tom, shading his eyes. "There's more men in the boats, amidships. Looks to be the *Antelope*."

He watched distant figures scramble down the brig's companionway, leaping recklessly into the two or three small boats bobbing close under the ship's hull. Others, already there, struggled to lift an object from the water. Again the scream floated across the tideway, shocking in its intensity.

"D'you hear there? Give way together," shouted Tom.

The command was superfluous. The galley was already slicing through the river's murky water at a speed few could match. Tom glanced at the *Antelope*. A platform had been lowered to the water's edge and a body laid on it. He watched as it was swayed aloft.

"Ahoy, *Antelope*!" Tom cupped his hands to his mouth, his voice carrying over the screams of a man at the extremity of his suffering. Half a dozen heads turned towards him. "In the King's name, we're coming alongside."

The galley turned into the tide, her bows throwing up a foaming wave of white water.

"Easy all. Stand by to ship starboard oars. In starboard oars." The slick, polished movements came with naval precision, the product of Tom's hard-driven training. The galley slid effortlessly in towards the brig's larboard side.

"Tisdale!" Tom looked along the length of the galley to his barrel-chested crewman at bow-oar. "Take up the hitcher and clap on the main chains."

"Aye, sir. Main chains it is." Tisdale reached across with the boathook, caught the massive iron chains supporting the brig's mainsail shrouds, and hauled the police boat close inboard.

Tom didn't wait for it to come to rest before he leapt to the companion ladder and ran up the ship's side with practised ease. On the deck, a young man lay on a crude wooden platform that had been used to raise him from the river. His right leg was tucked beneath him, an arm thrown carelessly over his face. Shuddering sobs racked his body. Tom kneeled down and eased the boy's arm away from his face.

For a moment he was too shocked to react. He looked up at the tight circle of men surrounding him and then down at a grey, barely conscious face.

Just three days had elapsed since he'd last seen Jacob Newman.

Boylin turned left out of Jerusalem's Coffee House and headed up Cornhill, his mood lighter than it had been in days. His meeting with the merchant had gone remarkably smoothly. The agreed price for the sugar was better than he'd anticipated and the place of handover quickly settled. If the scrub had meant to haggle about the details then he'd shown little appetite for it — surprisingly little appetite — thought Boylin. There had been only one matter on which the merchant had been adamant, insisting on a further delay before he'd accept delivery. Something about needing to make the necessary arrangements for its reception.

Boylin shook his head. He hadn't liked it. Hadn't liked it at all. The sugar had been hanging around for too long, especially since someone now knew where it was. Still, the important thing was that he'd found a buyer. It was time he celebrated.

He'd see if Miss Tompkins was at leisure.

A moment of doubt overtook him. She hadn't seemed overly pleased to see him the last time they'd met. He brought a hand up to the side of his face and traced the mosaic of taut skin with his fingers. Perhaps she no longer found him attractive or, then again, perhaps she'd not forgiven him for what had happened . . . He dismissed the thought. Had she not given him joy at their meeting, and smiled as she did so? He quickened his pace. He would renew the friendship. They would walk and talk and laugh as they used to do. She'd not refuse him.

Of that, he was now quite sure.

Tom studied the pale, unconscious face of Jacob Newman lying on the makeshift stretcher. The boy looked in a bad way.

"What happened to the lad?" Tom's eyes swept the crowd of silent onlookers. There was no answer. He looked back at the boy, carefully taking hold of the damaged limb and laying it next to the other leg.

"Get me some canvas strips, God rot your souls," said Tom, glaring at the unmoving mass around him. "And stand back. Give us some air, for all love."

The circle of men shuffled back and Tom felt the injured limb, his probing fingers finding the jagged shape of a protruding thigh bone. He looked up at the expectant faces.

208

"You there." He signalled a ruddy-faced, jug-eared man in his early fifties. "Place your finger here, by the hurt. No, not there. Here! The Devil take you man, have a care. Good! Don't move. I want no mistake when I come to bind the leg. I must know precisely where the hurt lies."

"How did this happen," he asked again, when he had done all that he could to make Jacob comfortable. Again the same determined silence.

"What happened to this boy?" Tom looked coldly at his jug-eared assistant.

"He were in the maintop with . . ." The man dropped his gaze. "He must've slipped."

"Who was he with?" Tom persisted, his anger rising. Another silence.

"I were." The voice came from the back of the group. Tom swung round to see a thickset man of about thirtyfive, his grinning lips drawn back over a row of blackened, stump-like teeth.

"And you are . . . ?"

"Sure it'll be Shamus O'Malley and that's a fact," said the man.

"What happened, O'Malley?" said Tom.

"It were like you were told, mister," said O'Malley. "The lad and me were in the maintop when he fell. There weren't nothing nobody could do to save him."

"He was in the water. How did he come by a broken leg falling in the river?"

"Sure, he hit the larboard rail on his way down," said O'Malley. "It were then he fell in the water."

Tom looked down at the boy's ashen face, acutely aware that time was not on his side. Any further questions would have to wait. He had to get the boy to a hospital.

"Where are the coal-whippers?" he snapped.

Half a dozen hesitant hands were raised.

"Then catch hold of the whip and stand ready. I mean to put the boy into yon galley. Ready?"

"Ready, aye, ready," came the instant response, the men relieved to be doing something. Anything.

"Sway away!" Tom felt the platform shudder under his feet and lift free of the deck. "Clear of the rail. Lower away."

"Where are we heading, sir?" said Sam, as soon as the platform had completed its descent and been securely lashed athwart the galley.

Tom squinted over the wide expanse of the Thames. For a moment he couldn't remember where he was; his mind still on the deck of the brig. Had the boy slipped from the rigging? Or been pushed? There'd been no wind that might have caused his fall and it was certain he'd not been drinking. And anyway, how could a man in the maintop end up in the water — and not on the deck — unless he'd been pushed?

"Make it Execution Dock, if you please," said Tom, studying the faces lining the *Antelope*'s rail. O'Malley was not among them. He looked back at his crew. "With luck we'll find a carriage to get us to the accident hospital. Let's hope so."

For several minutes, a silence hung over the galley, disturbed only by the sound of the water rushing along

210

her sides, and the measured breathing of the crew as they sped towards the river stairs a few yards south of the police office, at Execution Dock.

"Did you know the big fellow you were speaking to just now, your honour?" Sam tried to keep his voice light.

"O'Malley? The one who said he was aloft with Jacob? No, I've not seen him before. Why d'you ask?" said Tom.

"Oh, I just wondered. 'Tis nothing."

"You think he had something to do with this?" Tom nodded in the direction of Jacob's mute frame.

"I'd say it were possible, sir," said Sam. "Did you know the lad is Gabriel Newman's brother?"

"Aye, I did. He came to see me three nights ago and told me who he was."

"I didn't know that," said Sam, frowning. "But it's beginning to make sense."

"What is?" said Tom.

"I saw that cully, the one you spoke to on the brig just now, outside the police office three nights since."

"Are you sure it was O'Malley?" Tom's heart missed a beat.

"Aye, I'm sure," said Sam, recalling a previous encounter with the same man in an alley off the Ratcliff Highway. "Saw him when we came off the river at the end of the late-turn patrol. I wanted a word with him, but as soon as he saw me, he legged it."

"I see," said Tom, and then, as if an afterthought, "What did you want to have a word with him about?"

Sam hesitated, studying the blade of his oar. "He's . . . he's Boylin's muscle. I wanted to know what he were doing outside the office in the middle of the night."

Tom fixed his friend with a curious stare. Sam was holding something back. He let it go and turned to the unconscious Jacob. It had been a risk leaving the boy unprotected. He'd known that. He should have kept a closer eye on him, at least until he'd sorted out a better way of keeping him safe. He sucked his cheeks. If Jacob died, all his evidence would die with him.

Tom was suddenly uncomfortable, as though his concern for the boy had more to do with his value as a witness than any genuine interest in his welfare. He tried to put the thought out of his mind. Of course he cared, but it would be idle to pretend there was not an added dimension to his concerns.

He looked across at Jacob's pallid skin, listening to his shallow breathing, and wondered how long he'd got.

CHAPTER
FIFTEEN

The front steps of the London Hospital were crowded with the usual sorry assortment of people. It was always the same on Mondays, the day when patients were discharged and new ones admitted. Tom had never been able to understand the arrangement — keeping perfectly healthy patients in the hospital while keeping sick ones out, seemingly for no better reason than a more orderly changeover on Mondays.

He steered his little party clear of the crush, momentarily surprised by the sight of a dozen or more sailors. Then he remembered Peggy had told him of the constant trickle of wounded seamen the Navy brought to this hospital after every battle. Occasionally so many would arrive as to threaten to overwhelm the hospital's capacity to cope. He'd almost forgotten the war, his horizons now limited to the Thames, and a thin stretch of foul-smelling land on either side . . .

About to turn away, he spotted Peggy talking to someone in the crowd. A warm glow enveloped him and he recalled the afternoon they'd spent at Vauxhall Gardens, strolling the sunlit avenues and watching the other promenaders while listening to music in the great rotunda. Afterwards, they'd shared a meal in one of the pavilions and, as evening fell, had stood watching the display of fireworks before heading back to the river for the long journey home.

"Your honour . . .?" Sam raised his eyebrows in a questioning arch.

"Yes, I'm coming."

He glanced back at Peggy just as the crowd parted. On the step below hers — his face wreathed in a smile, his arms spread wide as though imploring some favour of her was Boylin.

Tom felt a jolt of shock and apprehension in his stomach.

"We must hurry, your honour." Sam's voice brought him back to reality. He wrenched his eyes away from Boylin and waved the crew on.

The receiving room was crowded as it nearly always was, the habitual atmosphere of quiet resignation punctuated by the sighs and groans of pain. The crew found an empty space and, while Sam went in search of a physician, Tom's thoughts returned to what he'd seen on the main steps of the hospital. There seemed little doubt that Peggy and Boylin knew each other and, from the happy expression on Boylin's face, knew each other intimately.

"What, pray, have we here?" A voice close to his elbow cut across his thoughts and he looked up to see a thickset man of about his own age standing next to where Jacob was lying.

"And you are . . .?" said Tom.

214

"I'm sorry, I should have introduced myself." The man bent over Jacob's prone body. "My name is Headington. I'm an assistant surgeon at this hospital. Now, if you will excuse me . . ."

Moments later, his examination done, the surgeon hurried away to one of the consulting rooms, returning a minute or so later with a tall, hook-nosed man in his mid-fifties. Tom remembered him from his first visit; remembered the same aloof expression, the same austere authority.

"What, pray, is your diagnosis, Mr Headington?" said William Blizard.

Tom listened with interest.

"My opinion, sir," said Headington, "is that it's a fracture of the femur and will require immediate surgery."

"Do you though?" Blizard's aloof tone bordered on rudeness.

"Well . . . that is, sir . . ." Headington's voice trailed away, a bleak and nervous look on his face.

"Be so good, sir, as to have the object moved to the consulting room," said Blizard, probing Jacob's injured thigh with the tips of his fingers. "And pray present my compliments to the duty physician. I fancy it is Dr Hamilton this morning. Ask him to spare me a moment, if he's at leisure."

Tom looked at his crew as the injured Jacob was carried away.

"Sam, lay along to the police office, will you? Present my compliments to Mr Harriot and inform him that I remain with this injured lad in the hope of discovering what happened to him. Kemp, Tisdale. You can also go."

He watched them leave and then ambled over to a bench from where he could see what was going on in the consulting room. He wanted to keep an open mind about what might have happened on board the *Antelope*, wanted to avoid reaching conclusions that couldn't be justified by the facts. But time and again his mind returned to the man who'd been in the maintop with Jacob, the same man Sam had seen outside the police office a few nights before, at the precise time he, Tom Pascoe, had been talking to Jacob inside. His thoughts rolled on. Nothing fitted. Why, for instance, had Sam hesitated when he'd been asked about O'Malley? What was he concealing?

The door to the consulting room opened and closed, and Tom looked up to see a third man join the pair around the injured boy. Then Blizard was beckoning the porters. A decision had obviously been reached.

"Take this object to the cutting-room. I shall be operating directly."

Tom rose to his feet and walked over to the door of the consulting room.

"Forgive my intrusion, sir," he said, "but may I ask if it is your intention to operate on this lad?"

"And who, sir, might you be?" Blizard looked sharply at Tom's soiled coat and breeches before catching sight of the tipstaff in the river surveyor's hand. His expression softened. "I see you are an officer of the law, sir, a member of the new marine police establishment, if I'm not mistook. But now that I think on it, have I not seen you about this hospital before?"

"Aye, in all probability you have, sir," said Tom, suddenly impatient. "But the boy . . . I brought him to the hospital. Do I understand you intend to operate on him?"

"Aye, sir. I propose an amputation."

"There is no other way?"

"I regret the necessity extremely," said Blizard, looking down at Jacob and shaking his head. "I've consulted with my learned colleagues, Dr Hamilton and Mr Headington here, and we are all three of the same mind. Perhaps in the years ahead it might be possible to save the leg of a man injured in this way. But for the present I must work within the limits of our present knowledge. It has to come off."

Tom nodded, strangely affected by the news.

The thin face of the chief clerk peered at Harriot from the open door of the magistrate's office.

"Sir Sydney Devall to see you, your worship."

"Did he say what he wanted?" said Harriot, looking up from some papers he'd been working on.

"It appears he wishes to speak to you about a murder, sir."

"Very well. Best you show him in, Mr Yeardley." Harriot rose to his feet as the merchant entered the room. "This is indeed an unexpected pleasure, Sir Sydney. What can I do for you?"

"The pleasure, sir, is mine. As to what you can do for me, sir, I bring some intelligence which I believe will be of interest to you."

Harriot waved his visitor to a chair and himself sat down, his fingertips resting on the edge of his desk.

"The fact is, sir," said Devall, "I believe I have information relating to a case of murder."

"Pray continue, sir," said Harriot, with a small wave of the hand.

"Not above three days since, sir, a fellow comes to see me and offers to supply me with a substantial quantity of sugar. I believe that sugar may have come from the West India barque the *Swansong*, on which, I understand, one of the crew was vilely murdered and the mate seriously injured."

"I remember the case very well, sir," said Harriot. "Did you know this man? The one who visited you?"

"No." Devall paused, glanced at Harriot and then looked quickly away. "I'd never seen him before in my life."

"I see," said Harriot. "But you offered to do business with him?"

"I did, sir. It is not unusual in the City." Again, the quick, uncertain flick of the eye. "We conduct our business where we can, and he told me he owned a small warehouse to the east of London. I saw no reason to disbelieve him. It was only subsequently that I happened upon one of your handbills concerning the trouble on the *Swansong* and, of course, the plundering of her cargo of sugar."

"And you considered the two might be linked?" said Harriot.

"Quite so. Anygate, before my suspicions had been aroused, I had already arranged to purchase the consignment of sugar he was offering."

"Has the consignment been delivered, sir?"

"No. Not yet."

"Could you describe the physical appearance of the man who came to see you?" Harriot picked up a quill and dipped it into an inkwell.

"Why, sir, let me see, now . . ."

"This is very handsome in you, sir," said Harriot, when he had taken down the description of his visitor's caller. "If you will now tell me when and where you expect delivery of the sugar, we will take care of matters from there."

"Oh dear me, no, sir." Devall's hand flew to his mouth, his fingers playing with a tuft of black hair sprouting from his chin. "I beg you, do not involve me in this matter. I have no wish for it to be known that I was the source of your information."

"I regret there is no other way, sir," said Harriot. "Your description, excellent though it is, will not allow us to gain the evidence we need for an arrest. We must know when and where the delivery is to take place in order that we might be there."

"But, sir, you of all people should know these rogues are dangerous and desperate men who would doubtless think nothing of cutting my throat," said Devall, his face paling.

"Without your help, this man will almost surely go free," said Harriot. "Will you not help us, sir?"

"There might be a way, sir," said Devall weakly. "Pray allow me a day or so to make my enquiries. Then, sir, if I must, I shall return with the information you require."

At about noon, several days after Jacob's admission to the London Hospital, the old hat-seller passed down a narrow, rutted alley and stopped in front of a pair of dilapidated wooden doors. Curling his bony fingers round the lip of one of the nearest, he wrenched it open and was at once met by a blast of warm foetid air. He stopped and waited for his nose to grow used to the stench and his eyes to become accustomed to the dimness of the room beyond.

It was a large place of perhaps forty feet square, a kitchen of sorts with a beamed ceiling and earth floor which admitted so little daylight as to need candles, even in the middle of the day. A single length of stout rope was stretched across the room at about shoulder height and on this a number of men and women were supporting their emaciated bodies, draping their thin arms over the cord, their heads lolling against their chests, apparently asleep. Others sat on benches, their heads resting on the tables in front of them or staring vacantly into space. No one spoke and only the occasional cough and the slurping sounds of gruel being sipped from earthen bowls broke the silence.

The Jew's entrance caused not the least stir and before long he had found a vacant position in the corner furthest away from the door. He sat down heavily, the tin mugs and canisters hanging from his string belt clattering noisily as he did so. Soon he, too, had dozed off, the four or five hats he wore gradually slipping forward over his nose.

He wasn't sure at what point he became aware of the two men sitting next to him on the bench, still less of when he purposely began to take note of what they were saying. He understood, perhaps better than most, the value of discretion, and would generally make a point of shutting out what was not intended for his hearing. But it was the mention of the name Sam Hart that caught his attention. He remembered that one of the two men who'd rescued him from his flogging, an Ashkenazi like himself, had been called by that name.

Slowly, he half opened his eyes until he was able see two men. The nearest one wore a patch over one eye and his wax-like skin was stretched tight over one cheek, as though burned. He shifted his gaze to the second man and realised, with a start, that he'd seen him before. Knew to avoid him. He struggled to remember his name. O'Malley. That was it. There was no doubting the broad, flat face, the thick lips and the yellowish, pockmarked skin.

"What you bring me here for?" It was O'Malley speaking. "The place stinks. We could have nattered all cosy, like, at the Queen's Head."

"Will you be keeping your voice down," replied the older of the two men. "It ain't no concern of others what we say and that's the way I like it. We come here 'cos no one knows us, see?"

O'Malley grunted but said nothing.

"I want that scrub, Hart, dealt with once and for all," the older man continued. "He got away last time. You make sure he don't get away again. I want him turned off proper."

"He's as good as gone," said O'Malley, his leering expression exposing a few stumps of blackened teeth. "Now what about all that sand we got down on the Lea. Ain't you going to get it shifted? After what happened, like."

"Ain't none of your business," said the older man. "But since you ask, we're shifting it last week in September."

"Jesus, Mary and Joseph, will it be that long? Could you not be bringing it up sooner?" said O'Malley.

"No." The older man seemed unsettled by the admission.

"Well, have it your own way." A pause, then, "Will you be going yourself, now? For the sand, like?"

"I will."

The pile of hats on the Jew's head slid forward. He sat perfectly still, resisting the temptation to push them back. From beneath the brim he could see O'Malley looking in his direction. Fear surged through him. The next moment O'Malley turned back to face his companion, seemingly satisfied they'd not been overheard. The Jew closed his eyes. He'd seen enough.

"When you've done for Hart, you can do the same to Pascoe."

"Captain Pascoe? D'you take me for a fool? Find someone else to do yer dirty work," O'Malley's voice hissed in alarm. "I'll not be taking on Pascoe for you nor nobody. There's not a man on the river can best him. What's your game with him, anygate?"

"All right, all right, keep your hair on," said the older man. Then, suddenly, "What's up? What's afoot?"

The hat-seller felt the eyes of the two men boring into him. In his imagination, he could already feel the blows raining down on his head; his punishment for being there, for daring to have overheard what should have remained secret. A suffocating surge of fear ran through him, his heart hammering against the thin walls of his chest. Suddenly, he heard the scuffling noise of men climbing to their feet: they were leaving. He watched them go, noticing the shuffling, crab-like movement of the older man, and the aggressive, rolling gait of the younger, his arms arched clear of his sides. And then they were gone. The door to the street creaked to a close after them.

All was quiet again but for the snoring of exhausted men and women, old before their time; that, and the heavy drumbeat of his heart.

About the same time as the hat-seller was watching the two men leave the lodging house, Tom Pascoe was approaching the main gate of the London Hospital, determined to see young Jacob Newman. He had already delayed the formal interview too long. He needed a written statement. The boy's testimony was crucial to the Boylin investigation.

Turning in through the massive, wrought-iron gates of the hospital, he climbed the stone steps leading to the main entrance of the building. He guessed Jacob was probably in one of the two surgical wards on the second floor. He crossed the entrance lobby, mentally running through the questions he wanted to put to the boy. How long had he known Boylin? How well? Could he describe what Boylin had been wearing on the night he went aboard the *Swansong*? What exactly had Boylin said and done while he was on board? Who was with him? The list seemed endless. Still engrossed in these thoughts, he almost collided with Peggy as he rounded the corner of the lobby.

"Why, Tom! Give you joy," she said, her face flushing with pleasure. "What, pray, brings you here? You cannot have forgotten that your shipmate, Mr Simmonds, was discharged many days since."

"Joy, Peggy," said Tom. "No, I'd not forgotten. I saw him on the Monday he returned for his certificate. He told me he had kept his berth as mate on the *Swansong*. He was to have sailed for the West Indies a few days since. No, it was young Jacob Newman I wanted to see."

"I regret it extremely," said Peggy, "but Master Jacob is dead."

"What?" said Tom, his eyes widening. "How did it happen?"

"He never recovered his senses after the operation," said Peggy. "The porters took him back to the ward and a little later Mr Blizard came to see him. I could see the surgeon was worried but there was nothing he could do until the fever had past. Then —"

"Fever?" interrupted Tom.

"Yes," said Peggy, looking surprised at the interruption. "It's quite normal for an object to suffer the fever after such an amputation. Many succumb before it runs its course. It's just one of those things. I once asked the apothecary why so many develop it. He said it was one of the mysteries of medicine but doubtless we'd solve it, one day."

"Poor Jacob," said Tom, a faraway look in his eye. "Are you able to tell me anymore?"

"I was about to take my customary exercise in the garden," said Peggy, a light blush rising in her cheeks. "Should you wish, we could talk there. I find that Miss Squibb, with whom I normally walk, is indisposed."

"Of all things I would like that."

They crossed the lobby floor and descended some steps into the garden quadrangle at the back of the hospital.

"How did you come to know Jacob?" said Peggy, after they had walked a short distance on a stone path speckled with moss.

"I —" Tom stopped in his stride. For a fleeting moment he wondered if it was wise to tell her what he knew of the boy and his connection with Boylin. He could not rid himself of the memory of Peggy and the Irishman on the steps of the hospital and the implications of their relationship for his investigation. He wrestled with his doubts. Cynicism had become central to his outlook as a river surveyor, compelling him, of necessity, to question the motives and explanations of others. It was, he supposed, an inevitable consequence of the duties he performed, of

225

the kind of people with whom he dealt and of their attitude towards him.

Seldom, in recent weeks, had he been permitted to look up from the gutter of human misery, to examine life other than through the distorting prism of his own distrust. But had it always to be this way? He looked at Peggy, her guileless face turned towards him, and at once he knew his answer.

"He was the brother of a man I've had dealings with," he said. "Some time ago Jacob came to see me at the police office and told me of the activities of a certain rogue I'm interested in. I think the boy died as a result of the information he gave me."

Peggy's hand flew to her mouth. "Oh, Tom, you cannot mean he was murdered?"

"I suspect so, yes."

"But why? Just for talking to you?"

"It happens," said Tom, carefully. "Men will often do things for no better reason than that they can, particularly where there is no check on their conduct, no fear of detection. Jacob knew the risks he was taking when he approached me. He hoped his actions would make a difference and improve the quality of the lives of the people in this part of London. I have to believe I can achieve that for him or he will have died in vain."

"But murder?" said Peggy. "Men will commit murder for no better reason than that they can?"

"Not entirely," said Tom. "But without the certainty of punishment, there is little to prevent the worst excesses of human behaviour. Doubtless the person who did this felt Jacob's death was necessary for whatever reason. Perhaps he feared for his own downfall."

They walked on, a warm breeze rustling the leaves of the orchard at the bottom of the quadrangle.

"This rogue you speak of," said Peggy, breaking the brief silence. "Is he the man you suspect of killing Jacob?"

"Not directly," said Tom, thrusting his thumbs into the waistband of his breeches. "But I believe it was on his orders that Jacob was pushed from the rigging."

"How will you find out? Who actually did it, I mean."

"That's not the difficult part," said Tom, smiling grimly. "We already know who was with Jacob in the moments before he fell. The difficult part is proving the fall was not an accident and establishing the link between that and the man I believe to be ultimately responsible."

"And do you think you can do that?" asked Peggy, her long, delicate fingers brushing the sleeve of Tom's coat.

"I must," said Tom, remembering John Harriot's words about the consequences of failure. "Before it's too late and this nation suffers the consequences of one man's greed."

CHAPTER
SIXTEEN

"*L'shana tovah*," Sam gave the traditional Hebrew greeting at Rosh Hashanah — the Jewish New Year — to another small group of incoming worshippers on his way out of the door of the synagogue.

"And well over the fast," came the invariable reply.

Sam emerged into Duke's Place and glanced up at the ashen sky, great peaks of rain-laden clouds sweeping up from the Thames towards the north-east. With luck he might make it to where he was going before the heavens opened. He threaded his way through the tightly packed square. It would take him about ten minutes to reach his mother's home in King's Street for their celebration of Rosh Hashanah. She'd asked him to bring some apples and had promised him a honey cake to welcome in the New Year, symbols of the sweetness in the coming twelve months, she'd said to him. It was at times like this that he thought about the faith he'd left behind.

"If you please, master."

Sam turned at the sound of the broken English. For a long moment he struggled with his memory, his gaze sweeping over the cadaverous face with its coal-black eyes, and the shabby, ankle-length wool coat adorned with tin mugs and colourful rags.

"Yes, yes, forgive me, brother," said Sam, embarrassed by his forgetfulness. "I remember you now. *L'shana tovah* to you. Give you joy at this New Year."

"Thank you, good sir, and well over the fast."

It was difficult to understand the hat-seller's strangled diction spoken through a heavy German inflection. Sam inclined his head and waited for the old man to continue.

"I came here in the hope of finding you," said the hat-seller. "I have a message for your friend Captain Pascoe and, alas, a warning for you."

Sam was still out of breath by the time he found Tom. The two men settled into an empty police galley moored alongside the pontoon at the foot of the river stairs. It was the only place they'd been able to find that offered any privacy.

"There ain't no doubt about it," said Sam, surveying his superior sprawled in the stern sheets. "From the description the hat-seller gave me, he were surely speaking of Boylin, and he recognised the other fellow. It were that unpardonable scrub you saw on the *Antelope*, the one what you think pushed young Jacob out the rigging."

"O'Malley?"

"Aye, that's the fellow. Anygate, the old man heard them talking, clear as day."

"And you say they mentioned the *Swansong's* cargo?" said Tom, his eyes fixed on a newly erected gibbet a hundred yards downstream at Execution Dock, the lapping tide rattling the chains enclosing the fresh cadaver.

"Near as makes no difference," said Sam. "They was talking about some sugar they'd got out on the Lea. Boylin said he'd be collecting it himself in the last week of September. I'll warrant he's found himself a buyer for the stuff."

Tom grinned. Harriot had told him about the visit he'd received from a merchant claiming to have been approached by someone wanting to sell him sugar. The description the fellow had given had perfectly matched Boylin. What had been missing was the date on which the merchandise was to be delivered. Now he had it. He made a mental note to ask Harriot for the name of the merchant.

"No chance the old hat-seller would be prepared to testify to what he saw and heard, I suppose," he said.

"Moses Solomon? He might, sir," said Sam. "But he's a frightened man, and with reason. It's hard enough for him as it is, without going out of his way to stir up people like Boylin."

"Well, I can't say I blame him for being frightened, and I suppose it wouldn't do us any good," said Tom. "From what I've seen this past month or two, the judges seem reluctant to accept the word of —"

"A Jew?" said Sam.

"Sorry, Hart. No offence meant."

"None taken, your honour," said Sam, rather too quickly.

"Did he tell you anything else?" said Tom, changing the subject.

"Nothing you don't already suspect." Sam ducked, as a gust of wind brought a fresh shower of rain down round his head. "More threats to both our lives and —"

He stopped.

"And what?" said Tom, on the alert.

"Seems young Jacob was pushed out of the rigging on Boylin's orders."

"How d'you know?"

"The hat-seller," said Sam. "Seems he heard them mention it but he didn't think nothing of it. He told me as we parted."

"I knew it," said Tom, hitting the gunwale with the flat of his hand. "Poor lad. Had he lived he could've handed Boylin to us on a plate."

"And now we've nothing?" said Sam.

"Almost," said Tom, watching a lighterman out on the Lower Pool struggling to control his charge, his back bent against the rain-soaked wind.

"How d'you mean, sir?" said Sam. "We ain't got no evidence left. You said so yourself. The judges wouldn't believe the old hat-seller, and Jacob was the only other witness we had."

"Except we now know when Boylin intends to bring the sugar up from the Lea," said Tom. "We just need to be there when he does."

At three o'clock in the afternoon, Peggy finished removing the soiled mattresses from the beds on the ward and replacing them with clean ones. The morning rounds of the duty surgeon and the apothecary had been unusually slow, putting her behind with her duties. She would not normally have minded except that today was her half-day holiday and she didn't want to be late.

She surveyed the pile of mattresses on the floor. An hour to remove all the flock fillings, wash them, and set them out to dry in the empty ward next door. If it had been a sunny day she could have laid everything out on the grass in the garden. She sighed, picked up the first mattress and hauled it through to Harrison Ward.

At the stroke of four, her work completed, she went to her room and changed. Putting on a bonnet, she made her way down the stairs and out of the main door, her spirit soaring at the prospect of a few hours to herself. At the iron gate marking the boundary of her world, she turned left and began walking down the Whitechapel road towards the City.

"My dear Miss Tompkins! How pleasant it is to see you."

Peggy's heart missed a beat as she recognised Boylin's voice. In spite of everything that had happened, there was a part of her that was still drawn to him, to the charm and the dangerous unpredictability that was his hallmark. He sidled up to her, his grotesque face twisted into the caricature of a smile. She waited while he caught his breath.

"If you is at leisure, Miss Tompkins, I should consider it the greatest of favours were you to allow me to accompany you."

She smelt the staleness of his breath and the acrid stench of lime on his clothes as he drew closer. She looked up at him, her doubts resurfacing, fuelling the memory of what he'd done. She could not forgive him that. Whatever the reason for her present attraction, it could not outweigh her revulsion at his past sins. Not even his pitiful affliction was enough for that.

She paused, aware she was not being entirely honest. The shock she'd felt when she'd first seen the condition of his face had affected her more than perhaps she'd realised. She suddenly felt guilty — ashamed to admit that Boylin's outward appearance had altered the way she viewed him. "Of course, sir, I would be happy with your company," said Peggy.

Boylin moved closer, his body rubbing against her side. She moved away, already regretting her decision. He followed her, slipping his arm through hers.

"I regret, sir, you presume too much upon my friendship," she said, disengaging her arm and doing her best to keep the lightness in her voice.

Boylin's jaw muscles flexed as he looked at her with a hardened eye. Peggy knew she'd angered him. She glanced over his shoulder at the gates of the hospital. She'd come too far to go back. She looked around, her anxiety growing. What few people she could see seemed wholly occupied with their own affairs — children playing in the road, a couple of women chatting in the doorway of a house. Thirty yards away, the shambling figure of a rag-man was approaching them.

"Ol' clo! Ol' clo!" An unlikely pile of hats sat on the old man's head, a collection of brightly coloured rags tied around his waist, an ankle-length coat incongruous in the late summer heat. Peggy thought of asking him to escort her back to the hospital. She dismissed the idea as absurd. Boylin presented no immediate threat, and anyway, what could the hat-seller achieve that she could not? The old man drew closer. With a start, she saw his eyes fixed on hers. Then he was gone.

"We were friends once, Miss Tompkins," said Boylin, his small, indolent eye lingering on her breasts, his breathing quickening.

"Aye, so we were, sir," said Peggy. "But those days are past, and for reasons you cannot have forgotten."

"Another chance, Miss Tompkins, I beg you. At least you'll be owing me that."

"Owe you, sir?" Peggy's eyes narrowed. She knew what he meant. The heavy hand of obligation had rested on her shoulders ever since he'd persuaded her to accept his offer. She'd needed it, of course — the money necessary to pay the physician when her mother had fallen ill. Still, the idea of being in debt had made her uncomfortable, and she'd been saving towards the day when she could repay the loan.

"Could we not let bygones be bygones, Miss Tompkins?" said Boylin. "Will we not, in the name of friendship, be forgetting what it is you owe me?"

"That is kind of you, sir, but it is out of the question. I am presently able to repay you all but one shilling and fourpence." Peggy swallowed, hard. "The rest I shall give you after I'm paid on Saturday. I beg you should wait until then."

234

"The money is yours, Miss Tompkins," said Boylin, his voice pleading. "In return, could we not be coming to some arrangement, some favour perhaps?"

"And what favour might that be, sir?" said Peggy, suddenly alarmed.

"Oh, Miss Tompkins, will you be toying with me, now?"

"You forget yourself, sir." Peggy's eyes flashed. "I cannot but think that the sun has affected you. The money owing to you will be repaid at the end of this week. I shall, on this occasion, overlook your momentary indiscretion and beg that you say no more. As for our friendship, it is over, sir."

Boylin's reaction was as swift as it had been unpredictable. He lashed out with a balled fist, catching Peggy on the mouth. She reeled back and would have fallen had Boylin not grabbed her chest and half-carried, half-dragged her into an adjacent alley before letting go. She sank to her knees, dizzy with shock, tasting blood from the cut to her lip.

"Common slut that you are," shouted Boylin, slapping her face. "I'll be doing what I should have done long ago."

The explosive pain of the blow spread outwards from her cheek. Through the blur of her vision she saw Boylin wrench at the belt of his breeches and tear at the buttons. She watched him come towards her and felt his hand push hard against her breasts. She fell back, a jarring pain shooting up from the base of her spine as she landed, her head slamming against the surface of the alley. She saw him kneel above her and felt his hand fumbling with the hem of her gown, his face florid with excitement.

"No, no, please God, not again," she sobbed, looking wildly about her, revulsion sweeping over her at the prospect of what was to come. Then she caught sight of the child. He was no more than about eight or nine years of age and stood motionless at the corner of the alley, watching them. Too late, she realised Boylin, too, had seen him.

She watched the Irishman struggle to his feet and, with a roar of frustration, lumber towards the boy, his arms flailing the air.

"No, not the child. Don't hurt the child," screamed Peggy.

She saw the boy run to the other side of the alley, stop and look back at Boylin. The publican lunged at him, knocking him to the ground but the child sprang to his feet and was backing away. Again and again Boylin rushed at him and each time the youngster ducked out of harm's way. The boy was doing it on purpose, she thought, drawing the publican ever further from her, allowing her the chance to escape.

She climbed unsteadily to her feet and hurried painfully, back to the London Hospital.

CHAPTER
SEVENTEEN

Tom's fist hit the table with a crash. He stared down at Harriot, his shoulders shaking with a rage he could no longer control.

"Won't stand trial?" he shouted. "You tell me that Boylin assaulted Miss Tompkins and attempted to rape her but won't stand trial? What more evidence can the Grand Jury possibly want?"

"I know this must be hard for you, Mr Pascoe," soothed Harriot. "I understand entirely —"

"Understand?" Tom sank back into his chair in Harriot's office. "I'm exceedingly glad that someone understands. I certainly don't. Tell me, so *I* can understand, how it is that Boylin can injure two people, one of them seriously, and still he does not have to stand trial? Is he above the law? Can no one touch this man?"

"Calm yourself, sir," said Harriot, getting up from his chair and limping round to where Tom stood, leaning on the desk. He patted the younger man on the shoulder. "I own it must be difficult for you to understand. The fact of the matter is we don't know the identity of the boy who was assaulted, but the available evidence suggests he was not seriously hurt and certainly he's never reported the incident. So far as we know, after the initial assault, he escaped. That leaves us with Miss Tompkins as the only witness of what happened to her."

"Is that not sufficient? Is her word not enough?" said Tom.

"It appears not." Harriot shuffled some papers on his desk, as though unsure of what to say. "I suspect the Grand Jury was influenced by her financial relationship to Boylin."

"What financial relationship?" Tom's head twisted round. "I know nothing of this. Does she owe the scrub money?"

"I'm sorry, Mr Pascoe," said Harriot. "I was under the impression you knew. It is, of course, none of my business but, yes, it is my understanding that Miss Tompkins owes Boylin a sum of money."

Tom turned away, remembering the sight of Peggy and Boylin on the steps of the hospital, the smile on Boylin's face. There seemed to be more to their relationship than he knew. With an effort, he returned to the matter in hand.

"Supposing this were true, how would that affect Miss Tompkins' credibility as a witness?" he asked.

"The Grand Jury's deliberations are, of course, secret," said Harriot, "but I imagine it was influenced by Miss Tompkins' impecunious state, the corollary of which is her inability to pay her lawful debts. The inference is that she would have every reason to see Boylin blackguarded in an attempt to avoid her financial obligations. Nor, I regret, is that all."

238

Tom stared at Harriot, his mind in turmoil, waiting for the magistrate to continue.

"In the absence of any compelling evidence to the contrary, the issue of consent would also have been a factor in the jury's decision. It would have been his word against hers."

"What can be done?" Tom clenched his teeth and forced himself to remain calm, the implications of what his superior was saying clear enough.

"I regret there is nothing that can be done," said Harriot. "A grand jury has the power to dismiss an indictment without the evidence ever being tested in open court. They have done so in this case. The Bill of Indictment was marked 'Not True'. The case is over."

Boylin stood at the corner of Great Tower Street and Mincing Lane, his hands deep in his coat pockets, his head bowed in thought. The delay in getting rid of the sugar was becoming the source of increasing anxiety. He'd not slept properly since the night on the Lea when strangers had beaten his men and disturbed the barrels. He had to move it — and quickly. But that meant changing the date — and the date was the one detail on which Devall had been insistent.

Boylin glanced along Mincing Lane, his anxiety growing. There was a point beyond which it was not wise to push the merchant. It would not do to anger him more than was absolutely necessary. He'd made that mistake once before, in the early months of their relationship, and been made to regret it. He'd got away with a beating on that occasion, meted out by a few of the merchant's flash cullies. But he doubted the scrub would be so gentle with him again.

His face darkened. He didn't like the subordinate role that had been forced on him, but had accepted it as the only realistic basis on which his criminal activities could hope to flourish. Yet, as time went on and his own power and influence within the port had grown, he had begun to believe that the day might soon dawn when he would be free of the burden of subservience under which he currently existed.

He paced back and forth across the junction. The day of his liberation from Sir Sydney Devall might be close but it had not yet arrived. Going to the merchant's house, as he had intended, and trying to persuade him to accept the delivery of the sugar earlier than they had agreed, was asking for trouble.

Meanwhile, it still needed to be moved . . .

Boylin needed time to think. He turned west along Great Tower Street, unconscious of where he was going, his mind occupied with a problem that seemed intractable. Along street after street he shambled, past fine houses, expensive shops, and fashionable coffee houses. He'd gone some distance before the solution occurred to him. It was far from ideal but it did offer an answer to his present difficulties.

He caught the familiar scent of the river, and turned towards it. He'd take a wherry back to Wapping. Ahead of him, a small group of people stood by the river steps. He joined them as a sculler fetched alongside.

He'd move the sugar to his own yard in Shadwell.

And he'd do it tonight.

★ ★ ★

Thoughts of Peggy and what had happened to her flooded Tom's mind. Little else touched his consciousness. The sights, the sounds, the smells of the river passed him by; his duties performed as though by rote.

He sat in the stern sheets, mechanically watching the passing river traffic as the police galley headed up towards London Bridge under a September sky smeared with columns of drifting smoke from countless chimneys. He'd tried to see Peggy; had been to the hospital several times since Boylin's attack on her. But the answer had always been the same: Miss Peggy Tompkins was not at leisure to receive him. Nothing more. No explanation. No hint for the future on which he might pin his hopes.

A loud crack of canvas broke in on his thoughts. With that part of a sailor's mind that is forever on the changing pattern of the weather, he glanced upwards, noting the scudding banks of grey-black cumulus gathering low in the south-east. He frowned with a small, anxious furrowing of the brow that he reserved for occasions such as this. His eyes swept the horizon, alert now, studying the billowing mass of darkness, tracking its course and speed. He looked up-river. He was close to London Bridge now, and the western limit of his patrol. In a few moments he would go about and begin the long haul back to Wapping.

Suddenly, he was aware of a stillness in the air, a tranquillity that stood apart from the moments of peace at high water, when the sleepless river was calmed and the only sounds were those of tiny wavelets lapping against the wooden walls of the ships. He knew the meaning of the stillness, had experienced it a thousand times before, but never here, never on the Thames. He felt the freshening force of the breeze on his cheek as it swung round to the east. Then came another sharp crack of loose-reefed canvas and the low moan of the wind passing through rigging. Over Poplar Marsh, far away to the east, storm clouds raced towards the City.

In the Upper Pool, oblivious to the impending strife, life went on its untroubled way, the dull roar of fifteen thousand men at work undiminished. Mudlarks, rat-catchers, scuffle-hunters and the rest, all busy about their daily toil. If they had seen the signs, they gave no hint of it.

"Easy all!" Tom raised himself off the arms box and looked back through the amorphous web of masts and rigging that stood between him and the approaching fury. There was an urgency in his voice when he next spoke. "Away larboard. Give way together. Handsomely now."

The galley curved round, creaming the water as she picked up speed, a shaft of sunlight sparkling off the oarblades that rose and fell in perfect unison. Tom's eyes shifted to the east.

He watched it come in, saw the surface of the water torn up into an ugly, racing maelstrom, a hundred, then seventy-five, then fifty yards away. High above the surface of the water, ships heeled violently in the wind's path; sails were ripped from the yards; small boats were thrown onto the shore, or dashed against the hulls of larger vessels. And right behind the tempestuous gale, a

242

solid wall of hailstones the size of plums slanted in towards him.

Gust followed powerful gust, each one stronger than the last. The low, undulating moan that had accompanied the first onslaught now rose to a scream as the gale blasted through the rigging of the tightly packed merchantmen, wrenching and tearing at the furled sails. A long, jagged streak of lightning snaked earthwards, followed by the growling roar of thunder that quivered the timbers of the police galley.

All about him, three- and four-hundred-ton ships were being tossed around by a wind which seemed to shake loose the rain and send it drumming on the turbulent surface of the Thames. Tom looked up at the sound of a crash, louder than the rest, that enveloped him in its hellish noise. On the north shore, close by the Custom House, the roof of a building had been borne aloft as though it were a scrap of paper, and sent down with a sickening boom among the vessels moored off Botolph Wharf.

Tom searched the river for some protection from the worst of the weather. The risk of collision with vessels cut loose from their moorings or being crushed by falling masts was growing by the second. Ahead lay a line of barges, their squat shapes offering some protection, some hope of respite. He cupped his hands to his mouth and shouted through the din at his rain-drenched crew, urging them forward.

"Tisdale, take a turn with the bow-line," yelled Tom, as the galley made its third attempt to come up under the lee of a barge. "Steady! Back all! Now. Take the strain. Steady! Ship oars."

Then he saw the wherry.

He counted five on the small rowing boat being swept down through the great arch of London Bridge, staring as it disappeared in the deep, rushing hollow of water below the stonework. He held his breath and waited. Then she was up again, rocking violently athwart the tide, the raging waters licking at her gunwales. He willed her to make it through the arch, his entreaties thrown back into his face by the wind. A sudden squall lifted the wherry's stern clear of the water and dashed it against the timber starlings, as though some giant hand had caught her and flung her aside, her human cargo thrown into the raging foam.

"D'you hear there? Cast off fore and aft," Tom roared above the screaming clamour of the storm. "Clear the bows."

He watched Tisdale ram the blade of his oar up against the high-sided hull of the barge to which they had been tied and push hard.

"Give way together."

The galley leapt forward as the ran-dan formation of oars bit deep, her bows buried in a mass of flying spray. No more than fifty yards separated them from the helpless swimmers, but it might as well have been five hundred. The surging tide would see to that. He glanced up into the rigging of an anchored brig, the violent thrashing of her stays threatening to bring her masts on top of them. He steered a course into the central channel away from the falling debris.

Out here, in the full force of the ebb tide, their progress was slower than ever. Steam rose from the crew's bodies and rain poured down over their eyes as they bent to their oars, each wave lifting the bows of the galley before bringing it down with a shuddering crash so that they seemed to stand still in the water.

Tom searched the area beneath the bridge. Soon it would be too late. He'd once seen a shipmate fall and be swept to his death in this river. There'd been no struggle, no shout. The man had been sucked down by the broiling torrent of the tidal race and pressed below the keel of the nearest ship. They'd found him a fortnight later, dumped on the black foreshore off Cuckold Point, his body bloated, his skin — or what was left of it — the colour of mottled coal.

"Easy all." Tom scanned the river, his view of what lay ahead hidden by the torrential downpour. Faintly, he heard the cries of the drowning, snatched away by the melancholy groan of the wind. He leaned out over the gunwale, looking down first one side then the other, in a desperate search for the living. He wiped the rain from his eyes, his fingers stiff from the sudden cold that had accompanied the storm. For precious seconds he saw only the pattering of hailstones on the surface of the river.

"Over there, sir." Kemp was pointing with his chin.

Tom had heard it too, a scream over the storm's undulating howl. "Where away?"

"Larboard beam, about thirty paces," shouted Kemp.

Through the driving rain, the frightened face of a woman came into view. Next to her was a young child, its head dipping below the surface and rising again, coughing, spluttering, swallowing the foul water.

"Away starboard! Pull, damn you, pull." The galley raced into a tight, sweeping turn.

Suddenly, a jolt pitched the crew forward.

"Body alongside!" shouted Tisdale, lunging over the bow of the galley and catching hold of an arm. The weight dipped the gunwale and brown water washed in, slopping about the bottom-boards with its pungent smell of fish and rope and timber. "Looks like a goner to me."

"Which one is it?" yelled Tom. "The bairn or its mother?"

"Neither, sir," said Tisdale. "It's a man."

"Well, if he's alive, get him aboard," said Tom, again catching sight of the woman and child, now no more than fifteen feet away on the starboard bow. He glanced at Tisdale, still struggling with the floating body.

"For God's sake, Tisdale, lay along there, else we'll lose the bairn and its mother." The wind swept the words away.

Kemp turned to help his colleague, his massive paw catching hold of a pair of breeches and yanking the man into the galley.

"Is he alive?" shouted Tom.

"Aye, sir, by the grace of God," said Kemp.

Tom looked back to where he'd seen the mother and her child. They weren't there. He shielded his face from the falling hailstones, his eyes combing the brown waters, desperate for a sighting. But there was nothing. For five long minutes the galley dropped down on the tide, keeping pace with an imagined body; where the tide might have pushed it.

"I think we've lost the woman and her bairn, God rest them," shouted Tom, at last. "Best we get this fellow ashore before we lose him, too."

"Over yonder." Sam's calm voice brought Tom's head round with a jerk. "Fifteen yards astern. Larboard quarter. Looks to be a floater."

Within a minute they were alongside the floating body, its arching back barely clear of the water, its head and legs wholly immersed.

"Don't look to be the woman, nor her child neither," said Sam, plunging his hand over the side and catching hold of some clothing. He pulled a man's head clear of the surface. Then he stopped, the colour draining from his face.

"For all love, Hart, shift your bob." Tom was losing his voice. "Get him out or drop him. One of the two."

Sam didn't move, his jaws clenched, his eyes fixed on the face of the drowning man.

"It's Boylin," he said.

CHAPTER
EIGHTEEN

Charity Squibb sat on the edge of her bed and watched the rain lashing noisily against the window of the room she shared with Peggy Tompkins. She turned quickly at the sound of a sigh, a worried crease crossing her brow. Her fellow nurse — whom she liked to think of as her friend — had been unusually quiet, almost withdrawn, these weeks past. She'd not wanted to interfere but neither did she like to see the younger woman in this state of obvious unhappiness, especially if there was something she could do to help.

"Dear Miss Tompkins, whatever can be the matter that you look so . . . so . . . pale," she said, replacing the bottle from which she'd been drinking in the pocket of her apron. "Are you sickening for something?"

"Why, Miss Squibb," said Peggy, looking up from some tapestry in which she'd been absorbed. "It's good of you to enquire, but rest assured nothing whatever ails me."

"Only, you knows I have your particular happiness at heart," said Charity, vaguely disappointed at her colleague's response. "And I hear tell — not that I take a whit of notice of gossip, you understand — that you was the victim of a horrid assault."

Peggy looked away. She had imagined herself fully recovered from Boylin's attack. Of the physical consequences, there was now little sign and she had long since repaired the clothing torn by the frenzy of his assault. Mentally too, after an initial period of perhaps two or three nights when she'd had difficulty sleeping, she had convinced herself that the nightmarish incident had been relegated to a distant part of her consciousness. Her daily routine on the ward occupied her waking hours and kept at bay the self-loathing and disgust of which she was now only dimly aware. But now Charity Squibb's question pierced her brain like an arrow.

"I . . . I . . ." Peggy's lower lip quivered and she dropped her head lest the older woman should see the tears welling in her eyes.

She was too late.

"Oh, you poor creature." Charity was on her feet and by her friend's side, holding Peggy's head against an ample bosom. "I knows something were up, the moment I saw them bruises and the torn dress. I said to myself, I said, 'Mark my words Charity Squibb, something's awry with Miss Tompkins.' Tell Charity all about it, child. It don't do to bottle things up, you know."

"He . . . he tried to . . ." Peggy's voice faltered and she blew her nose before letting her hands drop into her lap, her fingers twisting and turning the handkerchief she held. For a moment longer she thought of that encounter with Boylin and realised how much she had wanted to talk about it with someone

249

who might understand how she felt. She'd never thought of Charity in that context. "I feel so dirty, so completely worthless. You understand, don't you, Miss Squibb?"

"Aye, I do, child." Charity smiled encouragingly.

"When I got back to the hospital after . . . well, you know . . . after it happened, I just wanted to wash myself." Peggy looked up quickly, her fingers splayed wide. "You know the bath in the basement? Well, there! It's the only place where I thought I could really be clean again."

She paused and listened to the storm raging outside. After a while she began to speak again.

"Except it didn't make me clean," she said. "I scrubbed every inch of my body and still I felt dirty. You do understand, don't you?"

"Aye, child, I do," said Charity again.

"I still have nightmares," Peggy went on. "I'm frightened of going out of the hospital gates lest I might see him again, and I couldn't bear that. Of all things, I couldn't bear that. And d'you know the worst thing? The worst thing is the way they — the men of the Grand Jury — wouldn't believe me. I felt — I feel — worthless, as if the fault were mine. Oh, Miss Squibb, please tell me it wasn't my fault, that I wasn't to blame for the wicked actions of that loathsome man."

"There, there," soothed Charity. "What thoughts you have. Of course you're not to blame and of course it weren't your fault. You must never think so."

In the distance, a thin, cantankerous voice called for a nurse and Peggy listened for the sound of the night-watcher's footsteps. A moment later, she saw the light of a candle under the door of the bedroom and heard the rustle of a dress. Then the silence descended again, wrapping them in its comfortable stillness.

"I'll never see him again," said Peggy. "I just can't bear —"

"No, my lovely," said Charity, "of course not! But then I don't suppose he'd dare show his face in these parts again."

"No, no, you don't understand," said Peggy, fiercely. "I mean Captain Pascoe. I couldn't bear his pity nor his touch. It wouldn't surprise me if he thought I made up the whole story. Oh, Miss Squibb, ain't life cruel?"

"Don't take on so, child," said Charity, squatting by her friend's bed. "Your Captain Pascoe is a fine man and I've a notion of how he thinks of you and you of him, and that's a fact. You don't want to be saying and doing things all in a rush what you might regret later on. So why don't you get a good night's rest and we can talk about it in the morning?"

Peggy felt her reserves of energy drain away. Her decision to end her friendship with Tom had not been taken lightly, or spontaneously. In the days since she'd been attacked, her thoughts had seldom strayed from the subject and Tom's likely reaction to it. She had determined to keep it from him, to hide her shame and her embarrassment in the hope it would simply go away.

She might have succeeded in her plans for secrecy but for the appearance of a watchman who'd happened along the Whitechapel road. His questions as to her wellbeing had eventually obliged her to tell all. After that, the ponderous wheels of the criminal justice system had begun to turn, awakening memories she would rather have left sleeping, trumpeting to the world her most private discomfort, exposing her to impertinent questions, incredulous responses and public humiliation . . . And for what? The young boy had escaped the scene and could not now be found, while her own word had proved worthless in the eyes of the law.

Peggy ran her fingers through her hair and lay down on her bed, fully clothed. Maybe Charity was right. Maybe tomorrow, the two of them could talk again. Maybe . . .

Sam gaped in astonishment at the scarred face of the still-breathing body that lay at the side of the police galley. A single thought swirled through his mind: Joseph Boylin's life lay in his hands. The gift of life — or death — was his. He thought of what had gone before, of what Boylin had done, and his pulse throbbed with the intensity of his loathing. He loosened his grip, letting the body slip through his fingers . . .

Someone was shouting at him. It sounded a long way off.

Sam glanced up and saw Tom, his face contorted. He was mouthing something that Sam couldn't hear. He looked back at the bloated shape sinking below the waves, Boylin's long hair waving to and fro in the tide, his eye-patch falling away, a milky ball of translucent skin staring from where the eye should have been. A

252

thin stream of bubbles rose to the surface and burst into the fading light of the day.

"Hart! D'you hear me, Hart?" Tom was shouting again. "Are you mad? Clap hold of the fellow. Bring him inboard on the instant."

Strong arms pulled him aside and reached into the water. Sam looked on, as though a spectator in a drama in which he had no part. Boylin's body was being dragged over the gunwale and dropped into the bottom-boards of the galley. His face was ashen, his long hair matted across his face, his jaw slack.

"Does he live?" Tom's voice rose above the howling wind.

Sam listened for the answer, conflicting emotions stirring within him as the desire for an end to Boylin's existence battled with the moral code to which he'd been born.

"He's alive," said Kemp. "But whether he'll survive the day, I don't rightly know."

A week passed by. The man in the doorway stood stock-still, his unblinking eyes fixed on the house opposite. Just once did they move, swivelling to watch a growling street cat slink, low-bellied, across the deserted roadway, its tail twitching from side to side. The animal disappeared down an alley and the man's gaze returned to that which most interested him.

The door of the house opened, spilling into the night the last of the customers of the Queen's Head. None of them noticed the presence of the stranger in the doorway opposite. If they had, they might have remarked on the cold, expressionless eyes staring at the premises from which they had come, and they might have gone their various ways with a sense of foreboding.

Soon, silence returned to the street, and the stranger was left alone to his vigil, watching as the lanterns in the house were extinguished and the building blended into the darkness. His gaze shifted to a window on the third floor, the bedroom window of the man he wished to see. If Boylin were alive — and there were those who said he'd not survived the violent storm which had cost the lives of so many — it was to that room he would go. The stranger wanted to be sure. He wanted no mistakes for what he had in mind.

He stiffened as a faint light appeared in the window and grew stronger. It stopped, as though the lantern had been placed on a table, and a moment later the silhouette of a shambling figure passed across the ceiling of the room.

The stranger eased himself away from the doorway and stared upwards at the window, his fingers lightly caressing the point of a knife. A slow smile crossed his lips. There was no doubting to whom the silhouette belonged.

Soon the light in the room on the third floor was put out. The minutes ticked by and still Gabriel Newman remained where he was. At last, he stepped from the shadows.

In the distance, a dog barked.

Boylin rolled over onto his side. Something was nagging at him although exactly what it was, he

254

couldn't think. Certainly it had nothing to do with his discharge from the hospital, although that, too, was irritating him. He'd been thrown out far too early. Another few days to recover from his near drowning would have made all the difference.

Nor had it anything to do with the sugar still sitting out on the Lea — not that he hadn't fretted over that as well. He cursed the bad luck which had stopped him making the necessary arrangements for its removal. And now he was too weak to do anything about it.

The nagging sensation returned. Boylin leaned across to the tin sconce beside his bed, and blew out the candle. He'd remember what it was in the morning. He let his head drop to the mattress and closed his one good eye . . .

He dreamed he was in a small boat. There were other people with him, people he didn't know. The daylight faded. It was raining and a fierce wind was blowing. The boat was being buffeted, the water was choppy. Suddenly, a great jarring shudder, then the sound of splintering wood, and he was being lifted high above the waves, as though by a giant's hand. Now he was falling, falling, his body tumbling head over heels. He couldn't breathe, something was covering his mouth, his world was dark and threatening. He screamed. His eye popped open, his hands were clammy. A blanket was draped over his face. He swept it aside, his heart racing.

Slowly he relaxed, his eye closing once more, his consciousness slipping away again. The image of the storm returned to his dreams. Another boat. Men shouting. A face staring down at him. A face he knew. The image faded. It did not wake him.

How long he slept he did not know, but something had woken him. He stared at the ceiling and listened to the sigh of the wind. A door slammed. He jumped, his body tense, his ears straining. Something was wrong. He stared at the door to the room, his mouth dry. Somewhere in the distance he heard a dog bark. Suddenly he remembered what had been nagging him: he'd forgotten to lock the back door. He would have to go downstairs and see to it. He climbed from his bed and walked to the door of his room.

Crossing the road, Gabriel Newman's crouching shadow slipped down the passage leading to the rear of the Queen's Head. He stopped and listened. All was quiet; the moonlight catching the faint glint of steel in his hand.

He moved on, reached the back door of the tavern, stopped and looked back. Then he stretched out a hand and pressed down on the iron thumb-plate of the latch. It snapped open with a loud report. He froze, his eyes searching the windows above his head. Satisfied he'd not been heard he pushed open the door and stepped silently over the threshold, waiting there for his eyes to become accustomed to his surroundings. Closing the door behind him, he found himself in a small, bare room with a fireplace immediately to his left and a table and chairs in the middle. Set into the opposite wall was a second door. He crossed to it, eased it open and crept through into a much larger area filled with a number of long tables and benches. A row of beer barrels supported on wooden cradles stood against the wall on his left.

Newman skirted round the familiar furniture and made his way to where a pair of doors stood next to each other — the first barring the way to the cellar, the second hiding the stairs leading to the upper floors. Suddenly, a floorboard squeaked above his head, followed by the sound of footsteps descending the stairs. He pressed himself behind the door, and waited, his knife still in his hand.

A moment later, the door swung open.

"He's dead, you say?" said Harriot, clutching his pipe and removing it from his mouth.

"Aye," said Tom, waving his coffee cup for greater emphasis. "The matter is being dealt with by the Shadwell magistrates."

"Yes, I suppose it would be. It's on their ground." Harriot limped over to the sideboard and poured himself a fresh cup of coffee. "D'you know what happened?"

"The facts are still unclear," said Tom, "but it seems the whole household retired to bed at around midnight last night. A short while later Boylin remembered he'd forgotten to secure the back door of the premises and was on the point of going downstairs to lock it when he heard the pot-boy still moving about in his room. Apparently, he called him and ordered him downstairs."

"And that's where the fellow met his end?" said Harriot.

257

"Yes. His body was found in the taproom at the foot of the stairs with a number of stab wounds. The physician certified death at about three this morning."

"Do we know of any motive?"

"None," said Tom. "As far as we know, the deceased had no enemies. He was a man in his late sixties and had lived in Shadwell all his life. I've . . ."

Tom paused.

"Yes?" said Harriot.

"It's only my personal view," said Tom, "but I've an idea the man who died was not the intended victim. I think whoever murdered him was looking for Boylin and, in the darkness, thought it was he."

"Oh? What makes you say that?"

"The complete absence of a motive," said Tom. "There's no obvious reason for this man to have been the target. On the other hand, I'll warrant there are at least a dozen who'd be glad to see the back of Boylin."

"D'you have anyone in mind, sir?"

"Several."

"Including Hart?" said Harriot, watching Tom over the top of his spectacles.

Tom flinched. Yes, he'd considered the possibility. How could he not? He leaned over and put down his coffee on Harriot's desk, his hand trembling.

"Including Hart," he managed.

"What about yourself?" said Harriot. "Are you able to account for your movements? You, after all, have just as much reason as Hart to see Boylin dead."

"I know that," said Tom. "And, yes, I can account for my movements, should it become necessary."

Harriot blew out a cloud of tobacco smoke and nodded.

"What's your assessment of Hart? Could he have done it?"

Tom walked over to the mantelpiece and looked down into the empty grate. He thought of his friend, of the bond that had formed between them, of their mutual respect and admiration developed in the shared experience of the river, the moments of danger, of sadness, of boredom, interspersed with occasions of high drama and unbounded exhilaration. They were unlikely bedfellows, he and Sam Hart; men who, in the narrow, haphazard path of life had been thrown together as comrades; the Jew and the Gentile; the common labourer and a man bearing the King's Commission; an immigrant afraid of what the future might hold and an Englishman secure in the land of his birth.

Sam had taught him what it meant to be forever condemned as a stranger, forever banished to the outer limits of society. Whether Jew or Irish or Lascar, it was all the same; all suffered from the currency of casual brutality meted to the outsider, the deliberate marginalisation of all they had to offer, the cheapening of their worth . . .

He looked up, aware that Harriot was still waiting for an answer. He thought about the troubled expression that had so often inhabited Sam's features and, not for the first time, he contemplated the possibility that his friend's unhappiness was in some way connected to Boylin; that the difficulty between the two men was deeper and more profound than he had imagined. Gabriel Newman had hinted as much when Tom had interviewed him in prison. But was it enough to have driven Sam to murder? He wondered if he was allowing conjecture to cloud his judgement. He remembered the moment Sam had recognised the half-dead body he had pulled from the river, recalled the hatred etched into his every feature as he spat out Boylin's name.

Tom shuddered. It had taken every ounce of his will to intervene on Boylin's behalf and order him brought on board. Where the strength for his decision had come from, he didn't know. Perhaps his reaction had been driven by instinct rather than any moral prescription. He doubted whether he would have reached the same decision had he been given the luxury of time in which to consider the situation. Not even the thought of keeping Boylin alive for the gallows would have been sufficient reason to think of saving him. In that sense, he was as guilty as Sam in wishing the man dead. He stared into the fireplace, a sombre look in his eyes, self-doubt spinning inside his head, then turned back to Harriot.

"As you know, sir," he said, "Boylin has issued a number of threats against Hart's life, the history of which we've already discussed. For his part, Hart has never said anything to me about the situation and nor has he intimated any desire to see Boylin suffer. Indeed, the only time he has shown any animosity towards the fellow was at the precise moment he was in the process of saving his life."

260

"But that, sir, does not square with the facts," said Harriot carefully. "From what I hear, Hart had released his hold on Boylin and the fellow was sinking back into the water. Is that the conduct of a man bent on rescue?"

"There is no evidence to suggest that Hart deliberately released his hold on Boylin," said Tom. "You are to consider that there was a severe storm blowing and conditions were so hazardous as to make the retrieval of a body from the river exceedingly difficult."

"Be that as it may," persisted Harriot, "is Hart, in your view, capable of murder?"

Tom turned and met the magistrate's gaze.

"If you mean, sir, could he kill a man, then, yes, every constable must be prepared to take another man's life if the situation so calls. But if you are asking whether Hart is capable of doing so with criminal intent, as in the case of the pot-boy . . ." He paused. "I would have to say no."

For what seemed an eternity, Harriot gazed at his subordinate, puffing silently on his pipe, the rich aroma of burning tobacco filling the room.

"I don't think I have any real alternative," said Harriot at last. "I must pass such information as I possess to my colleagues at Shadwell for their consideration."

"You're aware, of course, Hart could hang," said Tom, a tightness forming in his throat.

"Aye, I know," said Harriot. "The thought had not escaped me."

261

CHAPTER
NINETEEN

Gabriel Newman shivered in the keen wind, his gaze fixed on the two luggers moored alongside the quay. He was hardly aware of their existence. The vessels just happened to be in his line of sight, as incidental to his view as the River Lea in which they floated, or the empty wastes of the Plaistow Levels stretching away into the night. He stood there for the sole reason that Boylin had ordered him to do so.

Behind him, in the wharfinger's hut, he could hear the publican's harsh, high-pitched squeal, issuing orders to the others. He wasn't interested. When the time came, he'd do what he was told — as he had always done. Anyway, he already knew that Boylin wanted to move the sugar up the Thames to Limehouse. There it would be landed and taken by cart to a yard in Shadwell that Boylin owned.

Newman tucked his hands under his armpits, hugging his chest. His brother had died on Boylin's orders. Why, he neither knew nor cared. It was enough that Boylin was responsible. Something had snapped inside him when he'd found out.

It hadn't been easy getting to the truth of Jacob's death, the path littered with the whispered half-truths of men afraid of the consequences of indiscretion, or too drunk to make sense of what they'd seen. But one detail had remained constant throughout: all of them had spoken of the stranger who'd tried to save the lad's life. "He were a big cully," someone had told him. "Had the voice of the quarterdeck an' all. Came aboard like a man born to the sea, he did. You should 'ave seen the lads jump to it when he spoke. But he were gentle as a lamb with your Jacob."

No one knew who the stranger was or where he had come from, their minds corroded by drink, their ability to recollect all but gone. Newman scratched the stubble on his chin. There was a vague familiarity about the description of the stranger he could not, for the moment, identify; his own mind a blurred confusion of memories. He started at the sound of his name being called and looked round to see Boylin standing in the doorway of the hut.

"Aye."

"You're coming with me, mister." Boylin waved a hand in the direction of the boats. "The others will go first. We'll follow. Will you be shifting your bob now? I'll not be carrying this sand in broad daylight on account of you."

Newman stumbled to the edge of the wharf and stepped aboard the second of the luggers, wondering who else knew the sugar was being moved tonight. If the talk at the Queen's Head was anything to go by, there weren't many who didn't.

He had a bad feeling about this job.

★ ★ ★

The police galley lay close to the north shore of Bugsby's Reach, her hull shrouded in darkness, the crescent moon hidden by low cloud. Ahead, a yellow light glimmered from Trinity Buoy House. Beyond that was Bow Creek, where the Lea joined the Thames.

Tom was only half-listening to the sounds of the river: the sucking and gurgling of the spring tide sweeping round the multitude of obstructions that stood in its way, the occasional thud of barges thrown together by the rushing water, the squeak of mooring lines under tension. He was thinking of Sam Hart and the murder of the pot-boy at the Queen's Head.

Despite his public declaration of support for his friend, Tom could not rid his mind of a lingering doubt. The expression on Sam's face when he'd initially pulled Boylin from the river seemed to replicate perfectly Tom's own feelings towards the publican; the same fierce loathing, the same desire for vengeance. But was that enough to condemn him? Did it mean he was capable of a premeditated act of murder? Tom didn't trust himself to answer the question.

A faint sound — a splash — came from the direction of Bow Creek. Tom tilted his head, instantly alert. It came again, quietly at first but growing louder by the second: the slow plopping of oars entering the water. He held his breath. The oars had been muffled, probably with cloth round the blades and thole pins — standard practice for those anxious to hide their presence. A surge of adrenaline passed through his veins.

264

"Hart," whispered Tom. "Check the lantern, will you? I've a feeling we'll be needing it shortly."

"Aye, sir." Sam bent forward and eased open the shutter of the storm lantern at his feet. He checked the linen wick, the flint and the tinder box. Then he shook the lantern itself, listening for the slurping sounds of the fish oil. "All correct."

"Thankee," said Tom, cupping his hands behind his ears and listening to the approaching sound, his hopes rising as they had done so often in the last three nights only to have them dashed. He'd begun to doubt the accuracy of the information given to Sam by the old hat-seller. And besides there was a limit to the amount of time he could stay away from his beat and the West India ships whose captains had paid for his protection. He'd already made up his mind that this was to be the last night he'd lie in wait for Boylin. He grimaced as he remembered Harriot's reaction when he'd told him he was still engaged on the observation.

"Your instructions, sir, are to investigate the prodigious depredations being visited upon this port. You cannot have forgotten the consequences of failure and yet you choose to waste your time on the lower reaches," the magistrate had thundered. "You have not one grain of evidence to support your contention that this man Boylin is in any way concerned with the matter."

"It is my judgement that the observation should continue," Tom had argued, an icy edge to his voice. "You have asked me to undertake an investigation. In order for me to do that effectively, I find I must commit

265

my crew to a period of observation beyond the normal limits for which we are responsible. You would honour me, sir, were you to refrain from interfering with my operational decisions."

"With a view to what?" said Harriot, his cane beating against the side of his leg. "Arresting a man you suspect of plundering your old ship? I repeat — time is not on your side. The consequence of any failure on your part to bring to justice the persons responsible for this plunder is the rising of this nation in open rebellion. The situation, need I remind you, is desperate."

"And without evidence," said Tom, stung by the criticism, "we have nothing."

It had not been a good meeting.

Tom raised his head. The approaching boat was closer. He waited for the second vessel. If this was Boylin, there should be two craft, not one. He wished he'd positioned himself closer to the mouth of the creek where he could at least have seen where the boat was coming from. The splashing drew level with the galley, less than fifteen yards out in the channel. Tom hesitated, his nerves taut as backstays. He didn't want to miss the second lugger, but neither could he afford to lose this one. The sounds receded up the reach.

"D'you hear there?" Tom's familiar preamble was delivered in not much more than a whisper. "Cast off bow line . . . Shove off . . ." He paused as the galley drifted clear of the moored barges, then, "Give way together. Gently now."

The galley came about, the steady, rhythmic beat of her own oars slapping the thole pins as she gathered speed for the chase. Tom thought of the coming minutes. There was no telling how many men were on the boat or how they would react to his presence. He guessed, from the size of the craft he'd seen on the Lea, there might be three, possibly four, crew on board. And likely they'd be armed.

Three minutes went by, then four. A shadow loomed ahead, low in the water and darker than its immediate surroundings, flecks of white water running down its side. The gap had narrowed. No more than thirty yards separated them. Another two minutes passed. Now Tom could see the shape of a man sitting in the stern, black against the grey-blue of the sky. The figure turned, as if aware for the first time of the presence of the pursuing galley. A hoarse whisper and then the frantic spattering of oars digging deeper, pulling harder, the stroke ragged, undisciplined. A stream of expletives cut through the night.

"They mean to run," said Tom, suppressing his excitement. A pause, then, "They're trying to hoist the lug sail."

The police galley surged forward. Tom screwed up his eyes against the spray, watching every move the lugger made. He knew few craft could hope to outpace him but that would change if his quarry succeeded in setting sail.

"In the King's name, we are police. Heave to!" Tom's voice boomed across the water.

A heavy splash on the larboard side of the lugger sent up a plume of white water, quickly followed by another, and then another. Moments later, two barrels floated by. Tom swore under his breath, the evidence needed to convict Boylin disappearing before his eyes. If he stopped for the barrels, he'd lose the lugger and if he didn't, he'd lose the evidence. Neither option looked good. He looked up the reach. Ahead of him lay the submerged sandbanks of Blackwall Point jutting out towards the middle of the river. Immediately opposite, in the bight, were the big ships of the East India fleet riding at anchor, their black hulls all but invisible against the night sky. And between, lay a navigable channel too narrow to call. He knew he'd be taking a high risk boarding the lugger now — even without the added problem of a following tide.

He slid off the arms chest, pulled the cutlasses and pistols from their holding racks and passed them to the crew.

He was going to board.

The pulse at his temple throbbed as he wondered how many of them would live to see the dawn.

A chill ran down Boylin's spine. He bent forward on the thwart, his mouth hanging open, listening to the shouted command from beyond the mouth of the creek. He knew the voice. Could never forget it. He waited, hearing the splash of the lugger's oars unbearably loud in the stillness of the night.

"Stop your rowing, damn your eyes, stop."

Pascoe had known where to find him. It was as though the fellow was in the lugger with him, as if the surveyor's hand was reaching out to take his shoulder in an iron grip — a grip that would see him hang. Dear

Mother of God, he didn't want to hang. His face was suddenly bathed in a cold sweat. He wiped it away and shivered. More than anything he wanted to curl up and go to sleep. Perhaps then Pascoe would leave him alone. He drew a pistol from below the blue apron he always wore and studied it with an unseeing eye, the palm of his left hand caressing the barrel.

"What is it you'll want us to be doing?" Newman's dismembered voice came out of the night.

"What?" Boylin remembered where he was and his stomach churned anew. From far away came more shouts, angry and confused. Boylin listened intently, his sweating fist closing round the butt of his pistol as a fresh thought came to his mind: Shamus O'Malley was on that boat. O'Malley, who knew too much about him to be left alone with Pascoe. O'Malley, who couldn't be trusted to keep his mouth shut. He looked down at the gun in his lap and self-pity welled within him. He reached a decision.

"Put me ashore," he ordered.

"Will I be seeing you at Limehouse Hole?" said Newman, putting the tiller over and heading for the west bank of the Lea.

Boylin seemed not to have heard him. He turned his head towards the sound of the distant shouting. Then he looked back.

"I'll be wanting some time to think," he said quietly.

"Stand by to board." Tom altered course to bring the police galley alongside the lugger. "Sam, hook us on and stay with the galley. Kemp and Tisdale, you come with me, cutlasses drawn. Pistols to be used only on my command. Is that clear?"

"Aye, sir," said Tisdale.

"Cutlasses it is, your honour," grunted Kemp.

"Ship starboard oars."

A crashing roar of wood on wood shattered the silence of the night as the two vessels ground into one another. Shouts, threats, bellows and more shouts erupted. Tom leapt across to the lugger, slipped on the wet deck and steadied himself. A sudden movement to his left. He turned. Two dark shapes rushed toward him. He crouched, ready to spring out of the way. The flash of a descending cutlass blade. He parried the cut then lashed out, jabbing the gilded metal crown of his tipstaff into a man's mouth. There was a grinding sound of breaking teeth. Then came a splash as the man toppled into the river. Tom ignored him, his eyes swivelling towards the second figure.

A faint click. Tom recognised the sound of a pistol being cocked and, instinctively, he ducked. A blinding flash of gunfire spat towards him, momentarily reducing his vision to a bright ball of light; a ball whistled past his ear. He drew his sword and thrust it at the man's neck. A scream of agony, then he felt the warm blood hit his face and saw the figure sink to the deck. He leapt forward. The body was quite still.

Tom looked round frantically, adrenaline still scudding through his veins. The furious noise of fighting had gone, the sound of gunfire and the clash of steel replaced by the sobbing, rasping, choking sounds

270

of exhausted bodies, their heads hung down, their backs bent.

"Tisdale? Kemp? You all right?" Tom rested his hands on his knees, his chest heaving.

"We're well, your honour," said Tisdale. "We've got three scrubs here what's as gentle as lambs. Only needed to clout 'em once."

"Is Boylin one of them?"

"No, your honour, he ain't."

Tom looked down at the body at his feet. It wasn't Boylin either, and nor was the man he'd tipped into the Thames. He was sure of that. Tom's shoulders slumped. He'd chased the wrong boat. He thought of returning to Bow Creek and searching for it, but dismissed the idea. If Boylin had been on it, he would have gone by now and, anyway, he could hardly deal with any more prisoners. He flicked back the canvas sheeting covering the hold; the barrels were still there, all but a few.

His relief was short-lived. While he might have succeeded in recovering the sugar from the *Swansong*, he still had no evidence to prove Boylin's involvement in the original theft. He straightened his back and looked along the length of Bugsby's Reach, towards Bow Creek. The faintest glimmer of grey far down on the eastern horizon signalled the coming of dawn. Soon the river would be filled with the comings and goings of men and ships and barges. He looked round at the faint splash and rumble of oars being worked.

"So there you are, Hart," he said, turning to watch his friend scull the police galley towards him. "I was beginning to wonder where you'd got to."

Sam grinned. "I regret my absence, sir. With your permission, I'll just land this here cully what I found paddling about in the water."

"Who is he?" said Tom, just able to make out the shape of a man's head above the gunwale, his arms lashed firmly to the forward thwart, the rest of him still in the water.

"Why, you above all should know," said Sam. "You, it was that gave him his ducking! I brought him back, since I doubt he'd have returned of his own accord."

"Very droll," said Tom. "What's his name?"

"I asked him the same question since I couldn't make out his face on account of the dark," said Sam, passing a line across to the lugger. "He reckoned it weren't none of my business. Changed his mind, though, after I ducked him once or twice."

"And?" said Tom, impatiently.

"It's Shamus O'Malley, your honour. The same rogue what pushed young Jacob out of the *Antelope*'s rigging. I reckon he should be able to tell you a thing or two what's of interest, like."

Gabriel Newman's heart beat harder the closer he got to the mouth of Bow Creek. His hooded eyes darted from shadow to shadow, his ears strained for the least sound. He, too, would have liked to get out of the boat with Boylin and walk across the Isle of Dogs to

272

Limehouse. He, too, would have welcomed the chance to avoid Pascoe.

And he might have suggested as much but for something in the way Boylin had looked at him: an empty, implacable stare, devoid of any feeling or emotion, as though a point had been passed in the publican's mind that would not again be visited, his decision irrevocable. He'd watched him stand motionless on the foreshore, his face turned towards the departing lugger, his pistol held limply in his right hand.

Newman lost sight of him as the lugger inched her way out of Bow Creek into Bugsby's Reach. He licked his lips and stared into the inky blackness, his nerves at breaking point. He watched the bows veer round to the west and point up to Blackwall Point, only the gentle plopping of the oars disturbing the silence. Soon he had passed the Trinity buoy and, after that, the ships of the East India fleet. He found the calls of their night watchmen strangely comforting.

He slouched in the stern as they rounded the point, the broad stretch of Blackwall Reach laid out before him drenched in the pale silvery light of a crescent moon. His thoughts dwelt on what the future might hold.

He could guess. Another job, another night of suffocating fear, the ever-present threat of arrest and the seemingly inevitable gallows. He wished he could stop and walk away from it all: from Pascoe, from Boylin, from the violence — and the fear that went with it. Yet he couldn't. He'd already tried to rid himself of

Boylin's crushing influence, to throw off the dead hand of subservience, but, as in so much else, he had failed. Even his attempt to kill the publican had failed. He was inextricably bound to him by a lifetime of acquiescence — and the need for work. Without Boylin there would be no work. And without work he would starve.

The tide had long since turned by the time they passed the seamen's hospital at Greenwich and entered Limehouse Reach, the ebbing current slowing their progress. In the eastern sky the first hint of grey heralded the approach of the new day; ahead, Newman was able to make out the bell tower of St Anne's Church. Soon the journey would be over. A few hundred yards and he'd have reached the steps at Limehouse Hole.

He began to relax.

Suddenly, he heard it: a barked order. Not loud, but an order nevertheless. For a second he thought it had come from one of the men-of-war they'd passed at Deptford Creek. Then he realised his mistake. The sound had come from the opposite direction. He held up his hand to stop the rowing, his head cocked to one side.

Silence.

Then there it was again, distant and indistinct.

He turned his head toward the sound and waited, his pulse beating fast. No one used the river at night. No one except villains — and the police. The sound grew louder, more distinct — the thud and squeal of oars, the splash of blades entering the water. Newman stared, willing himself to see through the grey-black gloom that played tricks with the human eye.

Seconds ticked by.

The foaming white of a bow-wave came into view. He sat transfixed, cold sweat against his skin. Now he could see the outline of an onrushing vessel, the shoulders of its crew bending and straightening in perfect unison.

Newman tried to swallow, his tongue sticking to the roof of his mouth, his throat like sawdust. He felt the urge to run, to row for the shore and disappear into the night. He tried to move, but couldn't; his arms like lead, his legs as though in chains.

The police galley was a bare thirty yards off his larboard bow. One turn of the ogler's head and Newman and the rest were done for. He risked a glance at the figure in the stern, hardly daring to breathe. It wasn't Pascoe but one of the other surveyors whose name he didn't know.

The rushing sound reached its peak and then was past them, speeding into the night. He waited for the clatter of the thole pins to recede and then motioned the crew towards the stairs at Limehouse Hole. Twenty yards from the shore, he picked up his storm lantern and opened the gate for a second. There was no response. He repeated the signal and waited for Boylin's answering flash. There was none.

Newman glanced back down the reach, the hairs on the back of his neck beginning to rise. He'd not a moment to lose. The police patrol would soon be back.

He brought the lugger to the stairs and called softly. He knew there'd be no answer.

Boylin watched the lugger pull away from the river bank and disappear from sight. He stood motionless for a minute or so, his back erect, his hands clenched by his sides, his eye fixed on the point where the boat had vanished. He looked down at the pistol still in his hand, his index finger resting on the trigger. He'd forgotten the weapon was there — cocked, primed and loaded. He raised it, as though curious to see its shape, turning it over in the palm of his hand. He traced its outline with his fingers, feeling the coldness of the metal.

The nights were cooler now and an early autumn wind brushed against his face, sighing as it travelled between the reeds at the water's edge. He looked up at the thick clouds racing across the heavens, heavy with the threat of rain and ringed with the ghostly light of the hidden moon. The sight brought Peggy to his mind. She belonged to Pascoe now. Of that, there was no doubt. The thought tormented him, eating away at his raddled brain. He turned to look again at the mouth of the creek as if expecting Pascoe to appear, to see him walking across the marshland towards him.

His eye dropped to the gun. He'd feel nothing, hear nothing. His difficulties and his torment would be at an end. Cold fingers clutched at his heart as he contemplated the seductive sheen of the gun's barrel. Better this than the weeks of waiting for the inevitable rope, a life without joy or hope. He raised the muzzle to his temple, his breath held tight, his lungs bursting with the effort of squeezing the trigger . . .

The explosion, when it came, seemed far away, the echo reverberating across the Isle of Dogs and chasing a thousand birds into the night sky. Boylin looked down at the gun still in his hand, the hammer drawn back, the barrel still cold. Plainly, the gun had not been fired. Plainly, he was still alive. For a moment he stood nonplussed, staring stupidly at the weapon, unsure of whether he felt joy or anger at his temporary deliverance. He raised his eye and looked across the marsh to where the sound of gunfire had come from, to where the dark waters of the Thames flowed down from Deptford to Blackwall Point. And it was then that the old fear returned. Pascoe had caught one of his boats; he would soon come looking for him.

Spots of rain began to fall, bending the reed stalks and splashing his upturned face. He sagged to his knees, a sob of frustration escaping his lips. He knew he'd not the courage to try again, to put the gun to his head and end his life. The moment had passed. He thought of Shamus O'Malley who, even now, would be in custody, and his stomach somersaulted. It wouldn't be difficult for Pascoe to make him talk, to make him confess to the murder of Newman's young brother, Jacob. And once he'd got that far, it would be a short step for O'Malley to involve Boylin. There was much that O'Malley could say in return for his life.

How had it come to this? Boylin blinked back his tears of self-pity and rage and tried to think. Someone had talked. Newman? He'd not the bottom for it. The wharfinger at the lime wharf they had just left? Unlikely. He, like Newman, had not the courage for it.

Boylin stared into the blackness. A name crept into the back of his mind and edged its way forward. Boylin dismissed it. It was absurd. But the name crept back, this time with greater force, refusing to leave him. He recalled his last meeting with Sir Sydney Devall at Jerusalem's on Cornhill, his delighted surprise at the merchant's agreement to all his demands.

All except one.

The date on which the sugar was to be delivered.

Boylin adjusted the patch over his blind eye, his hand shaking as realisation dawned: Devall had betrayed him. It was *he* who had insisted on a delay in the delivery of the sugar. It was *he* who had set the precise date on which it was to be handed over. Boylin had not liked it but had grudgingly accepted it, relieved he would soon be rid of the stuff. Certainly he'd not thought in terms of betrayal.

But now it all began to make sense. Devall had never wanted anything to do with the sugar. He'd agreed to take it knowing he'd never have to go through with it.

Boylin climbed slowly to his feet, wiping the mud from his knees. It was Devall who'd talked, who'd wanted him caught. It had to be.

The corners of Boylin's mouth lifted a fraction. He knew what had to be done.

Tom led the way into the Rainbow Coffee House on Cornhill and headed for the first-floor dining room with John Harriot close on his heels.

"I won't say I told you so, Mr Pascoe," said Harriot, after the two of them had seated themselves in one of the empty stalls, "but your three nights spent away from your normal duties do seem to have been a trifle wasteful, wouldn't you agree?"

"I can't say that I would," said Tom, suppressing his annoyance. "We've recovered a substantial amount of sugar stolen from the *Swansong*, and made a number of arrests."

"Are you certain the sugar is from the *Swansong*? Or even that it's stolen?" said Harriot. "Lord Portland presses for news on the main investigation. The decision on the taxation issue must be made before the end of October. If we fail to put a stop to all this plundering of the port, we could all be in for a very bumpy ride."

"I regret to hear that," said Tom, beckoning a passing waiter. "But, yes, I am quite sure the sugar is from the *Swansong*. The identifying marks on the barrels exactly match those shown in the ship's manifest."

"I remember, now," said Harriot. "You had some trouble persuading the authorities to show you the document. I believe they wanted written authority. But what about Boylin? Where was he?"

"Probably in the second boat," said Tom. "Shall we order?"

"Forgive me, Mr Pascoe," said Harriot, when the waiter had taken their order and left, "but this entire operation was intended to capture Boylin, was it not? He is, after all, the man you suspect of being largely responsible for plundering the port."

"You're partly right," said Tom. "I certainly want to lay Boylin by the lee. I'm satisfied he was responsible for the murder of my old cook and for the larceny of the *Swansong's* cargo. As to the rest, I'm no longer sure. In fact I can't find any record of large quantities of goods being stolen that can, in any way, be linked to Boylin."

"Good God, sir. Are you telling me that at this late stage we may have been wasting our time?" said Harriot, raising his voice against a clamour of noise coming from the street outside. He paused, an irritated scowl on his face. Then, "Oh, for heaven's sake, will someone please discover what all that racket is about?"

"There's a mob a'coming along Cornhill," said a nervous-sounding voice from a seat near the window.

"Master Landlord!" Tom's voice cut through the babble, joined now by the frantic pealing of the bells of a dozen churches. "Pray, be so good as to find out what the fuss is about. Then perhaps we can enjoy the hospitality of this excellent place."

Two minutes later, a breathless and excited landlord waddled back up the stairs. "I can hardly believe the truth of it, your honour. It's a most glorious day for England. Oh, sir, it's wonderful, to be sure."

"For God's sake, man, spit it out," said Tom. "Pray, what's so wonderful?"

"Admiral Nelson, sir, he's flogged the Frogs, I mean the French, sir. Dished them completely. Oh, listen to all the cheering and the church bells, sir. London is going mad, sir. People is laughing and singing for the joy of it."

280

Tom Pascoe, John Harriot and the rest of the room rose as one and hurried to the windows. A solid mass was moving up Cornhill in the direction of St Paul's, cheering, shouting, beating drums, blowing trumpets.

"I see a number of people are brandishing broadsheets, Master Landlord," shouted Tom, above the crash of cannon fire coming from the Tower. "See if you can persuade someone to part with his. We might learn the truth of this matter."

In moments, a newspaper had been thrust into his hand and Tom quickly found what he was looking for.

"Give you joy, sir," he said, passing the broadsheet to Harriot. "It seems Admiral Nelson caught the French fleet off the North African coast, near Alexandria, and thrashed it. It says here the official dispatches were delivered to the Admiralty this morning by Captain Capel of the *Mutine*."

For a minute, the two men stood at the window staring down at the tightly packed multitude as it wended its noisy way, the sense of relief and excitement at the long-awaited victory pushing to one side their concerns of the moment.

"Did you ever serve with Admiral Nelson?" asked Tom, his eyes still on the crowd.

"No," said Harriot. "I was only a lad when I was shipwrecked and left the Navy. I doubt I knew the time of day, never mind the names of senior officers, however exalted. What about you?"

"I knew of him, of course, but I regret I never met him," said Tom. "This victory comes not a moment too soon, I fancy. Boney has been having it all his own way for far too long."

"Where were we?" said Harriot, after the two of them had returned to their seats. "Ah, yes, you were about to accuse the Administration of exaggerating the scale of theft in the port. And worse still, that we may have been barking up the wrong tree."

"Not quite," said Tom, leaning back as the waiter spread a snowy-white cloth on the table in front of them. "What I'm saying is that according to local records, the volume of goods stolen, while significant, is nowhere near the volume mentioned by the Secretary of State."

"How can that be?" said Harriot.

"We've —" Tom paused while the waiter returned with several large blue-patterned plates laden with spatchcocked eel, roasted pigeon pies and a liberal helping of roast pork in a thick gravy. When the man had left, Tom went on, "We've been asked to find the person or persons responsible for the substantial drop in the value of goods being landed at the King's Beam. We both thought that what the Secretary of State was talking about was the straightforward plunder of shipping and we looked at who might be responsible for that. Boylin fitted this picture and we have dutifully gone after him."

"Please, do start," said Harriot, waving at the food on the table. "You were saying?"

"There's no doubt in my mind that Boylin is up to his neck in villainy," Tom continued. "Two separate witnesses have come forward to implicate him in murder and larceny. It is our misfortune that one of those witnesses is now dead and the other, a Jewish hat-seller, is to all intents and purposes valueless as a witness. Nevertheless, as I have already said, the volume of goods Boylin is suspected of taking is too low to have interested the Secretary of State."

"So we are looking in the wrong direction?" said Harriot.

"Not entirely," said Tom. "What I'm saying is that there is no evidence of any increase in the number of ships or lighters being attacked. On the contrary, since the beginning of July, when we began patrolling the port, there has been a substantial drop in this type of offence."

"Which should have led to an increase in revenue to the Administration, not the reduction Lord Portland complains of," mused Harriot.

"Exactly," said Tom.

"So where's it all going from?" said Harriot.

"I think the bulk of it is disappearing after it's been landed. It's the only way so much can be plundered without us knowing."

"What are you saying, Mr Pascoe?" said Harriot, looking suddenly grave. "All goods pass through the King's Beam as soon as they're brought ashore. Any losses at that stage would implicate customs officers."

"I regret, sir, that is exactly what I'm saying. It won't be the first time that we've come across game officers."

"You're making a very serious allegation. How many d'you think are involved?"

"I don't know, four or five officers perhaps."

"That many?" said Harriot. "And you think they've been bribed?"

"Aye, I do," said Tom. "They can earn a year's pay in a single day working for the likes of Boylin. And the more they allow through, the more they get."

"You're suggesting . . . what? That officers under-record the weight of the goods landed and allow the balance to be stolen?"

"Yes. It's not difficult. The quays are always pestered with a great crowd of people, not to mention the carts waiting to carry away the landed goods. I doubt anyone checks what customs officers choose to record at the Beam."

"How would they get round the way-bill?" said Harriot.

"Simple," said Tom. "The way-bill only records what leaves the ship and is loaded into the lighter. But since there is then a two- or three-week delay before that lighter reaches the quayside, any shortfall can, if necessary, be explained in terms of the goods having been stolen in transit. The customs authorities are simply interested in what actually reaches the King's Beam and not in the investigation of any theft. In any event they lack the resources necessary to find the villains responsible, so the shortfall is never recorded."

"An interesting theory," said Harriot. "But in order for it to work, the scheme would require an organising mind. Could that be Boylin?"

"I think he appears somewhere in the equation," said Tom. "Of course, he couldn't do it all on his own. In addition to the game officers, he'd need a receiver to fund the operation and have the contacts necessary to buy the goods afterwards."

"Like the gentleman you saw visiting him in the Queen's Head, on the night of the rat fighting?" said Harriot.

"That's the one. But just at the moment, we don't know who he is," said Tom. "Why, sir, are you smiling?"

"Because I'm not sure that's any longer the case," said Harriot, remembering a recent visitor to his office. "Does the name Sir Sydney Devall mean anything to you?"

CHAPTER
TWENTY

Newman sat at one of the long benches in the taproom of the Queen's Head, staring at the group gathered round Boylin. He still didn't know where the publican had been in the last two days. All he knew was that the scrub was here, large as life and twice as ugly. He couldn't deny there had been long hours when he'd been convinced Boylin was dead, and had rejoiced in the possibility. He'd not dared to ask him where he'd been. He knew, all too well, how the publican would react. It was the same reason he'd not asked him about the death of his brother, much as he wanted to know.

"Will you be calling yourselves sons of Irishmen?" Boylin waved a finger at his audience, the veins of his neck bulging through layers of flesh. "Will you not stand like men and fight for the Tree of Liberty? What is it your fathers and brothers are dying for in Ireland?"

There was no subtlety in the rasping rhetoric. It was the same crude call to arms, the same references to Irish liberty and the sacrifices of men like Keogh, Roche and others, that Newman had heard many a time before. He looked at the obsequious group huddled round Boylin, drawn to him as moths to a burning candle, their mood increasingly hostile and impatient of events in Ireland.

Newman sipped his beer and let his eyes travel round the room. At some other time he, too, might have been caught up in the excitement of the publican's harangue, but not anymore. He continued to stare at the assembled men with a growing sense of unease: Boylin was planning something. Why else would he stir the republican pot? Why else rouse the men's anger? Newman's curiosity subsided. What Boylin chose to do, or not to do, was his own affair.

Then, the image of an old man popped into Newman's mind; an image that was often with him. Sometimes, during the night or in the early hours of the morning when sleep was at its deepest, it would haunt him and he would awake, his body bathed in sweat. He wished it would go away; wished he'd not been on the *Swansong* the night the old man had died; wished he'd not seen what had happened.

But he *had* been there, watching as Boylin caught hold of the old man by his hair, smashing his skull against the rail and tipping him into the Thames.

A mile to the north of where Gabriel Newman was sitting, Tom Pascoe was approaching the London Hospital in Whitechapel. He stopped opposite the main gates and then crossed the rutted highway and entered the hospital grounds. He still wasn't sure if it had been sensible to come. Peggy had made it plain that she no longer wished to continue their friendship and, whatever her reasons, she was entitled to believe he would respect her decision. In any other circumstances, Tom would have done so, but a visit from Charity Squibb earlier in the day had persuaded him that a visit was called for.

"This ain't none of my business," she'd said, "but I'm afeared for Miss Tompkins. She's taken on so about the vile assault upon her person and made herself ill. I've tried speaking to her but she won't listen to no reason. She'll listen to you, though."

Tom mounted the stone steps to the front hall of the building and turned right down the central corridor, past the apothecary's room to the main stairwell. From here he climbed to the second floor.

"Nurse Tompkins?" A shabby, overweight woman of about sixty stood at the entrance of George Ward. "You just missed her. Matron allowed her and Nurse Squibb the afternoon off. She's in her room though. Shall I be calling her?"

"Is ..." Tom wavered, his desire to see Peggy tempered by his reluctance to disturb her. "Is she at leisure to receive visitors?"

"God love us," said the woman. "How should I be knowing if she's at leisure without me calling her?"

"Tom?" He heard his name before he could respond to the woman, and turned to see Peggy standing in the doorway of her room.

His heart missed a beat.

"Give you joy," he greeted her, watching as she glanced away from him, an expression in her eyes that he could not read. "I see, Miss Tompkins, that I intrude upon you."

288

He moved towards the stairwell. "Forgive me, I should not have come."

"Don't go! That is, unless you wish to." Peggy raised a hand as if to stop him. "I heard voices. I thought it was you."

"Of all things, I don't wish to go," he said, turning back to face her.

"I am grateful for your concern, Tom," said Peggy, the hint of a smile on her pale face. "And I find I am at leisure for some little while if you still wish to speak with me. But you must allow me to bring Miss Squibb. It would not be proper else."

The three of them descended the stairs to the garden quadrangle where once, on a summer's afternoon, they had walked before. Now, though the sun still shone out of a cloudless sky, it was a cold wind that blew from across the flatlands to the south-west and rustled the dying stalks of the flowers.

When they reached the southern extremity of the garden, Tom laid a hand on Peggy's arm and drew her back while Charity moved on alone. More than anything else he wanted to understand what had happened to their relationship to cause a gulf to open between them. In the few months since they had first met, she had come to mean so much to him, and if he had not known it before, he knew now that he loved her.

"I hope, dear Peggy, you'll not think me forward, but since . . . well, since . . ." Tom trailed off, unsure of how to continue.

"It was, I own, wrong of me to treat you as I have," said Peggy, wrapping her cloak around her. "I should have seen you and explained the altered state of my mind, except I barely understood what was happening myself. All I can do is try to tell you something of my past. Perhaps, then, things might seem a little clearer to you."

"There is no need," said Tom, gently.

Peggy held a finger to his lips. "There is every need, Tom. I want you to know why I acted as I did; why it has been difficult for me to meet with you and talk with you, as once we did."

She moved a little away from him, her hands still clasping her cloak around her, her head bowed. Then she stopped and looked back at him.

"Do you remember that you once asked me how I came to work at this hospital?" she said.

"Yes, I do."

"I told you that I had left my father's house in Kent to take up an appointment as a governess to a family in London?"

"Yes."

"At first, all went well there and I dearly loved the children for whom I cared. The routine of the house seldom varied and the master was scarcely at home. When he was, he would occasionally receive visitors for the conduct of his business. One caller in particular appeared to have seen me and taken an interest in me."

Peggy bent down and plucked a dead stalk from the side of the path, twisting it around her finger. When she stood up, she said, "Unused as I was to the attentions of the opposite sex, I allowed myself to believe that his interest in me was entirely honourable. In any event, I confess I found myself looking forward to his visits, when we would exchange pleasantries in the hall before the formalities of his business with my master took place. In the course of the following weeks, we became — how shall I say? — intimate, and would often walk together around the bookshops of St Paul's. And that is how I imagined the relationship would progress.

"At about the same time," she went on, her body beginning to tremble, "I received news that my mother was suffering from the ague and required the attentions of a physician. Alas, my father had not the means to pay for such treatment, nor even for the help of an apothecary, and he turned to me for help. Naturally, I very much wanted to assist in whatever way I could but I had no funds. My suitor became aware of my predicament and at once offered to loan me a sum of money, and that was the real start of my present difficulties.

"One day, I was in the house with the children when he arrived and, seeing that I was alone, he entered the nursery where I had my room. I immediately asked him to leave but he refused and began to force his attentions upon me. I resisted and he struck me and would, I believe, have continued if my mistress, fortunately, had not returned to the house, whereupon he was forced to desist."

She stopped and gazed down through the golden leaves of the orchard towards the faraway Thames. Tom waited for her to continue, his fists clenched, his anger threatening to choke him. She looked up at him with a sad little smile.

"Since I knew this man to be an acquaintance of my master," she continued, "I thought it best to say nothing of the incident to my mistress but to offer, instead, my immediate resignation. By the greatest of good fortune I discovered that the employer of a fellow governess was intimately connected with the London Hospital, and through him I was recommended for a position at this establishment.

"I had been here three years before I again saw my suitor. Although he once had been the object of my deepest affection, I scarce recognised him, such was the disfigurement of his face. I think, dear Tom, you have already guessed that the man was Master Boylin."

Tom's stomach lurched. Yes, he'd already guessed it, but it was still a shock to hear his name uttered. He looked at the pale face beside him. "And your master in London? Pray, what was *his* name?"

Peggy's brow furrowed in surprise. "Why, it was Sir Sydney Devall . . . Why d'you look at me so?"

"Forgive me, dear Peggy," said Tom, recovering quickly. "I interrupted you. You were saying, I think, that you again saw Master Boylin after a period of some years?"

"Yes," said Peggy, "It was near the end of my evening duty. I was accompanying a cadaver to the dead house when I heard my name called. It was dark, and I could not see who it was until I shone the light of my lamp onto his face. I confess I was shocked at his gross appearance, much changed as it was from what I remembered. Not wishing to appear uncivil, I exchanged a few words with him. At length he asked if he could call upon me again. I regret it extremely but, in the name of civility, I was compelled to agree. He has taken full advantage of that weakness of mine and has visited me on several occasions since then. The rest, I think, you know."

"Dear Peggy," said Tom. "Nothing you have told me could possibly affect my feelings for you. You should not imagine for a single moment that I think ill of you in consequence of your experiences. Indeed, quite the opposite. I would regard it as a singular honour should you allow me to call you my friend."

"You're a dear man," replied Peggy, her eyes bent to the ground, "and some day you'll meet someone with whom you can be happy. When that day comes, I may regret this moment, but truth to tell, I cannot love you as you deserve, nor care for you or comfort you in your times of need. In short, I'm without the tenderness of my sex that you have every right to expect. And if you were to ask me why, I could not reply since I do not know the reason. I can only tell you what I feel."

Tom felt as though his heart was being crushed. There was something so final about the way she spoke, as though she had long anticipated this moment and prepared for it. There seemed nothing left to say.

Abruptly, she turned away from him, and before he knew it she'd run the few yards that separated them from the steps to the hospital lobby. In a moment she was lost to his sight. Behind her, trailed the faithful Miss Squibb, a bewildered expression on her broad face.

Peggy did not stop running until she reached her room on the second floor, where she flung herself onto her bed. She lay there for some moments, sobbing violently, her head buried in her pillow, unable to think of anything except the consequences of what she had done.

She rolled over and stared at the ceiling, drawing her sleeve across her eyes as she struggled with conflicting emotions of sorrow and relief, unable to make any sense of the seeming paradox of her feelings. She had wished for Tom Pascoe's presence more than anything, and yet had pushed him away. His smile was a balm to her troubled soul yet his touch was anathema. How could she tell him that she wanted him as a friend but not as a lover, as someone to whom she could confide her innermost thoughts but who must remain at arm's length; how could she explain the love she bore him but the revulsion she felt at her own body? How could she tell him of her absence of trust in all men?

A light knock on the door and Charity's head appeared, an anxious look on her face. "Do I disturb you, Miss Tompkins?"

Peggy struggled up on one elbow and retrieved a handkerchief from the pocket of her gown.

"Oh, dear Miss Squibb, no, you do not disturb me." Peggy blew noisily into her handkerchief. "Is Tom . . . Captain Pascoe, gone? Is he well?"

"Aye, he's gone right enough," said Charity, "though, in truth, I can't speak for his being well."

Peggy looked up quickly, her eyes wide. "But he is all right? Tell me he is all right."

Charity didn't reply at once. Instead she came over to the bed where Peggy lay, and looked down at her colleague. "I don't know if he be all right or not, child. Wouldn't surprise me none if he weren't and that's a fact." She paused as though expecting an interruption. When none came, she went on, "What you do with your life ain't none of my concern, but I'll tell you this, Nurse Tompkins, it just ain't right what you're doing. It ain't right at all. Oh, I'm not talking about your Captain Pascoe, nor any other man, neither. It's you, my lovely, what's worrying me to an early grave. You got to look after yourself. Come now, you know your old friend Charity Squibb will help you in whatever way she can, but you've got to help, too."

"It's no good you going on at me, dear Miss Squibb," said Peggy, her handkerchief to her eyes. "I can't help the way I feel; not after what happened with that odious creature, Master Boylin. I know the fault does not lie with Captain Pascoe, yet it makes no difference. I cannot bear him knowing of the things that have happened to me, nor of what he thinks of me. I am ashamed of what happened, and cannot face him though, in truth, I love him dearly."

A great sob escaped from her, and long moments passed while she hid her face in her hands. Charity moved away from the bed and stood by the window, watching the scudding clouds sweep across a sky of pale blue. There was nothing more she could say. Perhaps, in time, her room-mate would recover. She thought of Captain Pascoe and sighed. Perhaps by then it would be too late . . . She hoped not. She turned and looked at Peggy's prostrate form and shook her head.

CHAPTER
TWENTY-ONE

Sam was sitting cross-legged on the table in the constables' waiting room. He glanced across to where Tom was warming himself by the fire.

"You say Sir Sydney Devall has been to see Mr Harriot?"

"Aye," said Tom, lifting the tails of his coat and feeling the heat through his breeches. "According to what he told Mr Harriot, he had a visit from Boylin who offered to sell him the sugar from the *Swansong*. The odd thing is that Sir Sydney pretended he'd never met Boylin before."

"Strange." Sam stretched and yawned.

"Yes, and it gets stranger. When Mr Harriot asked for details of where and when the sugar was to be delivered, Devall became quite agitated. It was only later that he agreed to make a few enquiries and let Mr Harriot know the result."

"Let me guess," said Sam. "He never did, did he?"

"No, he didn't," said Tom.

"By-the-by, have you seen him in the last few days?" Sam asked.

"Who? Devall? No. Should I?"

"There's been some whispers," said Sam. "Didn't make no sense until now. The talk on the river is that Boylin's got it in for someone, a gentleman what he intends to turn off."

"And you think it's Devall?" said Tom, staring at his friend.

"It's possible," said Sam. "We already suspect the merchant is involved in this case. Perhaps the sugar were supposed to have been taken to his warehouse the night it were stolen, but he refused it on account of all that trouble on the *Swansong*. That might answer why the sugar was still in Boylin's possession when we found it on the Lea."

"But if Sir Sydney Devall originally turned down the sugar, why would he still be involved?" said Tom.

"Because Boylin won't have many receivers what is capable of handling such a big amount."

"So you think Boylin was forced to approach Sir Sydney again and try and arrange a new delivery date?"

"Aye, I do," said Sam.

"And now something has happened to make them fall out with one another . . ." mused Tom. "*That* would explain why Devall went to Mr Harriot with an offer to help." Tom whistled. "I little thought him so reckless. He will know, as well as anyone, what Boylin is capable of."

"And now Boylin's found out," said Sam.

"Aye," said Tom. "It seems that way."

Sir Sydney Devall couldn't remember when he'd enjoyed himself more — or worked so hard to close a deal. He drained the last of his coffee and looked around the dining room at Jerusalem's, surprised to notice it was now almost deserted. He removed a watch from his waistcoat pocket and snapped it open. Half past eleven; far later than he'd imagined. He would call immediately for a hackney carriage to take him home. He looked at the time again, and his self-satisfied smile faded. There would be no carriages at this hour. He would have to walk — despite the threats made on his life.

He'd ignored the rumours at first. Like most people in his position, Devall had made enemies over the years and had learned that such talk seldom came to anything. Even threats that went beyond idle chatter rarely progressed to the point of real danger.

But this time it was different. He'd known that from the moment he'd discovered who was behind the threats. The terror he'd felt had been physical in its force; had caused a blurring of his vision, a queasiness in the pit of his stomach. Even after the corporal manifestations faded, the mental anguish persisted, feeding his mind with ever darker imaginings that threatened to overwhelm his sanity and rob him of his slumbers.

His power to influence events was largely illusory these days. There had been a time when he could have swatted away men like Boylin with a nod in the right quarters. But not anymore. He'd forgotten — or ignored — the necessity of the persuasive art of violence and its unbroken link with terror. The risk that Boylin would discover what he'd done, had always been present in the background of their dealings. And then there would be consequences. There had never been any doubt about that. He wondered how the publican had found out . . . not that it mattered. What mattered was that he had.

Devall called for his hat and cloak and walked to the door of the coffee house. Outside, a thick fog shrouded the street. He looked back into Jerusalem's, now empty of its customers. Even the man with whom he'd been doing business had left. He would have to go.

He glanced nervously up and down Cornhill before crossing the road, and his thoughts went back to the beginning of his relationship with Joseph Boylin. The co-operation had begun with minor depredations within the port, when he'd agreed to accept small amounts of coffee, tea and sugar that the Irishman had plundered from newly arrived ships. Soon, they had progressed to larger amounts. Gangs of perhaps ten or twelve men would board the vessels at night and terrorise their unfortunate watchmen into silent acquiescence to their thievery. Boylin had been a willing disciple in those days, anxious to prove himself equal to the tasks the merchant set for him.

It had, Devall conceded, been Boylin's idea, in the early summer of that year, to involve a few trusted customs officers in a scheme that allowed for a vast increase in the volume of stolen goods able to be handled in comparative safety. The partnership in which he, Devall, had taken the major share, had seemed an ideal arrangement from which both men could reap rich rewards.

But now . . . Devall shivered in the night air. He had, of late, grown increasingly irritated at Boylin's greed and his demands for an ever larger share of the spoils. But it had been the publican's veiled reminders of just how much he knew of the merchant's business that had proved the last straw for Devall, the point beyond which he was not prepared to tolerate the insolence of a lesser man, fearful though he was of the possible consequences.

Devall reached the junction with St Michael's Alley, the fog now so thick he was barely able to see half a pace in front of him. He slowed down, aware of a sudden anxiety whose cause he could not identify. Then, turning into the alley, he thought he heard a footstep close behind. He spun round and reached for his sword; the rasping sound of steel on steel, as he drew the blade from its scabbard, strangely comforting. He waited, trembling, his eyes staring into the shifting strands of greyish-white, swirling as though disturbed by someone or something.

He jumped as a rat scuttled out from the building behind him and brushed against his leg.

He should never have gone to the magistrate. He knew that now, could see the folly of his decision. Perhaps if he were to return and retract his statement, Boylin would let bygones be bygones, welcome the opportunity of working with him again. Perhaps . . . He faltered. He knew what he hoped for was impossible.

A minute slid by in silence, then another. Devall expelled a lungful of air and wiped his brow with his handkerchief. Carefully, silently, he moved on, his back pressed against the side of the alley, his eyes probing every shadow, chasing every flurry of the fog. Somebody *was* there, he was sure of it, though he saw nothing

He caught the faint sound of an accordion playing and men singing, and then lights — dim in the fog — came into view. The next moment he was outside a building, a familiar sign over its stone lintel: Jamaica Coffee House. He sighed with relief. Inside would be men he knew, West India merchants like himself, men he could talk to. He listened to the distant hum of conviviality as he stood at the door, tempted to join the company and forget his terrors. But to what end? Sooner or later he'd have to come out again. Strange how quiet it was, here on the outside . . . He started at what sounded like a stone being kicked. Again he pressed his back to the wall and waited. Nothing. He must have imagined it. He pressed on towards Lombard Street.

Then it happened.

The scream died in his throat as the sharp point of a knife pricked the skin of his neck while a powerful arm encircled his head, drawing him roughly to the side of the passageway and slamming him against a wall. He opened his mouth to speak, but no words came. A knee rammed into his stomach and he sank to the ground. He mumbled a prayer while fingers rummaged through his pockets, taking his notebook, his silk handkerchief — and then his sword.

As suddenly as it had happened, it was over. Devall lay still, listening to the rapidly fading footsteps, hardly daring to hope that his relief at still being alive would not prove short-lived. He knew he was still at risk. Whoever had attacked him could not have been the person whose footsteps he'd heard — the attack had come from the opposite direction. Cold drops of sweat coursed down his back as he climbed unsteadily to his feet, his knees and elbows aching from the force of his fall. He *had* to get home . . .

Devall ran stumbling to the end of the alley and turned into a deserted Lombard Street, his lungs bursting. By the time he reached the bottom of Mincing Lane the fog had lifted and he could see the branches of the plane trees stark against the black October sky. The lantern above the gate of his home was tantalisingly close, its light spilling a pool of gold onto the road. He looked to see what lay beyond it, but could see only the dead leaves stirred and scattered by a breeze. He looked behind him, a swift, frightened glance to check that the rustling vegetation had not masked the sound of someone's approach. Then he crept towards his house, his back flat against the walled boundaries of his neighbours' properties. Once he thought he heard a cough, a small, stifled sound from the other side of the road. He froze and waited for it to come again, but there was nothing. He looked at the lamp over his own gate. Less than twenty yards to go. He could make it . . .

The merchant rushed forward and pushed at the heavy wrought-iron structure. It didn't move. He pushed again, shaking it with all the force he could muster, blood rushing to his head, pounding in his ears.

He yanked at the bell-pull and heard the distant tinkle within the house. An age seemed to pass before the front door opened and the flickering light of a candle appeared. He stared over his shoulder into the darkness. Giddy with fear, he watched his butler move ponderously towards him, stop at the gate and fumble with the keys. Slowly, the gate swung open. Devall stumbled into the courtyard and again looked back into the street. On the far side he thought he saw a shadow move. He ran the few yards to his front door.

"Has everyone retired?" said a still-trembling Devall.

"They have, sir."

"Very well. Bring me a brandy in the library. Then you may go."

Fifteen minutes later, Devall sat back in his favourite chair by the fire, nursing his second glass of brandy. He was still shaking. He glanced at the carriage clock on the mantelpiece. Nearly one-thirty. He didn't feel ready for bed. Tomorrow he would see the Wapping magistrate and inform him that he'd made a mistake, that the description he'd provided was of an acquaintance wholly innocent of any depredation. After that, he would arrange to see Boylin . . . He took a sip of his brandy and felt his eyelids begin to droop. He must, he thought, be more tired than he'd imagined.

At the library window, the drapes moved a fraction and a floorboard creaked. In his chair, Sir Sydney's head dropped forward and his eyes closed in sleep.

The courtroom, on the ground floor of the police office at Wapping New Stairs was crowded, the stench vile.

Newman squeezed himself into a corner at the back of the room and looked nervously about him. He did not want to be here; he knew there'd be trouble. He glanced over to where he could see Boylin whispering to a number of lumpers and coal-heavers. He could guess what was being said. Boylin would be stirring them up, getting their support. He'd talked of little else since O'Malley's arrest; had left no doubt in anyone's mind of his determination to prevent a committal to the Old Bailey. Newman's heart beat faster. He knew Boylin too well to believe he'd stop now. He watched the publican move to another group. He'd been doing the same thing for the last quarter of an hour.

Newman turned at the sound of a commotion at the front of the court. A door had opened and a squad of half-a-dozen watermen constables appeared, fanning out to form a line in front of the mob, their arrival greeted with loud jeers. To one side of them, standing by the door through which they'd come, Newman recognised the tall figure of Master Pascoe.

Again the door opened. The crowd erupted into cheering. O'Malley was being brought in, together with the others with whom he'd been arrested. He grinned, rolled his shoulders and waved before turning to face the magistrate's table.

Newman edged his way closer to the street door. When the trouble started, he wanted to be out of harm's way. Suddenly, the room fell silent. The magistrate, Mr Harriot, had limped in, exchanged bows with his clerk and sat down.

"Carry on, Mr Clerk, if you please." Harriot looked tired.

One after the other the witnesses stepped forward, took the oath, and gave their depositions — the merchant whose sugar it was, to prove ownership; a clerk from the Sugar Exchange who testified that the sugar originated from Barbados "on account of its fineness'; another clerk from the Marine Society office to establish the markings on the barrels as those from the *Swansong*; Tom Pascoe with evidence of possession and arrest.

"Slow down!" complained the magistrate's clerk more than once. "I am obliged to take down what it is you are saying. You are, sir, speaking too quickly."

Finally it was done.

Harriot cleared his throat. "Shamus O'Malley, Michael Flaherty, John O'Connor and Joseph Finnigan, the offences with which you are charged can only be dealt with at the Quarter Sessions before a judge and jury. On the facts before me, I consider there is sufficient evidence to commit you to stand your trial and . . ."

The rest of the magistrate's words were drowned by the angry howl of the mob, which surged towards the waiting line of constables.

Newman scrambled for the street door. It wasn't his fight. He looked back to see Master Pascoe standing in front of the mob, his sword drawn, his voice rising above the clamour.

"In the King's name, stand back," said the voice of the quarterdeck. "I warrant I'll cut down the first man that moves."

306

Newman heard no more. He had already slammed the door behind him and was running down the passage leading to Wapping Street.

It was some hours later when Tom knocked on the door of Harriot's room and walked in. The magistrate was sitting by the fire, his head enveloped in a cloud of tobacco smoke, his face drawn and grey from lack of sleep.

"Thank you for coming." Harriot waved away the worst of the smoke. "You've heard the news, I suppose?"

"You mean the business this morning?" said Tom. "Yes, I was there, sir."

"No, I'm afraid it's worse than that," said Harriot. "Sir Sydney Devall was murdered sometime last night. The details are a little hazy but I understand it was a pretty messy business."

"I'm sorry to hear that," said Tom. "I knew he was in some danger, of course, as did many others. Have there been any arrests?"

"No," said Harriot. "Boylin is the prime suspect but there's no evidence to implicate him at the moment. Seems he can account for his movements during the night. More to the point, I regret Sir Sydney's death means you've lost another witness in your case."

"Aye, the thought had just crossed my mind," said Tom.

"Speaking of Boylin," said Harriot, "is he likely to try and carry out the threat he made in court, this morning?"

"About burning the police office down?" Tom scratched the back of his head. "He's a desperate man with a great deal to lose. I'll warrant he's worried O'Malley will turn King's Evidence and give us all we need to hang him, so yes, I think he will. And when he comes, it will be with several hundred men who owe him their loyalty."

"Has O'Malley said anything yet?"

"Nothing at all," said Tom. "But Boylin doesn't know that and it's my guess he'll do anything to make sure the fellow keeps his mouth shut."

"Including starting a riot?"

Tom didn't answer. He rose and walked to the window, where he looked out at the Thames, covered now in a low-lying mist. Only the masts of the ships and the spire of St Mary's church were visible through the blanket of white, reducing the habitual bellow of the port to a dull whisper. Tom drew a slug of tobacco from his coat pocket and bit into it.

"Yes," he said, at last. "As I say, I think Boylin's gravely concerned about his own future. According to my informants, he's been whipping up the men with talk of what's going on in Ireland. So far as that goes, I've certainly noticed a change in their mood. They're more sullen and aggressive than in the past. Not that Boylin's a whit interested in what's going on over there. In my view, anything he says on the subject is done for another purpose."

"Do not make the mistake of underestimating the impact that events in Ireland are having on the Irish in

London," said Harriot, stabbing the air with the stem of his pipe.

"I don't," said Tom. "But the situation we are facing has nothing to do with events in Ireland, tragic though they undoubtedly are. The Irish who work within this port have no political views whatsoever and seek merely to feed themselves and their families."

"I think, sir, you are missing the point," said Harriot. "The Irish blame us, the English, for causing this uprising in their homeland. As they see it, they've been oppressed for years and made to suffer. In the —"

"Naturally the Irish blame the English for their ills," interrupted Tom, his irritation rising. "Who else would they point the finger at? Certainly not themselves. Yet it is, in large measure, the Irish gentry who are to blame for the suffering of the people. It is the same here in London. The men who work on the river are not paid for the work they do and are, instead, sent out to plunder the ships in order to survive. The money due to them is kept by the very masters who encourage and profit from the depredations and who compel the men to drink at their own establishments. And who are these masters? Why, they are Irish publicans, like Boylin."

"I hear what you say," said Harriot, "but you would do well to recognise what drives these men. Yes, of course, they are abused and mistreated by their own but that's hardly the issue. It's their perception of reality that's important, not the reality itself. These men face the certainty of the gallows if they're caught rioting. That's no small consideration, and I believe that whatever Boylin has told them about the necessity for fighting, they will have accepted it wholly and absolutely."

"You have the right of it, sir," said Tom, anxious to call a halt to the argument. "I regret I spoke in haste."

"You have nothing to reproach yourself for, Mr Pascoe," said Harriot, mollified. "I've often been accused of doing the same thing myself."

He leaned forward in his chair and chuckled. "It's funny, is it not, Mr Pascoe, that we've been concerning ourselves with the prospect of open rebellion should you fail in your investigation. Now it seems we are to have one for the opposite reason."

Harriot's expression turned grave. "By-the-by, I'm afraid I've some more bad news for you. My Shadwell colleagues tell me they have sufficient evidence to charge Samuel Hart with the murder of the pot-boy at the Queen's Head. I regret it extremely, but first thing tomorrow morning, he will be arrested and taken to Shadwell."

Tom swayed back in his chair, as though he'd been punched.

Joseph Boylin got up from his chair in the back parlour of the Queen's Head and walked to the door of the taproom. There was no going back now. Not since this morning when he'd threatened to burn down the police office. He scowled at the memory of what had happened. He might have succeeded in getting O'Malley out of there — almost certainly would have done — but for Pascoe. It was him the men had been wary of. Holy Mother of God, there'd not been a single God-fearing Irishman with enough bottom to take him on. First one and then another had turned and run rather than face Pascoe. It was then his anger had got the better of him and he'd threatened to burn the place down.

The flash cullies — his flash cullies — were out, rounding up the lads from as far away as Ratcliff and Limehouse in the east and Southwark and Rotherhithe on the other side of the Thames. He'd teach that bastard Pascoe what it meant to get in the way of Joseph Michael Boylin. He opened the door and went in.

The taproom was full.

By eight in the evening the sun had long set on the courts and alleys of Wapping. The cold wind of the morning had gradually increased in force and now propelled whirlpools of dust and rubbish between the high buildings of a deserted Wapping Street. Tom Pascoe turned on his heel and walked back down the passageway to the front door of the police office. He'd counted fewer than a dozen people in the street in the last five minutes — seamen mostly, although a few had been local traders hurrying home. He couldn't say he was surprised. Word would have got around of what had happened; Boylin would have made sure of that.

He walked into the courtroom and bowed to the Bench where Harriot was still working through the day's list of cases. Doubtless the magistrate would be at it for several more hours — unless something happened to stop him. He heard the door open behind him and turned to see Tisdale.

"Anything?" Tom raised a questioning eyebrow.

"Nothing, sir," said Tisdale, knuckling his forehead. "All the men what's available have been posted like what you said; two each by the front door and the back gate, but they ain't seen nor heard nothing."

Tom looked at his watch. Five past eight. He suddenly remembered he still hadn't spoken to Sam about his impending arrest. He felt an uncomfortable lurch in his stomach. He couldn't put the matter off any longer. He should have told him the moment he'd known he was to be investigated. As for Boylin's threats this morning, if anything was going to happen it would have done so by now.

Then he remembered the silence in the street outside. He'd give it another half-hour before he stood the men down. Meanwhile he'd find Sam and warn him about the morrow.

CHAPTER
TWENTY-TWO

Sam Hart looked down from the top of the river stairs at the hundreds of lanterns bobbing up and down on the tideway — one for each ship lying at anchor — their long ribbons of light shimmering in the fast flow of an ebb tide. He turned up the collar of his jacket, hunching his shoulders against the cold wind. Out on the reach, the noise of the port had been stilled and nothing but the occasional shout of a watchman disturbed the peace of the evening. He turned to look at Tom, standing next to him.

"I'm to be arrested for the murder of the pot-boy?"

He'd known for some time that he was suspected of the death at the Queen's Head — word had got around as it always did — but he was disappointed that Tom had not thought fit to tell him immediately. Later, when someone claiming to have overheard the conversation between Tom and Harriot had told him that his friend had failed to defend him as vigorously as he might, the disappointment had deepened to a sense of betrayal that he found difficult to shake off.

"I'm deeply sorry, Sam, but, yes, the Shadwell Magistrates want to see you tomorrow when you will be formally charged with the murder."

"Could Mr Harriot not have asked me where I was that night?" Sam stared out over the water. "Before he reported the matter, like? Perhaps I might have put his mind at rest."

"I regret it extremely . . ." Tom's voice faded into an awkward silence.

"I had nothing to do with the death." Sam let out a long sigh. "I don't expect you to believe me but it's —"

"I do believe you, Hart."

"It might have made a difference if you'd said so."

Tom shrugged. There was nothing he could say. Nothing, anyway, that might assuage Sam's feeling of betrayal. For a moment or two neither of them spoke. Then Sam said, "You once asked me why I gave evidence at your inquest. D'you remember?"

"I remember," said Tom, seeming relieved to be talking about something else.

"It were on account of something what happened before ever I set eyes on you." Sam paused, and then in a low voice he went on, "Not so long ago I were engaged to be married. Hannah Pinkerton, her name was."

"I didn't know," said Tom.

"No, I never told you. Nor nobody else, neither," said Sam, a catch in his voice. He let his head fall forward and a hand passed over his eyes. "Her father were against the marriage on account of me being a Jew, but it made no difference. Hannah was determined we should wed.

"Then one day, she comes to me and tells me her father was in debt and she'd have to help him. I offered

314

her what I could but she refused to take it. Said she would find some other way of getting the money she needed. The next day she were gone. Disappeared, like."

Sam glanced over his shoulder as the front door of the police office slammed shut and a shadow moved down the pathway towards Wapping Street. He turned back to Tom.

"I saw her father and asked him where she'd gone. At first he refused to speak to me," said Sam, wiping the palms of his hands against the side of his canvas slops. "But before long he relents and tells me he knows nothing of her where-abouts. We searched, him and me, high and low, but it were many months before we found her. By then, she were prodigious ill and the sickness had ravaged her, taken away her beauty and, aye, her youth an' all. I were only able to recognise her by the bright red dress she wore. That and her blue shawl."

Tom's eyes widened, but he said nothing.

"I took her back to my room and watched over her," Sam continued. "I couldn't afford no apothecary. All I could do were to sit with her and hope. The fever came to her on the third day and by the next morning she were gone."

"How I wish I'd known," murmured Tom.

"What were that, sir?"

"Nothing, Sam. Nothing," said Tom. "Please go on."

"Before she died, she told me what had happened to her." Sam was quieter now, more intense, his face turned to the sky, his eyes moist. "It were Boylin's doing, your honour."

He glanced at Tom, as if to ensure he was listening. "That was who her father owed money to. Boylin. Hannah went to him and offered to work for him to pay off her father's debt. He found her work all right — as a doxy. Threatened to have her father committed as a debtor unless she did what she were told."

"Christ!" Tom clenched his fist. "The bastard forced her into prostitution?"

Sam said nothing for a while, the memory of Hannah filling his head, the sight of her bruised and battered face, her swollen lips, before him. He saw her eyes pleading for the help he couldn't give. A sharp pain twisted at the base of his stomach. With an effort he began to speak again.

"Hannah were frightened her father would never get out of the Marshalsea if he were committed there. Otherwise she'd not have done it. She died in my arms and I thought my world would die with her." Again Sam paused and wiped his eyes with the sleeve of his jacket. "I didn't know the cause of her fever until her inquest. It were then I learned it were the syphilis what killed her."

The muscles in Tom's face flexed and tightened.

"I wanted to avenge her," Sam continued. "Boylin never knew she were my girl but that made no difference to the way I felt about him. I wanted to kill him and I came close to doing it that day of the storm and, aye, on another occasion, too. But that don't mean I killed the pot-boy, your honour."

"I am so deeply sorry for your loss," said Tom, resting a hand on Sam's shoulder.

"It's the gallows for me now, ain't it, sir?"

"It don't look promising," said Tom. "But I warrant I'll not rest until I find the man responsible."

In the courtroom at the Wapping police office, the clerk was the first to hear the roar of a mob. He held up his hand for silence. The bellicose clamour was getting closer, demanding attention. The door of the court opened and Tom stepped in.

"A mob, sir, is approaching from the direction of Shadwell and I suspect it has us in mind."

"Very well, Mr Pascoe," said Harriot. "Are the men ready? How many can we muster?"

"Five constables including myself, sir. The only other persons in the building apart from you and Mr Colquhoun are his three guests and the Chief Clerk's staff. About fifteen in all, plus the prisoners. I've given orders for the shutters to be put up and the main gates locked."

"Good," said Harriot. "Does Mr Colquhoun know?"

"He does, sir. Two of his guests are taking to a boat while the third is on his way to the roof where he intends to stay. That reduces our number to a dozen. Mr Colquhoun will be down directly. I shall issue firearms to the men and position them in the event we come under attack. In the meantime, I suggest all members of the public leave the building forthwith."

"Very well, Mr Pascoe," said Harriot. "Mr Clerk, clear the court, if you please."

"Your honour?" It was Sam. He was looking at Tom. "Tisdale reports the mob has reached Old Gravel Lane and is starting down Wapping Street. Says it numbers around four or five hundred, armed with cudgels and the like. No sign of any firearms at the moment."

"Issue all the men with pikes in addition to their hangers and muskets," said Tom. "Brief the two men by the front door and those by the main gate about the situation. They are to remain at their posts until I tell them otherwise. I want all the rest of the men in the constables' waiting room. Is that clear?"

"Clear, aye, clear, sir." Sam turned to go, his long, plaited hair swinging behind him, all memory of their recent conversation put to one side.

"Gaoler," said Tom, seeing the elderly constable standing by the door, "how many prisoners do we still have in custody?"

"Four, your honour. The scrubs what's to blame for all this hoo-ha."

"Very well," said Tom. "If you've not already done so, put them all in the holding cell until this is over. I shouldn't wish to have them running loose."

The thunderous roar grew louder. Tom stuffed a pistol into his belt and, with Harriot at his side, made his way along the corridor to the front office. He glanced at the magistrate. The limp had gone from the older man's step, the years shed away, a gleam of excitement in his eyes.

"You realise, Mr Pascoe," said Harriot, "that you and I are the only two men present who've ever smelt gunpowder burnt in anger. I suspect that won't be true by the day's end."

"I make no doubt of that, sir," said Tom.

The two men strode into the front office, a single, tallow candle spluttering its light onto the frightened faces of those present. Tom stepped forward and addressed the men.

"These are solemn times," he said, raising his voice against the clash and bellow of a crowd that had reached the outside of the building. "No one should be in any doubt about the gravity of the situation in which we find ourselves. Most of you are aware of the intention of this rabble to rescue four men presently held in our custody. It is, of course, our intention to deny them that objective. Their release would serve only to embolden the mob outside these walls and give it heart for further outrages. We must put out the fire that others have lit, or watch the consequences of our failure spread throughout London."

A furious battering on the main door of the building made the men jump.

"Let me know what's happening, Hart," said Tom glancing over his shoulder to where Sam stood by the door to the corridor. He watched as his friend headed out of the room. Moments later he was back.

"Some of them scrubs are at the main door, trying to kick it in," said Sam. "The rest of the mob is in Wapping Street. They don't look too happy."

A stone crashed against one of the shutters, breaking the window-pane behind it and sending shards of glass scything across the room. The missile was followed by others, and those inside took refuge from the flying splinters. Tom put his head close to Harriot's ear.

"I'll be taking two men to the first floor," he shouted above the din. "It's time we put a stop to this. I doubt the shutters will take much more."

Without waiting for a reply, he beckoned Sam and Tisdale to follow him and raced up the stairs. Once into the front room, the three of them ran to the windows. Below, the densely packed mob filled the narrow confines of Wapping Street and stretched away to the east, towards Shadwell. More had entered the passage leading to the front entrance of the police office, while those behind packed the alley that ran down the side of the brewhouse opposite. Tom ducked out of the way as cobblestones thundered against the walls and windows of the building. Behind him, Harriot came into the room.

"Load and prime your pieces," called Tom. He turned to the magistrate. "I regret it extremely, sir, but the situation is now critical. May I have your authority to fire down on the ringleaders?"

Harriot looked out through the window and nodded, a fresh gleam of battle in his eye. "Carry on, Mr Pascoe."

"Choose your targets with care, my lads, and make your shots count," said Tom, kneeling at the window and shattering the glass with the butt of his musket. "Present your pieces. Steady . . . steady . . . fire at will."

Outside the dung wharf, off Wapping Street, Gabriel Newman was sweating profusely. He'd been at the back of the crowd with Boylin when he'd seen the sheets of flame erupt from the upper windows of the police office and heard the thunderous roar of the muskets. He, like the rest, had sprinted out of range and now stood waiting to see what would happen next. From the front of the crowd someone was shouting.

A man was dead.

A collective sound rose into the air, a fevered, strangled groan, amplified by the high buildings. Hands were raised in the air, some clutching lengths of timber, others waving pikes and bludgeons. The noise grew in intensity, those in front urged on by those behind. Newman found himself being swept along by the crush of bodies, his arms pinioned to his sides, his feet barely touching the ground. He struggled to breathe. To his left, he saw a man fall and get trampled underfoot, his screams of terror barely heard above the din of riot. Fifty yards short of the police office, they halted, those behind rushing headlong into those in front.

Newman saw a gentleman in a grey wig now coming out of the police office, half a dozen men on either side of him. Newman recognised Master Pascoe and, further along, Master Hart. They were armed, the gaping muzzles of their guns pointing at the crowd, the long barrels of their sea service pistols tucked into their belts. A wave of apprehension swept over him. He wished he hadn't come. He wished he'd stood up to Boylin as he'd intended.

He looked again at the grey-wigged gentleman. It was Mr Colquhoun. He'd seen him in court from time to time. Someone had once said he was the superintending magistrate. Next to him stood the other magistrate, Mr Harriot. Newman watched Colquhoun pick his way through the debris to the middle of the street. From there, he faced the crowd and began to read from a sheet of paper. Newman strained to hear him.

"Our Sovereign Lord the King chargeth and commandeth all persons being assembled, immediately to disperse themselves . . ."

"Will he be reading the Riot Act, now," breathed Newman, as a howl of derision drowned out the rest of the magistrate's words.

Another surge, and Newman was propelled to the front rank. He looked wildly about him and tried to force his way back. He caught sight of Boylin several yards behind him and to his right. The publican was holding a pistol in his hand and was aiming it at someone in the police line. Newman jerked his head round, trying to see who it might be. It was almost impossible to tell. It looked as if it might be Master Pascoe, but then again, maybe not. He looked away but something made him turn back and look afresh at the tall man with the yellow hair and the faded blue coat of a naval officer. Newman's memory stirred, a vague notion that he was missing something.

Snatches of a half-remembered story came to him. "He came up the side like a man born to the sea . . ." Newman fought to retain the moment, clutching at the vanishing memory. "He were a big cully . . . had the voice of the quarterdeck . . ."

It meant nothing, yet it meant everything. The words drifted in and out of his mind, tantalisingly close yet beyond the reach of his fuddled brain. The mob was roaring again, pressing forward. Newman saw the guns of the police line rise once more to the shoulders of the watermen constables and felt the blood drain from his head as he cowed and waited for the ear-shattering explosion he was sure would follow. Abruptly, the baying howl of the crowd ceased and a breathless silence descended on the scene.

"Steady lads. Present your pieces."

Newman recognised Tom's voice without needing to look up. He shot a glance at Boylin and saw him again raise his pistol. Surely the mad bastard would not shoot now. Not with a line of armed men facing him. Another strand of a remembered tale sidled into Newman's head, ". . . he were gentle, oh so gentle, with your Jacob."

Then the realisation hit him. He stared at the man in the uniform of the King's Navy, the blue coat frayed and dirty, the gold buttons dulled with age. He looked at the creased and rugged features, the hair tied back with a black silk ribbon and at once he knew who it was who'd tried to save his brother's life.

Newman's eyes swung from Pascoe to Boylin and back again in frightened fascination. His mouth opened and he screamed his warning, again and again. He felt his eyes bulge and his throat constrict with the effort of the shriek, all to no avail. Around him, the raging pack swayed to and fro, the din so loud it hurt. He threw another terrified stare at Boylin. Still the publican held his gun, now pointing it, now bringing it down to his side as if to keep it hidden. He wished he'd finished the job he'd started that night in the Queen's Head when he'd knifed the pot-boy instead of Boylin.

He looked back at the police line, gauging the distance between Boylin and Pascoe, weighing up the chances of the river surveyor being hit. He knew little of guns but enough to know that chance played its part in whether you lived or died. He found himself mumbling the Lord's Prayer, then stopped. It had been a long time since he'd turned to the Almighty. It didn't seem right somehow to pray when you needed Him and ignore Him when you didn't . . . on impulse he began again, his inhibitions put aside. Why, he didn't know. He knew only that the man who'd gained him a Royal Pardon and striven to save the life of his brother might yet forfeit his own at Boylin's hands.

He had to act. He had to put a stop to Boylin's murderous ways. Come what may he would tell Pascoe of how he'd been on the *Swansong* the night the old man, Denny, was murdered, his body tossed into the tideway like so much rubbish. He'd tell him where the sugar stolen from the *Swansong* lay hidden, of Boylin's attempts to sell it to Sir Sydney Devall, and of the prodigious quantities of tobacco and silk and wine and timber that was slipping through the King's Beam — all of it on Boylin's orders. He would tell him as soon as the riot was over.

A movement near the police line caught his attention. Sam Hart was running, heading straight for the mob, his cutlass drawn, his long pigtail streaming out behind him. Newman craned his head, trying to see. Had Hart seen Boylin's gun? The howl of the crowd rose to a crescendo, every eye bent to the flying figure, weaving, dodging between the hurled bricks and stones.

A pistol shot.

Newman looked for Boylin. The publican was still holding his gun but he'd not fired. It was someone else shooting. He knew others in the crowd had brought guns. He looked back at Sam Hart, saw him stumble, pitch forward, crumple to the ground. Out of the corner of his eye Newman saw Boylin again raise his pistol, his thumb pulling back the hammer, the barrel aimed at Pascoe.

Newman moved forward.

The jeering roar of the mob drowned the sound of the explosion. Newman felt the stab of pain in his chest and looked down, his eyes widening in surprise, his hands clasped tight around the front of his shirt. Blood oozed between his fingers and the red stain on his clothing spreading outwards. He felt suddenly cold, light-headed, separated from events. Around him the mob was dropping back, He tried to move with them but felt tired, his legs weak. The air about him was suddenly cool. His mind refused to function, to explain what had happened. Then Boylin was standing in front of him, a scowl of rage on his face. Why he was there, smoke drifting from the mouth of his pistol, Newman could not understand. He watched as the publican edged away.

How quiet it was. He could see the crowd, their arms waving, their mouths open, but no sound came to his ears. Dimly, he felt strong arms binding him, pulling him along, his feet dragging uselessly on the surface of the road, stumbling amongst the detritus of riot, the hot, stale breath of men on his face.

Then he passed out.

CHAPTER
TWENTY-THREE

Tom stood alone amidst the rubble of Wapping Street, his face and clothing covered in a fine layer of black dust, his eyes red-rimmed, his hair dishevelled and hanging loose about his shoulders. He looked at the smashed windows of the police office and the brewhouse opposite, at the pall of dust that still hung in the night sky, the litter of pike staves and lengths of timber, the discarded footwear and the broken paving. Hardly a square inch of the road surface did not bear evidence of the night's mischief.

Sam injured. Several of the mob dead. How many he didn't know — three, perhaps four.

Someone barked an order. Short and crisp. Tom turned to see Harriot departing with a file of militia — the Radcliff Volunteers — who'd arrived to help, the clatter of their boots on the cobblestones quickly fading as they disappeared in search of the riot's ringleaders.

He was relieved not to be assigned a specific role. There were things he wanted to do, things he had to do. He thought of Sam. He'd seen him go down and had tried to reach him, but Harriot had held him back. When next he'd looked, his friend had gone; taken, someone had told him, to the London Hospital, his condition unknown.

Now he waited for news. That was the hardest part, the mental strain of not knowing. He wondered what had caused Sam to rush headlong at the mob. He must have seen something. He'd ask him as soon as he got the chance, but for the present he had to find Gabriel Newman. Before it was too late.

He thought of the moment he'd seen Newman fall. Behind him, half-hidden by the crowd, he could have sworn he saw Boylin. He'd been holding something. A pistol? Tom wasn't sure. And even if he had been, how would that explain what had happened to Newman?

Unless . . . Tom stared at the ground. Unless it was a mistake. Unless Boylin had not meant to shoot Newman and the lumper had simply got in the way.

"Sir?" Tom turned at the sound of Sam's voice. "Hart. I'm mighty glad to see you. Have they patched you up?"

"Aye, it were only a flesh wound in the shoulder. I thought you might have need of my services, so I told them I was leaving. Miss Peggy were proper cross with me but she let me go."

"She's not the only one who's cross with you," said Tom. "You could have got yourself killed. What made you do a stupid thing like that?"

"Saw some cully what had a gun in his hand. Leastways it looked that way to me. I thought to get him before he could do any mischief."

"So he shot you," said Tom. "D'you know who it was or what he looked like?"

"I regret it extremely, sir, but it were all I could do to keep out the way of them stones what were being thrown at me. I'd no time to look at the cove's face."

"It wasn't Boylin by any chance?"

"I couldn't swear to it either way, sir. As I says, I were trying to stay out the way of them stones. Anygate —"

"You sent for us, sir?" Tom looked up to see Tisdale and Kemp approaching.

"Aye, so I did," said Tom. "I want to find Gabriel Newman. If he's still alive I've a notion he'll want to talk to us. We'll start with the house in Union Street where he usually sleeps."

Within minutes, the four of them were heading north up a deserted Old Gravel Lane, their progress watched by frightened eyes from behind a score of darkened windows, a cold, damp wind gusting up from the Thames, tugging at their coat tails and chilling their fingers.

They had reached the Ratcliff Highway before they saw any semblance of life — a shifting throng, shambling, hurrying, creeping among the shadows, shy of all it encountered. Tom knew many of its members: the drunks, the thieves, the crimps, the cut-throats and the prostitutes who frequented the Highway. Others — the sailors, the fops and the plain curious who, if they were lucky, would survive the night and tell the tale of what they had seen — he did not. But all of them recognised Tom.

"Evenin', Master Pascoe."

"Awright governor?"

"Godspeed, Your Honour."

The greetings and salutations drifted in on the putrescent air as silhouettes melted away on his approach. A squad of well-fed seamen trotted past on the other side of the road, led by a midshipman, himself no more than a boy. They paused at the sight of the police patrol, and then went on, the midshipman nodding his salute, his shrill, pubescent voice clear above the din of the crowd as another unfortunate soul found himself pressed into His Majesty's Navy.

At the corner of Union Street Tom stopped and looked down into the blackness, where neither the light of the stars nor the moon could penetrate. He waited while his eyes grew accustomed to the gloom and then moved into the narrow alley, feeling his cautious way amidst a collection of abandoned carts, broken chairs and the occasional rotting carcass. It was quiet here, after the noise and bustle of the highway, the eerie silence disturbed only by an occasional cry from behind a blackened window, the soft murmur of a prostitute plying her trade, and the scuttling din of a startled cat.

The derelict house before which they now stood, was no better and no worse than its neighbours. A four-storey brick-built structure that had, at some time in its history, been supported on either side by other buildings but which had long since collapsed. Now it was propped in place by large timbers set at angles to the crumbling walls. No light shone from its windows and no door stood at its entrance. Tom looked up at the roof, its pitched outline sharp against the vaulted sky. There was no sign of life up there, under the eaves, where Newman often slept. He stepped over the threshold, gagging at the powerful stench of human excrement.

"Tisdale, there! Fetch up the lantern, on the double." Tom pressed the sleeve of his coat to his nose and waited while Tisdale fumbled for the flint-and-metal strike. "You stay here with Kemp. Should you see Newman, clap hold of him till I get back. Hart, you're coming with me."

He peered up the flight of stairs. Several of the treads were missing. So were the banisters. And from somewhere up above he could hear a strange buzzing sound, like that of bees entering the hive, a low hum that seemed to reverberate around the staircase, swelling and reducing in a kind of rhythmic tempo. He raised the lantern. The light wasn't strong enough for him to see what it was. Quietly, he beckoned Sam and the two of them crept towards the landing where Tom again lifted the lantern.

Every inch of the landing was packed with the sleeping forms of men, women and children, their thin, skeletal frames covered with strips of sacking and old carpets, the air filled with the sounds of fitful coughing, of snoring and the cries of the very young. No one could move without disturbing his neighbour, no sound could be made without it being heard throughout the landing.

Tom stepped over the slumbering bodies, letting the lantern shine on their exhausted faces as he searched for Newman. The landing was followed by each of the three rooms on that floor and then by the floor above.

Everywhere, the scene was the same; bodies huddled together with no space for privacy or modesty.

And still there was no sign of the man he'd come to find.

Abruptly, he remembered Newman telling him that he was often compelled to live in the garret. But how to get there? He looked around. Tucked away at the end of a short passage was a dilapidated door he'd not previously seen. Stepping over more bodies, he pulled it open.

Behind was another flight of steps, much narrower and steeper than those he'd so far climbed. Tom thought for a moment. It was unlikely anyone would survive a winter's night up there, where little stood in the way of the chill winds that blew up from the Thames and the sky could be seen through the gaps in the tiles. On the other hand . . .

He sighed. He'd not forgive himself if Newman was up there and he'd left without looking. He mounted the steps.

Here, as on the floors below, the entire area was covered with what seemed to be a patchwork of rags, pieces of canvas and sackcloth beneath each of which lay a human being. Leaving Sam by the entrance, Tom ducked his head below the eaves and climbed over the mass of dormant figures, his lantern swinging ahead of him, examining the face of each in turn.

"'Ere, what's your game?"

"Bugger off afore I clout you one . . ."

"Spare a penny for me little 'un, your honour . . ."

He counted over sixty adults and children beneath the sloping roof, but of Newman there was no sign. Disappointed, he began retracing his steps and had almost reached the stairs when he heard a soft intake of breath coming from behind a chimney stack to his left. Tom swung the lamp into the dark corner and, at first, saw nothing except the morass of anonymous faces.

Then he saw him, the lantern light dancing across the pitted skin of Newman's white face like the image of some nightmare, his sunken eyes moist with pain.

"I've been looking for you," said Tom.

"I'll not have been doing anything, Master Pascoe, so help me God," whispered Newman. "I were trying to stop Joseph Boylin."

"So you did get in the way," said Tom, easing himself into the cramped space next to Newman, the hard edge to his voice softening. "You did it on purpose. Let me take a look at the wound."

"Mary, Mother of God, be with you, sir." Newman closed his eyes and began to cough. When he had stopped, he looked down at his blood-stained shirt, his hands clamped across his stomach. "I feel awful cold, so I do."

"Here, take this," said Tom, taking off his greatcoat and draping it over the Irishman's thin shoulders. "Now let me look at that hurt of yours."

He leaned forward and examined the wound, a neat hole in the middle of the stomach from which strips of Newman's shirt hung, driven into the body by the force of the shot.

"Why did you do it? We both know Boylin was trying to get me," asked Tom, sitting back on his haunches and regarding the face opposite.

"You . . ." Newman coughed up some blood — bright red and frothing. "God bless you, sir, you tried to save me brother's life. I'll not forget that, so I won't."

"Aye, he was a fine lad," said Tom, again surveying the wound he dared not touch. It would likely make an already serious situation worse. "But you've got yourself into a pretty pickle now. How d'you feel?"

"I'm not long for the grave, Master Pascoe, and that's a fact."

"Nonsense." Tom tried to sound confident. "Master Hart will fetch the physician and you'll be fixed up in no time."

"Bless you, sir," said Newman, letting his head sink back onto a strip of carpet that passed for his pillow.

"D'you feel able to talk?" asked Tom, after Sam had left them.

Newman's hooded eyes blinked in the light and he looked down at the red stain on his shirt, his fingers picking at the pieces of cloth around the wound. In the silence that followed, Tom wondered if he'd heard the question. Somewhere, a small child began to cry, a harsh, discordant screech of hunger and discomfort, its mother's exhausted voice doing what it could to soothe him. At last, Newman looked up.

"What is it you'll be wanting to talk about?"

Through a gap in the tiles, Tom could make out the first hint of the emerging dawn. There wasn't much time. They both knew that. A large part of him wanted to stop now, stop questioning Newman, give him some comfort and solace in the last moments of his life. But that wasn't possible. Newman was his last chance. He had to take it.

"About Boylin," said Tom, his eyes searching Newman's for the reaction he hoped was there. "I want to talk to you about Boylin."

CHAPTER
TWENTY-FOUR

Boylin sat up in bed, the loud hammering at the front door jolting him from his sleep. He shot a glance through the window of his room, saw the light grey of the sky, tinged with the pink of the rising sun. He didn't need to ask what the noise was about, he'd been expecting it. On the floor below, the housemaid was moving about. She could open the door. Give him time to think.

A fresh round of hammering made him jump. He swung his legs to the floor and struggled to the window, the floor-boards cold beneath his feet. He could make out three, possibly four men, gathered outside the Queen's Head. His heart pounded. What to do . . . Run? But where to? The old country? They'd never find him there. His spirits lifted and then drooped. It was too late for that. He'd never make it out of the house. He closed his eye, saliva dribbling from his mouth, his hands trembling at the thought of what was to come.

He moved away from the window into a corner of the bedroom, his back sliding down the wall until he squatted on the floor, his hands covering his ears, his eye closed. Below, he heard the front door crash open and then the sound of running feet coming up the stairs.

A banging on his door.

Then a voice he knew well, one he loathed and feared above all others.

Sam lounged on one of the only two chairs in the constables' waiting room, his head lolling back, his eyes closed, listening to the general noise and clatter of the street outside the window. The remains of a gutted candle stood in its tin sconce on the table, an untidy heap of melted wax around its base.

"What do we do now?" Sam brought his head forward and stared moodily at the far wall. "Now that Gabriel Newman's dead, we'll have to release Boylin, won't we?"

"Yes, we might have to," said Tom. "But not just yet. I want him to sweat for a while."

"What for?" said Sam. "With Newman dead, we can't use any of what he told you in evidence, and that means we've got nothing."

"Newman's dead right enough and, yes, most of what he said can't now be used in court," said Tom. "But there's a morsel that can."

"And what morsel would that be?"

"Hardly worth mentioning, I grant you," said Tom, smiling. "But since you ask, it's the bit where Newman admits to killing the pot-boy at the Queen's Head."

For a second, Sam didn't move. Then his head jolted forward and he stared disbelievingly at Tom.

"Newman admitted to the killing? Just like that?"

"Not quite," said Tom. "I told him we had some witnesses who'd seen him in the vicinity of the Queen's Head on the night of the murder. He knew he was dying and when I suggested he might want to get things off his chest he admitted it *was* him."

"What if you'd been wrong?" said Sam. "He'd have known you were trying to trick him."

"Yes, he would've done," said Tom, with a wry smile. "But it don't often fail. Anyway, the point is, the magistrates will accept the signed declaration of a man who knows he's dying even if the trial occurs after his death."

"Did he say why he did it?"

"Aye, he did. And as we thought, it wasn't the pot-boy he'd been after. It was Boylin. He'd wanted to kill the scrub ever since he discovered that he'd been responsible for his brother Jacob's death."

"And the rest of what Newman had to say? Can that be used? The bit about what Boylin's been doing?"

"No, we can't produce that in evidence. The court will only accept what Newman said about his own involvement, not what he says about anyone else."

"So we're back where we started," said Sam, throwing his hands in the air.

"Not quite. You're in the clear over that business with the pot-boy," said Tom.

Sam pushed back his chair and got to his feet, unsure of how he felt. There was an empty void where there should have been relief and happiness, a sense that something was missing. He'd still not come to terms with Tom's failure to support him when he needed it most. A part of him wanted to question the foundation of their relationship. He wondered if it were possible for true friendship ever to exist between a Jew and a Gentile, whether the cultural differences between them were not too great to be overcome.

He gazed at the burning coals in the fire grate, felt the heat warming his face. He sighed and turned away, the mood of despondency lifting. With time, he'd get over his sense of betrayal and perhaps learn to see things from a different perspective.

"I own, I shan't be sorry to have seen the last of that cloud," said Sam, glancing at Tom's wide, honest face beaming with pleasure. "But I regret it extremely that we've lost the case against Boylin."

"It *would* be a pity to lose all Newman's evidence, wouldn't it?" said Tom, rubbing the stubble on his chin, his eyes half closed. "Perhaps there is another way."

The afternoon shadows lengthened in the courtyard of the police office as the sun sank towards the horizon. Soon it would be dark and they'd have to light candles. Tom didn't much care for this room. He could smell the rotting flesh of the drowned cadavers awaiting collection in the adjoining room — not really a room at all, more a space below the office to which the floaters were brought for identification, but it amounted to much the same thing.

Tom was writing on a sheet of paper. From time to time, he looked at Boylin sitting opposite him at the table and then, without a word, continued writing.

339

"What's your game?" Boylin's voice broke in on the silence.

"Not long now, old cock." Tom stared at the ceiling.

"You can't keep me here, you English bastard," Boylin was shouting again. "It's nothing I've done wrong."

"You've nearly finished telling me what you've been up to," said Tom, returning to his task.

"Fuck off, mister! I've not said a bleedin' word."

"What d'you mean?" said Tom, a look of mock horror on his face. "You've admitted to everything. It says so, here. My colleague will confirm that, won't you, Hart?"

Sam looked surprised but nodded his head nevertheless.

"You don't know nothing, Pascoe."

"Oh, but I do," said Tom. "I've written down everything you've told us. The details will, of course, be given in evidence at your trial. But you knew that, didn't you? We told you before you started talking to us. We warned you. Didn't you hear me caution you?"

"I'll not have said a fucking word." Tom watched the veins in Boylin's neck bulge. "I'll be seeing you in Hell, mister. You've got nothing on me."

"Let me see, now," said Tom, reaching for a separate sheet of paper. "Would you like me to read what Gabriel Newman has said about you?"

"He'll not be knowing nothing." Boylin's voice had risen to a scream.

"Really?" said Tom. "I'm afraid he's going to be in the witness box for quite some time, is our Gabriel.

Let's start with when you smashed my old cook's head on the rail of the *Swansong*. You didn't know Gabriel saw that, did you? You thought only Jacob had seen that and you took care of him, didn't you? Now let's go to the bit where Gabriel tells us where the sugar from the *Swansong* is presently stored. Your yard is just off New Gravel Lane, isn't it?"

Tom looked across at Boylin trying to gauge the effect of his words. Boylin had to admit his villainy and he'd only do that if he thought there was no point in lying; that Tom already knew everything.

"Perhaps you'd prefer to hear Sir Sydney Devall's statement."

"That scrub's dead. I made sure . . ." Boylin stopped suddenly.

"You made sure of what, Boylin?" said Tom.

"Sure, he's dead. The whole bleeding port knows that."

"Yes, he's dead," said Tom. "But he had quite a lot to say about you before he died. You didn't know that, did you? You didn't know he lived for over an hour after he was attacked."

Tom paused, his eyes searching Boylin's for any sign that the publican knew he was lying. There was none.

"Then there's your old mate O'Malley," said Tom, risking another lie. "You do remember Shamus O'Malley, don't you? He was the fellow who pushed young Jacob Newman out of the rigging on your orders. You must remember that. He's turned King's Evidence and he's got plenty to say that you won't want to hear, I'm sure."

Boylin's features were ashen now, his head bowed. When he next spoke, it was barely above a beaten, frightened whisper. "What is it you want from me? I'll help you if you help me."

"What makes you think I'd want to help you, Boylin?" said Tom.

"Sure, I can be telling you everything what's going on in the port, so I can."

"I already know," said Tom, scraping dirt from under a fingernail with a sliver of wood. "You forget. Sir Sydney and the others have told me all I need to know. You're going to hang, Boylin. There's absolutely no doubt about that."

"What is it I can be doing for you, sir?" pleaded Boylin, his hands tightly clasped. "I don't want to hang."

Tom sat back in his chair and folded his arms. "I don't need anything from you, Boylin, but if you want me to save you from the hangman, you can give me a signed statement and I'll tell the trial judge what a good boy you've been."

CHAPTER
TWENTY-FIVE

The noise grew steadily louder as they pushed their way up Old Bailey towards Newgate Street, a fine mist of rain lancing down out of a slate-grey sky, a sharp chill in the damp October air.

It seemed all London was here, a dense mass pushing its noisy way north, its progress slow, its ribald humour at its most coarse. Ahead, the grey walls of Newgate rose up through the drizzle. A scaffold lay against its west wall, its lower half draped in black baize, its sudden appearance shocking in its finality, as though damning all those who beheld it.

Joseph Boylin was to hang. A cold shiver passed down Tom's spine, a kind of dread of what was to come, as though he had no business to be here, that his presence debased the value of human life. He wasn't needed. His job was done. It had ended when he had finished giving his evidence at the Old Bailey. What happened thereafter was a matter for others to decide, not him. And yet he was here — with Sam — a willing participant in the unfolding theatre of death, as eager to witness the last, pathetic jerk of a human being as the next man.

He looked at the bobbing heads in front of him. He was as they were. He could claim no difference, no higher motive for his presence among them. The thought repelled him. No man's death, not even Boylin's, should be the occasion for public entertainment. He wondered what the Irishman was doing at this precise moment, what was going through his mind.

Anger? Fear? Remorse?

The first two, perhaps, but the third? He doubted it. To believe Boylin was capable of remorse was to invite the idea of a compassionate being, capable of recognising his culpability and confessing to it. The notion that Boylin would, of his own volition, have admitted to his crimes was absurd, a possibility Tom had been unable either to hope or wait for. The stakes had been too high.

Reaching a point opposite the Debtor's Gate, he and Sam turned in through the door of the Magpie and Stump. From the doorway they were able to look out across the wide expanse of Old Bailey, filled now with a dense, noisy crowd, crammed into every conceivable vantage point.

"Some years ago," said Sam, "some Jewish lads were hanged at Tyburn for the murder of a servant in Chelsea. It were a brutal killing but they were only convicted because one of their number turned King's Evidence."

Tom looked at his friend and waited for him to continue.

"The case led to much anti-Jewish feeling in this country and from then on, people wishing to insult us would shout out —"

344

"Go to Chelsea." Tom finished Sam's sentence for him. "I know. I asked Mr Harriot about it and he told me the story. Can you be suggesting there is a similarity between that case and this one?"

"Not exactly," said Sam. "But I know what it is to be regarded as a savage and a rogue, just as Boylin and his fellow countrymen are."

A growling roar interrupted them and Tom looked up. A hatch in the floor of the scaffold had been thrown open and a procession was coming through. He recognised the Sheriff and Under Sheriff dressed in ankle-length, fur-trimmed robes. Behind them came the black-clad figure of the Ordinary of Newgate, reading aloud from an open prayer book. Then came the stumbling, terrified figure of Boylin, his hands bound in front of him, a fixed caricature of a grin on his face. The palms of his hands faced outwards, his fingers splayed wide in a hopeless appeal to the crowd. Around his neck was a halter, a white nightcap on his head. The din of the mob increased, erupting into a chanting screech that filled the air and chased a flock of pigeons from their roost high above the Debtor's Gate.

"Hats off." The roar of the mob again. "Down in front."

Boylin was led to his place below the high beam, his chest rising and falling with the rapid intakes of his breath, his fists clenching and unclenching, his eyes darting from the crowd to the hangman and back again. Behind him was the second of the condemned. Shamus O'Malley was to die for the murder of Jacob Newman. There were only two this Monday morning.

Tom watched the halters round the necks of the two men being taken up and looped through the butcher's hooks screwed into the underside of the gibbet. He let his eyes fall back to Boylin's face. The Irishman had seen him, was staring at him. Tom felt awkward, as if caught peeping at something that should have remained private. He turned away.

When he looked back, the nightcap had been drawn down over Boylin's and O'Malley's faces. He watched the staccato breath of the men forcing the cloth of the nightcap in and out.

From the far side of Skinner Street, the bell of St Sepulchre's struck the hour, its booming waves reverberating painfully against Tom's ears. A low groan rose from the crowd and the hangman moved forward, his hand hovering over the locking bolt holding the trapdoor in place.

Tom looked away; the crowd fell eerily silent. A second later the squeal of the opening doors and the unearthly howl of the mob told him it was done.

Without a backward glance, Tom left, pushing his way through the grinning mob, east towards Whitechapel and the London Hospital.

He had delayed too long in seeing her.

GLOSSARY

Abaft — behind, to the rear of

Adze — the principal tool of the shipbuilder of old. Looks a bit like a garden hoe but razor sharp

Backstay — see Stays

Barky — see Barque

Barque and Barquentine — three-masted sailing vessels. Differing only in the configuration of their sails

Beam (on the beam) — at right angles to the vessel. See also King's Beam

Bight — the outer curve in the river, opposite to the Point

Blackstraps — long canvas bags used for carrying stolen coffee, sugar, etc. and suspended inside the trousers

Boat gun — a heavy, long-barrelled flintlock gun fitted with an iron swivel yoke for steadying and aiming purposes

Bottom-boards — planks of wood on the floor of a small boat. See also Ceiling planks.

Brail — temporary furling of sails

Break (as in fo'c'sle break and break of the poop) — point at which the deck levels change sharply

Brig and Brigantine — two-masted ships differing only in the type of rig carried

Bumboat — small boat used to carry vegetables and general provisions to ships in port

Capstan/capstan bars — means by which the anchor and other heavy objects were raised. Bars are inserted to give purchase for the men operating the capstan

Ceiling planks — planks in the hold of a vessel laid across the floor and up the sides to the level of the beams. See also Bottom-boards

Chains (1) (hang in) — the bodies of executed felons were sometimes placed in close-fitting cages and suspended close to the scene of their crimes as an example to others

Chains (2) (or chain plates) — the anchor points for the shrouds

Clew — the bottom corners (in a square sail) by which the sail may be hoisted to the yard for furling. Also, the line or rope by which the furling takes place

Clubbing — means of controlling a ship while dropping downstream. An anchor is thrown over her stern and dragged on the river-bed

Common Serjeant of London — the second most senior permanent judge at the Old Bailey

Cooper — a barrel maker

Copeman — a receiver of stolen goods

Crimp — an individual who makes his living "persuading" others to join the crew of a ship and delivering them (usually unconscious through drink) on payment of head-money. The "private sector" equivalent of the press-gangs of the Royal Navy

Cully — slang for a man

Dung Wharf — literally the wharf from which dung was

loaded onto barges and taken down river for disposal. The one mentioned in this story is thought to have been at Phoenix Wharf, a few yards up-river from Execution Dock

Fiddler's Green — a sailor's paradise where food, drink and the ladies are plentiful

Gig — a boat provided for personal transport

Hanger — a sword or cutlass

Hard — refers to the bottom of the river. Also means those parts of the river bed solid enough to rest the keel of a vessel

Hawsehole — the hole in the bows of the ship through which the anchor cable passes

Hitcher — boat hook

Hoy — a small, single-masted sailing vessel

King's Beam — huge scales placed at the Legal Quays to weigh merchandise on which tax was payable

Lascar — an Indian, but could be used to describe any Oriental

Legal Quays — the trading wharfs between London Bridge and the Tower where all goods on which duty was payable had to be landed

Lighter — a barge-like vessel used to convey a ship's cargo to shore

Lightermen — men licensed to control the lighters

Lumpers — men engaged to lade and unlade ships

Lumping — the action of carrying the cargo

Luggers — a "lug"-rigged sailing vessel for use in rivers and coastal waters

Maintop — top of the first length of the mainmast (counting from the deck)

Orlop deck — the lowest deck in a ship, usually used for cargo

Passing House — a house (usually a tavern) where men could find work on the river

Police Office (or Court) — following the abolition of the old (and corrupt) Trading Justices system in the late 18th century, a total of seven police offices were opened in London (at Queen's Square; Great Marlborough Street; Hatton Garden; Worship Street; Whitechapel; Shadwell; and Southwark), each one in the charge of three stipendiary magistrates who were given between eight and twelve constables apiece. On 2 July 1798 an eighth office was opened at 259 Wapping New Stairs under the charge of Patrick Colquhoun and John Harriot, with a patrolling force of around sixty watermen constables supported by a large additional group of men performing various functions. This new office and its staff were partly funded by the government with the rest of the cost borne by the West India Merchants and Planters Committee

Ran-dan — a rowing formation for three rowers

Rat lines — the transverse (tarred) ropes in the shrouds that act as a ladder for the crew to climb into the rigging

Sand — slang for sugar

Slops — strictly, baggy trousers worn by seamen

Skiff — strictly, a ship's working boat but extended to mean any small rowing boat

Snow — European, two-masted merchant vessel of up to 1,000 tons

Spring tide — the exceptionally high tide which occurs fortnightly as a result of the moon's gravitational pull. Opposite to the Neap tide

Starlings — timber stakes placed as a defensive ring around bridge supports

Stays — ropes supporting the mast of a ship. The forestay reaches from the bows to the mast. The backstay goes from the stern to the mast

Stern sheets — that part of an open boat between the stern and the rearmost rowing position. The space is usually fitted with a seat for passengers but in the police galleys of the late 18th and early 19th centuries, it was the place where the arms chest was kept. The river surveyor would use the chest as his seat

Tackle House Porters — a high-level Fellowship given the right of porterage of all non-measurable goods in the port

Taffrail — the after rail at the stern of a ship

Thole pins — wooden pins between which an oar is threaded

Thwart — the transverse wooden seat in a rowing boat

Topgallants (t'gallants) — the second highest sail on the mast (below the Royal)

Watchers — women employed in hospitals to "watch" the patients during the night while the nurses slept

Watermen constables — the name given to the first marine policemen

Wherry — a single- or double-crewed rowing boat used as a ferry

Yawl — a small two-masted sailing boat

ACKNOWLEDGEMENTS

I think it was Winston Churchill who once said that, for an author, the process of writing a book was like handling a mistress who quickly turned into a mother-in-law. I know what he meant. For me the really exciting part of being an author is the bit at the beginning — the research. Delving into original documents of the age was a voyage of discovery and I owe a huge debt of gratitude to those who freely gave of their time to help me understand the reality of 18th-century London life. I include the staff of the National Archives at Kew and the Guildhall Library in London, the curators of the Jewish Museum in North London, the Thames Police Museum at Wapping, the London Hospital Museum at Whitechapel and the Museum of London Docklands on West India Quay.

There were others, too. Helen Newman and her husband Captain Mark Boylin, whose names I stole as two of the characters in this tale and without whose help I would have struggled even more than I did. Mark, in particular, was a source of invaluable maritime knowledge. Kelly Falconer who bashed and cajoled me with advice on style and grammar in the early stages, cannot escape a mention. Neither, of course, can Sara, the long-suffering love of my life who also enthusiastically joined in with the bashing and cajoling. Finally, may I mention my agent Oli Munson for his belief in me, and my editor, the incomparable Jane Wood, for her wise help and advice in bringing the book into the light of day.

The mistakes along the way are mine. If I have got anything right, it is the result of the collaborative effort of many, many people.

P.J.E.

Also available in ISIS Large Print:

The Devil's Mask

Christopher Wakling

Meet Inigo Bright, young lawyer and artist, working in Bristol after the abolition of the slave trade. At odds with his wealthy merchant family and engaged to a girl he no longer loves, Inigo's dissatisfaction is complete when his boss, Adam Carthy, instructs him to investigate records of import duties for the newly formed Dock Company.

But the detail is in the devil's mask. Inigo's search leads him to *The Belsize*, a ship newly returned from the Indies, laden with rum, sugar, tobacco — and a chilling secret. Suddenly those in the city whose interests the secret protects move savagely to keep the truth hidden, at all costs.

Before long Inigo, his boss and family are implicated, a cover-up seems their only way out. But when he links the case to a charred corpse found in Clifton, Inigo discovers that there are other bodies to account for . . .

ISBN 978-0-7531-8932-0 (hb)
ISBN 978-0-7531-8933-7 (pb)

The Crimson Cavalier

Mary Andrea Clarke

Pre-Regency London: a hotbed of robbers, ruffians and imposters . . . A girl might as well put her faith in a highwayman!

Georgiana Grey is a sore trial to her upright brother Edward: independent, outspoken and determined to follow her own path regardless of the cost to her social position and reputation.

But the late 18th century is a dangerous time. Sir Robert Foster, a prominent but unpopular citizen, is murdered close to Georgiana's home, apparently killed by the Crimson Cavalier, a colourful and infamous highwayman. Georgiana has her own reasons to be certain the Cavalier is not to blame, and to Edward's chagrin, she sets out to track down the real culprit.

Georgiana discovers plenty of people with good reason to wish Sir Robert dead, but her quest for the truth is obstructed on all sides. As the net closes on the Crimson Cavalier, her own life could be at stake.

ISBN 978-0-7531-8534-6 (hb)
ISBN 978-0-7531-8535-3 (pb)

The Mysterium

Paul Doherty

A mysterious assassin prowls the narrow alleyways of London

February 1304, and London is in crisis. A succession of brutal murders shocks the city as it comes to terms with the fall from power of Walter Evesham, Chief Justice in the Court of the King's Bench. Accused of bribery and corruption, Evesham has sought sanctuary to atone for his sins.

When Evesham's clerk is found cruelly murdered, and then Evesham himself is discovered dead in his cell at the Abbey of Syon, it appears that the Mysterium, a cunning killer brought to justice by Evesham, has returned to wreak havoc. Sir Hugh Corbett is ordered to investigate the hideous murders. Has the Mysterium returned or is another killer imitating his brutal methods? As Corbett traces the ancient sins that hold the key to discovering the killer's identity he must face his most cunning foe yet.

ISBN 978-0-7531-8894-1 (hb)
ISBN 978-0-7531-8895-8 (pb)

Thou Shell of Death

Nicholas Blake

Fergus O'Brien, a legendary World War One flying ace
with several skeletons hidden in his closet, receives a
series of mocking letters predicting that he will be
murdered on Boxing Day. Undaunted, O'Brien throws
a Christmas party, inviting everyone who could be
suspected of making the threats, along with private
detective Nigel Strangeways. But despite Nigel's
presence, the former pilot is found dead, just as
predicted, and Nigel is left to aid the local police in
their investigation while trying to ignore his growing
attraction to one of the other guests — and suspects —
explorer Georgina Cavendish.

ISBN 978-0-7531-9118-7 (hb)
ISBN 978-0-7531-9119-4 (pb)

Nightshade

Paul Doherty

January 1304 and Hugh Corbett, devoted emissary of King Edward I, has been charged with another dangerous mission. Scrope, an unscrupulous manor lord, has reneged on his promise to hand over the Sanguis Christi, a priceless ornate cross he stole during the Crusades. Furthermore, he has massacred as heretics fourteen members of a travelling religious order, whose corpses now lie in the woods near Mistleham in Essex.

The King, determined to restore order and claim the treasure before the Templars demand its return, sends Corbett to Mistleham. But as Corbett reaches the troubled village, it becomes obvious that Scrope has other problems. A mysterious bowman has appeared, killing townspeople at random. Have the Templars arrived to wreak revenge?

As panic rises, can Corbett restore Mistleham to peace, and return the treasure to the King, before further blood is shed?

ISBN 978-0-7531-8320-5 (hb)
ISBN 978-0-7531-8321-2 (pb)

ISIS publish a wide range of books in large print, from fiction to biography. Any suggestions for books you would like to see in large print or audio are always welcome. Please send to the Editorial Department at:

ISIS Publishing Limited
7 Centremead
Osney Mead
Oxford OX2 0ES

A full list of titles is available free of charge from:

Ulverscroft Large Print Books Limited

(UK)
The Green
Bradgate Road, Anstey
Leicester LE7 7FU
Tel: (0116) 236 4325

(Australia)
P.O. Box 314
St Leonards
NSW 1590
Tel: (02) 9436 2622

(USA)
P.O. Box 1230
West Seneca
N.Y. 14224-1230
Tel: (716) 674 4270

(Canada)
P.O. Box 80038
Burlington
Ontario L7L 6B1
Tel: (905) 637 8734

(New Zealand)
P.O. Box 456
Feilding
Tel: (06) 323 6828

Details of ISIS complete and unabridged audio books are also available from these offices. Alternatively, contact your local library for details of their collection of ISIS large print and unabridged audio books.